More Than a Game . . .

From the start Coldiron spotted Barry as a winner . . . a perfect physical specimen . . . an unpolished diamond of a handball player. With training, he was unbeatable.

Until Barry became a ruthless hitter—with the skill and power to cripple a man . . . or even kill him.

And Coldiron had shown him how.

Killshot:

When one player, by virtue of perfect execution and precise coordination, drives the handball in such a fashion so it strikes the front wall low to the floor, allowing his opponent no possibility for a return shot.

> *The Arte of Handball*
> by S. O'Dwyer
> Dublin, Ireland, 1815

But There Is a Second Kind of Killshot:

When a certain breed of renegade player attempts to hit his opponent with such force as to maim or otherwise injure him . . . for life.

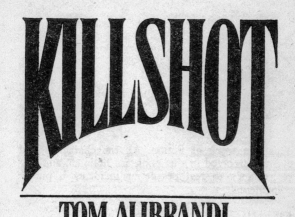

KILLSHOT

TOM ALIBRANDI

PINNACLE BOOKS   •   LOS ANGELES

KILLSHOT

An original Pinnacle Books edition, published for the first time anywhere.

First printing, January 1979

ISBN: 0-523-40375-5

Cover illustration by Paul Stinson

Printed in the United States of America

PINNACLE BOOKS, INC.
2029 Century Park East
Los Angeles, California 90067

This book is dedicated, with my purest love,
to Astrid.

ACKNOWLEDGMENTS

Carole Garland for believing in me as a writer and as a friend.

Gaye Tardy, my editor, for calling out my best by her unwavering faith in the story and in me.

Scott Penney for playing critic and friend.

Pinnacle Books for taking the gamble.

Alan Bonner for his creative zingers across the miles.

Bob Earll, as usual.

And to Chris, Patrick, Camille, Mike, Greeny, Dick, Pam, Pete, Jeff, and all the other Coldirons of the world. They are the happy crazies, and make this planet more livable.

Barry walked to the service area, a rectangle
five feet wide, bounded by two red lines, halfway between front and back walls. Extreme

Killshot:

"When one player, by virtue of perfect execution and precise coordination, drives the handball in such a fashion so it strikes the front wall low to the floor, allowing his opponent no possibility for a return shot."

The Arte of Handball
By S. O'Dwyer
Dublin, Ireland, 1815

But there is a second kind of Killshot:

"When a certain breed of renegade player attempts to hit his opponent with such force so as to maim or otherwise injure him . . . for life."

Chapter One

New Orleans, 1950

If it had been raining, as it had most of the day, the two men would've called a cab. Instead, they stepped into the dark and rain-washed street from the New Orleans Handball Club. The collars of their belted raincoats were buttoned high to protect their throats against the heavy and cold air.

The larger of the two, shoulders squarely filling his coat, was perspiring under a navy watch cap. His face absorbed the night, only high cheekbones and gun-metal gray eyes reflected the faint light.

The smaller man's hands darted and shoulders shrugged as he spoke quietly. Though nervous, he wasn't perspiring. Hatless, with receding hairline, he appeared older than the other man. They were both twenty-four years old.

"Slick as snot. You took it to him. Slick as snot."

"Yeh," the big man answered. His eyes were locked straight ahead as he walked.

"You did in their best; you gave the son of a bitch a handball lesson right in front of the old man. It was surely one for the boys."

1

"Fuck the causes."

"Okay, then. Two thousand dollars buys a bunch of Jack Daniel's Green."

"Give me the Green."

The smaller man wouldn't leave it at that. Too much had been at stake back there. "C'mon, man. You kicked ass out of that limp-wristed ham-'n'-egger. And lightened Bradford's wallet by two grand. When the news gets back to Boston, they'll be hoisting a few for you."

A smile found its way to the larger man's lips. They were thin lips, pulled tight over teeth stained from too many strong cigars and carloads of reheated coffee. He let his mind sip at the significance of the win, but it kept showing him dollar signs. Two thousand bucks for two hours' work wasn't bad. He'd had worse. Much worse. Now he was expecting better. Now, maybe the sport would be returning to the players.

"Let's hit it out of this burg," blurted the smaller man. "I don't trust that guy." His hands moved like the wings of a hummingbird.

"No need to worry, Danny. There won't be any trouble. We'll drop by Shinner's. Knock back a few." He was referring to a neighborhood bar owned by an old handball friend.

Had the two men not been so preoccupied they might've noticed the car that followed a half block behind. The 1949 Buick, black against washed asphalt, crept along unlit and unseen among the shadows. An occasional ribbon of streetlight flashed across three figures; two in front and one in back.

As the prowling car approached the twosome, the figure in the back seat nodded.

The man in the watch cap was the first to hear the Buick's throaty roar as it sprang toward them. He hadn't figured it would come so soon. He knew immediately who they wanted.

Engine noise and screaming tires soaked into the night. The car ate up the block and was on them in seconds.

"Keep going, Danny," the big man called. "Meet me at Shinner's." He broke into an alley, behind the balustraded, metal-faced buildings, which he hoped might be a way out. Danny dashed down the sidewalk and disappeared.

The man in the watch cap tucked his shoulders into his chest and ran full blast into the unlit, shaftlike cavity. Charging violently and blindly into the blackness, he held out his arms to fend off any post or other obstruction that might be waiting to cut him down.

The Buick turned the corner. Its headlights cut the night like giant flashbulbs. They also showed that the alley dead-ended into a twenty-foot, windowless wall.

The man skidded to a stop as his eyes caught a glimpse of something green against the blurred, even waves of brick. It was a doorway. He felt the glossy smoothness. No doorknob. It opened from the inside. Desperately he clawed at the joint between door and frame, nearly tearing out his fingernails. It was securely bolted.

"Cocksucker," he hissed.

The car's girth filled the alley's width. There was no retreat for the man. He inched deeper into the alley, prodded by the polished hood that was close enough to touch. His gray eyes frantically searched for a piece of lumber, garbage can, anything that would help him scale the wall in back of him. There was nothing.

He backed to the point where the T-shaped alley flared. He could go no farther. He braced himself against the wall for the fight, protecting his back. He waited for the car to reach the alley's wide part, where they would have enough room to open the doors. Adrenalin pressed against his lungs. He fixed his eyes on the three shadows in the Buick.

Only the car didn't stop. Confused, he vainly tried to straight-arm it away. It was then the rubber slug hit him in the chest, driving his lean body upright. It hit him like a golfer's tee shot. His head snapped against the brick wall. Blood soaked through the wool of his cap. He was out on his feet.

In an instant, he was torn from his semiconscious dusk by his own brain-searing scream as it rushed from his lungs in a wall of agony. The Buick's buttresslike front bumper ground to a stop against the bricks. His legs had been snapped below the knees like dried branches. The writhing man clawed harmlessly at the car's grill.

A well-dressed man stepped from the back seat, almost nonchalantly, as if to speak with a gas station attendant. Wide-brimmed black dress hat pulled low over one eye, he walked to the pinned man. Without expression, the shorter man examined his driver's work. Then he reached into the stricken man's coat, feeling for his shirt pocket, and removed the envelope containing the $2,000.

Through pain-blazed eyes, struggling to remain conscious, the big man studied the face of the one responsible for crippling him. He had only seen him once; that was earlier that evening. The hated rival's patrician good looks, square jaw, lean nose, and graying hair would be forever etched in his shocked mind.

The car door closed and backed away to a second throat-rupturing scream. The man fell forward, his once-powerful legs bent at a grotesque angle at the point where they were broken nearly in half. He lapsed into blessed blackness.

Chapter Two

COLDIRON, 1975

"Motherfucker," the man behind the wheel yelled at his gasping and sputtering white 1959 Ford Fairlaine. His name was Tate Coldiron. He was forty-nine years old—as near as anyone, including Coldiron himself, could guess.

His mother had been the Jewish wife of a clothing store owner in Broken Arrow, Oklahoma. She had left the haberdasher and had run off with a Cherokee Indian cowboy named Zachary Coldiron, to a life of easy passion, heavy drinking, and hard times. They had both been killed in a drunken auto wreck while their four-year-old son, Tate, lay asleep in a neighbor's house. The kid was subsequently raised by nuns in a St. Louis orphanage until he ran away at fourteen with a deep dislike for stern authority and Roman Catholics. He had earned his living mostly in and around athletic clubs ever since.

With each miss and catch of the engine, his car snaked slightly on the snow- and ice-covered off ramp. The Ford had begun losing power twenty miles outside Rochester. Coldiron had decided to get off the New York State

Thruway while he still could and have it looked at.

On his way to Cleveland and a Saturday handball tournament, a tow truck plucking him from the Interstate would've cost him an arm and a leg. He was two days and two hundred miles from his destination. He had twenty bucks to his name.

With mixed feelings he paid the toll and headed into Rochester. The previous hour he had fought high winds and had hardly been able to see the hood of his car. The snow had been coming straight at him. His eyes burned and ached from peering through the endless, swirling wall of white.

But the delay still bothered him. He hated to stop. Coldiron needed to get to Cleveland. The weekend tournament stood between him and vagrancy.

The storm was treating the city more kindly. The winds were slackened by buildings and trees. At 9:00 P.M., the streets were nearly deserted. Only an occasional taillight winked at him in the muffled darkness.

He spotted platinum lights of a service station through dancing bugs of snowflakes. Coldiron pointed his car toward the brightly lit service bay. He waited in the car for the attendant, a kid in his teens, who was sweeping up. The kid waited back.

"C'mon, maggot. I'm business," he said. He then climbed from a car whose appearance lost ground in the light. Its metal skin was riddled with rust and dents. The window on the passenger's side lacked six inches of closing.

The attendant saw the man approach the station door and casually moved to the office and locked the register.

Coldiron's menacing appearance didn't help his cause. He walked with a severe limp; the collar of his battered, gray overcoat was pulled high on his neck. Navy watch cap stretched over his ears, his taut, gray eyes guarded a nose that had been redone by a fist or two. It was his serious mouth that really got the kid's attention. Coldiron's lips were pressed and purpled with anger and cold. They were thin lips that looked like they kept his tight facial skin from unraveling.

"Fuckin' freezin' out there," he spit as he shuffled into the warm station. He stamped blue, high-topped gym shoes on the ceramic tile floor.

"Do something for you?" The sandy-haired, bearded kid kept an eye on the door. He decided to make a break if the guy tried anything. Walt on graveyard had been robbed twice in six months. The last time, some crazed black guy had peeled back his scalp with a jamb bar. Walt had spent a month in the hospital.

Key to the register in his pocket, the kid had ceded the station to the stranger.

"My car is acting up. You look at it?"

Even a nineteen-year-old college kid knew

8

that one. Start toward the guy's car and get it in the back of the head. He stayed put.

"What's wrong with her?" The kid had a helpful tone in his voice and fear in his eyes.

"Losing power. Best I could get was thirty-five. Hardly made it in here."

"I'm not a mechanic. You can leave it here for the night, though. The owner will look at it in the morning."

"I don't have until morning. Got to be in Cleveland first thing." Coldiron leaned against the porcelain wall. "You're the only station open for five miles and you're telling me you can't fix a car? What the fuck you do here?"

"Pump gas at night, mostly. If you want, mister, pull it in and I'll have a look. Might just be a frozen gas line. The wind'll do that."

Without answering, Coldiron shuffled outside, fell into the car and worked the ignition. It barely started.

"Over five bucks to fix it, and I put my shorts on backward," he mumbled. He reached over and patted his traveling companion. It was a quart of Jack Daniel's Green Sour Mash Bourbon. There was about four fingers left. It was all he had left to kill the pain in his legs until Cleveland.

Winters were the worst; his stems ached day and night from November to April. He could barely get into the car to leave Boston earlier that day. Once again he had promised himself to cut down on his drinking, win some coin

9

and move to Florida, where the sun would bake out the hurt. It was a vow he had made hundreds of times, whenever the ache got unbearable. And one he'd broken every time. He needed the instant relief of the Green more than he needed to save for Florida.

Coldiron would've gone to Cleveland on a stretcher. The $750 first prize in the Buckeye Invitational Handball Tourney would buy a lot of bourbon. Even without legs, he could wipe any pansy-palmed son of a bitch in Ohio.

Thinking of the easy money, Coldiron cursed himself for cutting it so close, leaving no money for an emergency. Listening to the Ford's irregular beat was the kind of anxiety he would rather have avoided. But things had been rough since New Orleans. It had been twenty-five years of grubbing for leftovers.

"Let's have a look," the kid said. He was beginning to feel less like a potential robbery victim. He closed the big overhead door behind the Ford.

Coldiron stayed in the car. He choked his bottle, spun the cap, and pulled himself a deep, burning taste.

The kid saw Tate's head roll back under the jug and gave the guy a "what-the-hell" look. Raising the car's hood, which weighed twice what it should have because of the two-inch blanket of snow and ice, he began pawing around the motor like he knew what he was doing.

"Gun it."

Coldiron goosed her. The rev was bad. The motor strained as though he were running molasses in it.

"Sounds bad," the kid said, peeking around the hood. "Might be valves. You got no compression."

"Kid's a fucking genius," Coldiron mumbled. "Can't make it up a flat grade and he tells me I got no compression."

"How long to fix it?" Tate said aloud. He reached into the pocket of his second-hand L.L. Bean brown corduroys and fingered the lonely twenty. Ten of it was entrance fee for the Cleveland tourney.

"Mechanic gets here at seven in the morning. If he can get the parts, you can probably have it back tomorrow night. Sometimes parts are tough to come by for these old cars. I know. I'm tryin' to restore a '55 Chevy."

"What'll it cost me?"

"Valve jobs run about a hundred and a half."

"Good Jesus." Coldiron hissed out ninety-proof breath the kid could've chinned himself on. He beat a tune on the cold plastic steering wheel with his palms.

Knowing the answer to the next one before he asked, he did anyway. "Think she'll make it to Cleveland like this?"

"Cleveland? You kidding? The curb would be a long shot."

Coldiron never heard him. He was already

11

figuring what he'd do next. Essentially broke for a quarter century, survival said always plan ahead. He quickly decided to stay the night and let them fix the car. He'd make some calls and try putting the touch on friends for a $200 stake.

"Where could I flop for the night?"

"Couple of motels in the next block."

"Anything cheaper?"

"The YMCA is three blocks north."

"That's more my speed. I'll call tomorrow and see how the car's coming."

The big guy pushed himself out of the car. Then he cranked open the back door and dragged a scarred suitcase across a vinyl seat, split and soiled from wear, and windows left open for weeks at a time. He balanced the suitcase against his thigh and moved into the forbidding Upstate New York night. He turned to the kid and finger waved. "Good night, kid. Tell them to get started on it first thing."

"Okay, mister." The attendant watched until the prints made by Coldiron's dragging gym shoes disappeared beyond the service station's orbit of mercury vapor lights.

It took Tate fifteen minutes to find the brick and limestone eight-story YMCA. The only life in front of the place was a wiry-coated and lean-legged dog. The mutt pranced across the street, lifted his leg, and laid a steaming line of urine across the cornerstone that read A.D. 1937. The brown dog turned to Coldiron. The animal wasn't big. His quickness and wide mouth made him look dangerous.

"My luck, the fucker is rabid," Tate drawled. He gave the dog a wide berth to the snow-packed stairs.

The Y lobby smelled of wet wool and warm Naugahyde. It was empty, except for a black man in soiled clothes and a hardhat reading a newspaper on an overstuffed couch. Whenever the guy shifted, air rushed from the cushions and made the sound of passing gas.

Coldiron was met by a nervous and tall desk man whose nose looked like a peeled potato. "Help you?"

"I need a room for the night."

Hairs hung from the bottom of the clerk's nose. "You a member of the Y?"

Coldiron grunted affirmatively and pushed apart his overcoat. Melted snow had leached into the wool. The coat felt like forty pounds. His high-topped gym shoes were thawing into puddles around his feet; something Potato Nose noticed. Tate laid his well-worn card on the desk and blew into his hands.

"Colder than a groundhog's pecker out there."

The clerk ignored the comment. He fingered the dog-eared membership card. "Thirty-eight consecutive years. Never seen one that old." Air whistled through his nose when he breathed.

"Six dollars for the night. In advance, Mr. Coldiron."

"No respect for seniority, eh?" As if to re-

13

lieve himself, Tate again parted his overcoat. He reached into his pants pocket and handed over the wadded twenty.

With the long and dainty fingers of a neurotic florist, the clerk picked at the bill. Coldiron's change came back the same way.

"How long you be with us?"

"A day or so."

"Enjoy your stay, Mr. Coldiron."

Tate nodded. He gathered his well-traveled suitcase up with his cantaloupe-sized fist. In the bag were his handball gear, clothes, and the bottle of Jack Daniel's. Except for the seriously ill Ford, everything Coldiron owned was in that bag. The possessions of a lifetime.

The old warrior looked forward to the warm room and some long pulls from his bottle to try and kill the pounding ache in his legs. And maybe help him forget his financial worries. At least until morning.

Chapter Three

BARRY WEST

Rochester Circuits manufactured semiconductors and integrated circuits for shipment throughout the world. Their plant was located on the city's south side, in a series of one-story brick buildings that covered twenty acres of an old onion farm.

By 4:00 P.M. Friday it was nearly dark. Night closed in fast and early in January. The building's narrow windows beamed golden slivers across freshly fallen snow.

The company's accounting division was located in Pod One. In the building, hundreds of cost experts and secretaries rode desks behind four-foot-tall partitions carpeted in various pastel colors. Divided into working divisions, the accountants of Pod One huddled over calculators and ledger sheets, amassing billing documents, production cost sheets, and payroll accounts. Their secretaries blazed away at wide-mouthed electric typewriters.

In one of the upholstered cubicles sat Barry West. He was twenty-six years old and a five-year veteran at Rochester Circuits. With the company since graduation from Ithaca College,

West was tall and lean; his blond hair was trimmed just within company standards for length. He wore his standard business uniform of white oxford button-down shirt, maroon rep tie, three-piece suit and horn-rimmed glasses that guarded intense blue eyes that were set slightly too close together for his strong and wide face.

West was busy checking cost figures for a new circuits board the company hoped to market the following spring. On the report a week, he had waded through thousands of calculations, cost projections, and profit margins for the presentation to the division chiefs the following Tuesday. Since it was scheduled to be typed Monday, he needed to stay at his desk until it was wrapped up. He had extracted a solemn promise from Margaret Burns, the secretary he shared with three other accountants, that the report could be typed in one day.

More than the fact that it was the end of a rugged work week and he'd be done with the boring report, Barry was anxious to leave the plant to get to his handball match scheduled for six o'clock at the Y. Playing the game since he was fifteen, he had distinguished himself as one of the better players in the Rochester area. Two trophies, signifying local tournament championships, watched over him from a nearby metal bookcase.

For the moment, his mind and energy were focused on the report. Living with the thing day and night for a week had clogged his mind with swirls of numbers and contract stipulations. He wanted the bundle of papers to be someone else's problem at quitting time. Margaret Burns's problem.

He was down to the final page. A few strokes of his company-issue mechanical pencil and it'd be done. He leaned back in satisfaction. Then Barry reached for the phone and punched a number more familiar to him than his own.

"Susan. Hi. How's your day?"

"Hi, back. Working my buns off. We go to press tomorrow." It was Susan Burnett, editor of *Woman's Weekly Magazine* and West's lover for two years. They'd met while working on a mutual friend's city council campaign. It had taken Barry a month to get up the nerve to call her for a date.

She continued, "Right now the fucking thing looks like a kid's paper doll clippings."

Her voice was a welcome change from the low murmur of office equipment, endless ringing of phones, and muffled voices of obedient men chattering like hamsters that was West's daily anthem from nine to five.

"Finish in time for dinner?" He talked close to the phone as though he was making a drug deal. "My match is at six. I should be done by eight."

"Doesn't look like it. Go ahead without me. Why don't you call me later? Maybe I can slip by your place for a drink."

"Okay. Talk to you later," he said and hung up. He didn't want to let on that he was disappointed, that he'd been looking forward to celebrating the completion of the report with her.

Barry took a moment to lean back in his swivel-reclining chair and think about her. With the wild cinnamon eyes of an unbroken colt, a perfect face, and hair that fell on her shoulders like night water, Susan could've looked as at home on the cover of her magazine as she did behind her editor's desk. He pictured the way she carried herself—with grace and dignity. Susan was nearly six feet tall. Some tall women appeared awkward. She was regal.

He did that a lot. Barry liked to fantasize about her. It helped the clock sweep around to five o'clock.

He had been pressing for marriage over the past six months. She loved him. They dated each other exclusively, but Susan wanted no part of marriage. At least not until Barry discarded some of his tired, Ivy League ethics, beginning with his allegiance to Rochester Circuits and his ongoing paranoia over possibly losing a job he didn't even particularly like.

Susan preferred seeing him two or three times a week, spending the nights in his bed, or with him in hers, but she had made it clear she wanted to remain single. She wished to retain the solitude and freedom of her own apartment and her own life. It was an attitude that had become more and more irksome to Barry. He wanted a stronger commitment.

At a quarter to five West dropped the draft on Margaret's desk. "I'll need ten copies Tuesday morning. Now don't let me down."

His secretary was a strawberry blonde with huge boobs that on her otherwise tiny figure looked like '59 Cadillac bumper guards on a Fiat—breasts that had sprouted considerably after a medical leave the previous year. Some of the guys in the office called her "glass packs." Behind her back.

"No problem. Will you be in Monday in case I have a question?" She tended to sound her words through her ample nose.

"All day, Margaret. Be a while before I'm up for parole." Barry gathered his overcoat and made for the door.

Margaret jammed the sheaf of papers into her desk drawer and muttered without anyone hearing, "No souls saved after four o'clock." She resumed her late afternoon work, a Harold Robbins novel.

Margaret was not alone. Fridays from three-thirty on at Rochester Circuits was a study of motion without accomplishment. The women's restroom door opened and closed like a baffle in the wind.

It took Barry a half hour to reach the Y. He spotted an empty space in front of the building, parked his car, and dashed up the flight of stairs, through the lobby and to the locker-room area. And to his long-awaited match with Dr. Tony Liccione, the Buffalo dentist and two-time state finalist.

The two had met several times in the past two years, each time West coming closer to beating the forty-year-old dentist. Liccione had been slipping. Age was stalking him. Reflexes no longer what they once were, he'd lost a step in speed. Barry felt the time was right to take him.

Reaching the entrance cage, Barry quickly scribbled his name and membership number on the daily tote sheet. He said to the little man behind the wire mesh, "What'dya say, Crackers?"

"Can't complain. Nobody in the fucking place listens, anyway. Hear you're playing Liccione." Crackers had been so dubbed because of the ever-present box of treats on his desk.

"News travels fast."

"I type the goddamned reservation list. Give 'em hell, kid." Crackers had the tone and look of permanent irritation. When Crackers had started calling West by his name the year before, Barry was sure he had arrived.

"Thanks." Barry timed his walk to Crackers's pushing of the button that electronically released the door. It was a security measure that kept the fags, winos, and petty thieves from wandering into the locker room.

The equipment room was a cavernous alcove with floor-to-ceiling racks holding wire baskets. It reeked of sweat and athletic humidity. To West it was a rose garden in bloom.

Carrying his basket of equipment to an empty locker, he began his transformation from accountant to athlete. Under the work-a-day uniform were the long, hard legs of a long-distance runner. West had wide shoulders, the tendons and muscles resembling sections of cable. He had the flat stomach of a lightweight fighter.

After tightly lacing his gym shoes, Barry walked through the locker room, carrying his sweat-stained handball gloves in one hand, and bouncing the hard, black ball on the concrete floor with the other. His presence had been completely altered to that of a strong and self-assured-looking competitor; even his horn-rimmed glasses had been traded in for contact lenses.

West was on his way to participate in a sport that offered him physical, emotional, and spiritual vacation from his job. It was a holiday he insisted on taking at least four times a week. Handball was a rush, an upper, for Barry, one from which he went through withdrawal symptoms of irritability, listlessness, and other mood changes if he didn't play regularly.

Excitement energized and renewed him as he jogged up the three levels of iron stairs to the courts.

Chapter Four

THE MEETING

Coldiron had been leaning, both elbows on the bar and head bent slightly over an empty double-shot whiskey glass, for a half hour.

"Fix me up with another double Green," he ordered.

The white-haired, grog-blossom-faced bartender moved toward him. Service was good. Only two other patrons and an "I Love Lucy" rerun on TV competed with Tate for the bartender's attention. At 3:30 Friday afternoon, it was still too early for office workers to be sipping before-dinner drinks.

As the barkeep plucked the bottle of Green from the rack, Coldiron reached into his pocket. He pulled out the lone dollar.

"On second thought, make it a draft," he said quickly, in time for the bartender to switch gears, replace the bottle of Green, and run beer into a tall glass. Coldiron almost laughed at the fix he was in. If it had been someone else, he might have.

Stuck in Rochester for a week, he had been unable to raise a dime on the phone. Room rent due, service station owner giving him heat about the repair charges on his car, Tate was now reduced to drinking draft, which was, in his opinion, one step above chilled urine.

If it wasn't for his daily workouts on the courts, three hours a day practicing, warming up, expelling his mounting frustration at being stranded, Coldiron was certain he would've gone bonkers. Soberly.

As it was, sitting in the bar, listening to Desi Arnaz jabber broken Cuban, nursing the draft, Coldiron was convinced the world had squatted and dumped on him. Fresh out of moves, he knocked back the beer, waved to the barkeep, and moved from the dimly lit joint like he was walking on glass. The frigid, damp weather and lack of Green were showing on his legs. He was certain his fragile bones were turning to powder with each step.

Tate tugged his watch cap down over his ears and closed his coat tight. He shuffled into a dusk that promised more snow. The white stuff had fallen every day he had been in town. The sun had not shown itself once. Someone at the Y had commented to him, "Weather's so lousy here, it keeps out the riffraff."

"I qualify. Wish the fuck it would've kept me out," Tate had retorted. "Goddamned cars've got to wear flags on their aerials, so you can spot 'em over the snowbanks."

Back at the Y, Coldiron made his way to the rear of the building. He caught the elevator to the one place where he hoped he might figure something out. Reaching the cage room, the sweet-sour aroma of stale gym clothes hit him. The humid warmth of the showers and steam rooms wiped at his face. His spirit was nudged up a notch.

Crackers was at the desk. The attendant was reading an *Argosy* magazine, continually reaching blindly into a box of gingersnaps.

Coldiron asked, "Any decent matches this afternoon? Like to see some 'ball."

The cage man looked at the quiet stranger. It was the cripple who had been around the club for about a week. Crackers liked the guy. He preferred people who kept to themselves. Coldiron had done that, signing up for courts at odd hours, like ten in the morning, eleven at night, when the place was deserted. And Tate had always been respectfully pleasant to the little guy.

"There's a good one at six." He turned the reservation sheet toward Tate. "West is playing Liccione on Court Two."

"That any good?"

"West is tops in town. Liccione ranks as one of the best in the state. Should be a tight one."

"Might as well," Tate said. "My broker's office is closed for the weekend." He signed the sheet and waited for the door to buzz open. He'd take the elevator to the gallery level and watch some handball. Maybe there, something would come to him.

West was already upstairs. He was waiting in the jailwalklike hallway behind the four courts. Noises like pistol volleys sounded through thick walls. The passage was gray, low, and long. The light bulbs seemed too weak to do what they were asked. It was a catacomb of sweat and subdued excitement.

Court Two would be free in ten minutes. Barry took the time to fall to the floor and reel off fifty pushups. The veins in his arms pumped up like garter snakes. Energy peaking, he paced quietly, without realizing, until he heard the determined-sounding footsteps chugging up the stairs. The cadence said short and powerful legs. Liccione had arrived.

At first sighting they sized each other up. It had been almost a year since they had last met. Lust for combat was quickly veiled with manners, macho handshakes, and backpats.

"Tony. How have you been?"

"Good. You?"

"Making it."

In their last meeting, in the Western New York Regionals, the dentist had bested Barry in the finals. But only after the younger man had extended Liccione to 32-30 in the final game. Ordinarily 21 points long, a game must be won by two or more points.

Liccione began swinging his stumplike arms in clockwise circles. "How much longer we got?" he asked.

"Their time's up." Barry peered through the quarter-inch-wide slit in the stockade door. Sportsmanship and the lights triggered by the opening and closing of the door dictated that oncoming players not interrupt a working point. Sudden darkness and a hard rubber ball traveling in excess of a hundred miles an hour might spell serious injury. Pausing until the point was finished, West rapped loudly on the door, then swung it open. The lights cut.

A greeting came from one of the guys leaving the dark court. "All yours. We have a date Monday at six, don't we?" It was Otto Rogers, an old college buddy and steady handball competitor of Barry's. The rangy, ex-pro football tight end had only beaten West once in the previous year. But Otto was a ferocious athlete who wouldn't quit. Their matches were always tightly fought.

"I'll be here," laughed Barry.

High-intensity lights, twenty feet from the floor and guarded by thick wire mesh, snapped on with the slamming of the door. The hardwood floor gleamed brightly from weekly waxings and the constant buffing of thousands of stops and starts of gym shoes.

Barry worked his hands into his red-backed, gray calfskin gloves that were stiff from constant soaking and drying. A pair lasted him about eight weeks. Or until the leather rotted and shredded from moisture and concussion.

He pulled the straps across the backs of his wrists as tight as he could stand it. The closer glove and hand were to being one, the greater control he had over his shots.

Both men were outfitted in white, all the way to their high-topped gym shoes. White allowed maximum sighting of the ball. It was a courtesy thing in private matches. Tournaments required it.

They began the warming-up ritual. Neither hit his ball, only tossed it repeatedly against the front wall easily; first overhand, then sidearm, and finally underhand. With each throw each man stretched his arms as far back as possible. Spasmodic or pulled muscles, even torn shoulder ligaments, resulted from improper warming up. Wordlessness hung in the air. Droning of exhaust fans and slapping of rubber against wood was all that was heard. These were men at work.

Fifteen feet above the players, in the gallery's shadowed seclusion, a lone man watched with unseeing eyes. The activity in Coldiron's head was far more furious than that below him. Thoughts zipped through his mind like blind birds flying into closed windows.

Missing the Cleveland tourney had left him no prospects for handball money until the Providence Invitational, two weeks and four hundred bucks away, which was how much it would take to bail his car out, pay the room bill, and cover expenses to Rhode Island. Even if he wanted to stiff the Y and donate his car to the service station, he didn't have bus fare to skip town. He was stuck.

Head propped in his hands, Coldiron pondered his next move. It had to come fast. That morning, Potato Nose had told him to come up with the room money by tomorrow or they'd move his stuff into the street and change the lock on his door. Camping out in January in Rochester was not Tate's idea of fun. So there he sat, while his mind attacked him for being a failure and a fool. He tried to concentrate on the two players.

The shorter of the two looked powerful. He was so hairy, he appeared to be wearing a full-length sweater under his gym outfit. The muscles in his limbs had little definition, running together like sections of salami. Bald to the temples, Liccione's head resembled a fur-lined ashtray, from Coldiron's vantage point.

The two began hitting shots, at first easy ones off the front wall, then the back wall, with both men placing the ball low to the floor. Low shots were the most difficult to return. When they struck the crotch of the floor and front wall simultaneously, the ball was killed and the volley ended.

Liccione drove a few against the ceiling, the ball glancing off the front wall and floor, so it bounded high and came down parallel to the back wall. It was a pass shot; an excellent move to slow down a game. If the ceiling shot dropped close enough to the back wall, an opponent had no room to position himself for a return. Even if a weak shot was managed, Liccione would be camped against the front wall for an easy kill. He owned the ceiling shot.

"Ready?" asked Barry.

"In a second." The dentist moved to the sidewall. He began beating his hands against the concrete to bring the blood to the surface of his palms and fingers. Some players ran scalding water over their hands before a match to get them to swell slightly. Barry was slapping his together, at first slowly and softly, increasing in velocity and intensity as if he were giving a rousing ovation at a Broadway hit. Cold hands meant bone bruises, which could spell the loss of a match and a long layoff.

"Ready," announced Liccione.

Barry tossed his ball to the dentist, who held it in one hand, with his own ball in the other at eye level. He dropped them to determine which one bounced best.

"Yours," Liccione called, indicating West's ball had more life. The dentist placed his in the back corner, safely out of play.

"Throw for serve?" Liccione asked.

Barry nodded. They moved to the back wall to decide the right to important first service. And the opportunity to run up a string of points before the other man broke a sweat.

"Yeh. Go for it," Barry answered.

Nearly parallel to the floor, Liccione fired the ball, hitting the front wall two inches from the floor. Barry followed. His toss struck the wall and floor simultaneously. A perfect throw.

"*Oooooweeee.* The kid's hot today. Your serve."

Barry walked to the service area, a rectangle five feet wide, bounded by two red lines, halfway between front and back walls. Liccione crouched near the rear wall and waited for West's initial offering.

The unnoticed figure in the gallery stirred with growing interest.

Barry bent into the ball, driving it against the front wall like it had been shot from a gun. The black blur skidded low along the sidewall, striking the back wall to Liccione's left. The dentist never made a move.

"Long," Tony called. It was no good. To be playable a serve had to strike the floor before hitting the back wall. Nor could it hit more than two walls before striking the floor, nor first make contact with the ceiling or sidewall and be a legal serve.

Tony readied for the next one. A second fault turned over the service.

West leaned into it and drove a beauty off the front wall that slipped along the sidewall, with just enough English so that it died in the back corner. Liccione tried to dig it out, but his return shot never reached the front wall. A point for West.

Liccione's experience and court savvy forced his younger opponent into repeated mistakes. He kept West hemmed in against the back wall with volleys of low and hard alley passes. These were shots that hugged the sidewall and made an opponent retreat to the rear of the court. Barry

30

was not allowed near the front wall during the first game.

The dentist's mistake was trying to run with the better-conditioned West. Though managing to stay with the kid in the initial game, fatigue found his legs in the second. Barry's shots began falling just out of his reach.

Liccione valiantly attempted to slow the game with ceiling shots and fisters; closed-handed drives that sent the ball bouncing crazily around the court. But West kept coming; he wouldn't let up on him; he made the older man chase every shot. The kid smelled blood.

Coldiron was still wracking his brain for a way out, paying the match only token interest. *Shit*, he thought, *a hundred would get me out of this burg. They can have the fucking car. I'll take the train to Providence, win some coin, and buy another short. Trouble is, where do I get the yard?*" Of the close-to-three-dozen alternatives he had come up with in the past fifteen minutes, that one seemed the most logical.

Then, as if Tate's eyes constricted into focus, he noticed something he had overlooked in his obsession with his plight. Right in front of him was his solution. Here was this kid, dressed to the teeth, kicking the shit out of a guy that looked like an escapee from a circus. The hot dog kid's fancy shoes, outfit, and calfskin gloves were worth more than $100 alone. He was a fat fish rolling right at Coldiron's aching feet.

At the match's conclusion, Liccione's face

was the color of margarine. He paced the floor in a hot walk, searching his lungs for air. Barry's superior endurance and youth had paid off. After splitting the first two games, he had taken the third and match-deciding tilt. He had beaten Tony Liccione for the first time ever.

His glove was dark with sweat when he offered his hand to Liccione.

"Good match."

"You too, Barry."

"I think I'm gonna hang around for a few minutes and work on some things," West announced.

"Doesn't look to me like you need to. Give me a chance to get back at you?"

"Anytime. I was lucky." Barry held down his elation.

"I'll call you the next time I'm in town." Liccione pulled open the door and left.

Barry waited until he was sure the dentist was out of earshot, then he let loose. "*Awwwright!*" One of the state's best handballers had had to ask him for a rematch.

He then turned to working on his lefthanded shot. A natural righthander, Barry's southpaw delivery had no sting to it. Something the guy in the gallery had noted with interest.

"A good player would've done in that old bald-headed fart without breaking a sweat. He runs like he's got one foot nailed to the floor."

Barry backed slowly into the center court area. He looked around. Seeing no one, he figured it must've been the groaning of the big fans. Sometimes they sounded like distant voices. He returned to his task.

"If you had any shots, you might make a decent bush league player."

Barry wheeled around. This time there was no mistaking it. He had heard a voice. There was someone in the gallery. He stared in irritated disbelief as a man stepped from the shadows and propped one foot on the gallery rail.

Coldiron continued, his voice ricocheting off the court's quiet, "If they hung you for being a handball player, you'd die an innocent man. *Hee hee.*"

Chapter Five

THE SCAM

"If I had this court reserved for another hour, old man, I'd be happy to hand you your ass."

"Well, I'll be damned. *Hee hee.*" Coldiron's laughter drifted down to the court to be sucked up by the fans like smoke. "Isn't that a coincidence? I happen to have this very court reserved for the next hour. Might I interest you in a little stakes match?"

"My pleasure, friend."

"How much you willing to put on your own nose, kid?"

"Be easy on yourself, pop."

"How's twenty-five bucks a game and fifty for the match sound?"

"Get your gear. You're on." Barry smiled at the guy. The extra cash would buy a nice night out with Susan.

"I'm on my way." Coldiron disappeared back into the shadows.

It took Tate just ten minutes to get to his room and shake out his equipment. There was a glint in those gray eyes as he donned his gym clothes. A hiss sounded when he peeled back the lid of a new can of balls, his last. It was the can he had been saving for his next tournament.

Next he ran his bare hands under water as hot as he could stand. His words came out as a croaky melody. "This guy is gonna be a piece of cake. A-a-a-ngel food."

Coldiron knew he was practically on that bus for Providence. He'd hooked a fish that was worth an easy hundred. He felt that maybe his luck had finally turned around.

West waited in the hallway, still wringing wet. Even his gym shoes and socks were discolored and soggy. He had been known to drop as many as ten pounds in a ninety-minute match, so demanding was the game he loved. And so ferociously he played it.

When he saw Coldiron make the turn into the hall and begin limping toward him, he almost laughed out loud. He was that certain he was the victim of a cruel joke arranged by a friend. Someone had sent a cripple to play him. The guy was probably a wino the practical joker had plucked out of the Y waiting room, some old drunk who had come in out of the cold they'd offered a couple of bucks to harass West. Or maybe his challenger was just plain crazy. All kinds of fruits wandered into the Y. Barry decided to carry the thing through and see. He had nothing better to do.

Coldiron's blue gym shorts and matching faded shirt both advertised the Boston YMCA. His left leg, the one in which the recurring

35

staph infection had necessitated six additional operations since New Orleans, was shrunken and badly bowed. Coldiron shuffled like he was suffering from chronic crotch rash. His wire-like hair had been slicked back with water, making his cheekbones appear to jut beyond his nose.

"You sure you want to go through with this?" West asked. He tried hiding his smile by covering his mouth with his hand.

"You got it."

West watched the old man warm up, while continually keeping an eye on the gallery for whomever arranged the debacle. He just knew it had to be a gag.

Coldiron did the usual. He took some short shots against the front wall, picked a few easy ones off the back wall, and lobbed a couple of ceiling shots to loosen his shoulders. He showed West nothing during the warm-up.

"You're actually serious, aren't you?" West poked.

"Ready anytime you are," Coldiron answered.

"Let's see your ball," the kid said. Tate bounced him an easy one. West picked it out of midair and drove a vicious shot against the front wall. It came away right on the floor. It was a perfect kill.

"Nice shot, hot dog."

"Thanks. Looks like your ball is new. Let's use it."

"Okay. Now let's see what you do for money."

"Want to throw for serve?"

"You take it. You'll need it. How many games you got left?"

"About one more than you do, old man," Barry laughed.

"Twenty-five and fifty. Right?"

"You know it. Hope the Senior Citizens Association doesn't find out about this."

"Me, too."

"You got a name, old man?"

"Coldiron."

"Mine's Barry."

Tate nodded and moved to the back wall. He got set for West's initial offering.

The younger man stepped into the serving zone, checked how his opponent was lined up, and attempted to put out of his mind that he was facing a cripple. On the off chance the match was for real, West decided to concentrate and get the thing over with quickly. He could use the practice, anyway. Besides, he hadn't issued the challenge. The goofy old guy had. He'd let it be Coldiron's problem.

He bent into his first one, laying the ball into the back left corner. It was an excellent serve—low and dying where the walls and floor met. He crouched and watched the front wall for Coldiron's return. His first serve went unanswered.

"One-zip," West announced. The ball rolled

back to him. He had learned something right off. The old guy had no left. He'd found the jugular vein early; it was a place he planned to go whenever he needed a run of points.

What he hadn't seen was that Coldiron had merely moved to the ball, checked that Barry was watching the front wall, and let the serve die in the corner. The old fox's plan was to make it close; he wanted to keep the kid sucking. Coldiron didn't want to scare his fish off until the bait was taken and the hook was set. He was going to play this kid for all he could get.

Barry eyed him, acknowledged the older man was in position, and readied for his next serve. It came to Coldiron's right; another low and hard one. This time West turned to watch. It was a careless move, one that took him out of position for a return. He would lose a split second to turn back to the front wall. Handball was a game in which an instant meant the difference between gaining or losing a point.

Or worse, by watching his opponent, he exposed his face to be hit by the return. Noses were broken, eyes cut, or eardrums burst because a player faced a shooting opponent. It was just that Barry was certain the old guy wouldn't touch his serve.

Coldiron reacted like a burglar. He dug the ball out of the corner with lightning-fast reflexes and drove it low against the front wall. *Thunk*. It was a perfectly executed killshot.

"Nice return," Barry acknowledged. In his walk to the back wall, he made the mental note that the old guy had a pretty fair righthanded shot.

Coldiron was up. He bounced the ball three times in front of him, using the time to see how West lined up. The kid was leaning to his left. He was telegraphing his weak portside.

Tate bent into his delivery. He executed a move so rapid Barry never saw it. Coldiron had twisted his wrist sharply upon making contact with the ball. The serve went to West's left; it wasn't particularly fast or difficult to handle. The younger man had the time and room for an easy kill. He would've, if the ball hadn't made a crazy right turn as it came off the floor. The ball headed to the sidewall, rather than continuing in its natural flight toward the back wall. West caught the hard rubber on the tip of his middlefinger, sending a sharp pain up his arm. The ball dribbled weakly along the floor.

"One apiece," Coldiron said.

West glared at the old man, took a deep breath, and silently scolded himself for not paying attention. He crouched low, locked his jaw, and waited. Coldiron gave him the next one in the exact same spot as the first serve. West moved carefully to the ball, measuring the spin and leaving himself plenty of time to judge the slice. Only there was no slice, no bounce, no nothing. The ball skidded dead like the server had a string attached. West almost threw his

39

arm into the gallery trying to change gears in midswing. He missed by six inches.

"Two-one."

Coldiron showed him three more. Barry never even got one of them to the front wall. Then Tate took a dive. He gave the kid an easy one off the back wall to kill. West was up, trailing 1-5.

Barry, remembering well Coldiron's right-handed kill, drove one into the lefthand corner. He got set and focused on the front wall. He heard Coldiron curse. The ball dribbled back to West's feet.

"Five-two," West said. The kid clenched a half smile. He'd lay everything in the left corner. The old guy was a one-armed bandit, or so Barry thought, watching Coldiron massage his left shoulder after the miss. Plenty of players had the good serve and strong righthanded shot. Only the great ones could kill it with either hand. He vowed he'd have Tate looking like a pretzel by the end of their match.

Coldiron won the first game, 21-18. The score would've been a lot worse if he hadn't intentionally blown a number of shots. He was being careful not to scare the kid off. It was the money, not the reputation the old guy was after. He won the $25. That's all he cared about.

Coldiron also captured the second game, 21-17. He had played around with the kid, he had teased Barry by laying the ball just out of his reach, but close enough so the kid tried for everything. Coldiron had had West running around the court like a crazy man, while giving him nothing easy. The kid had had to work for every point he got. Even when Coldiron had intentionally missed a shot, he had made it look as if he was straining, like it had been an authentic miscue.

By the end of the second game, West was breathing fire. Coldiron had hardly broken a lather. He was a master craftsman; he made every one of his moves count. To show the kid how fresh he was, he practiced some shots while West took a five-minute water break between games.

"I only got one more game left," West said as he dragged back on the court. He looked embarrassed. His shirt was soaked all the way through. It clung to his skin.

Since it was to be the last game, Coldiron finished it fast. He moved around the court with the agility and deftness of a high-rise steelworker. The ball moved as if he controlled it electronically; it landed wherever the Indian-Jew wanted it to. He threw everything at the kid in that final game; he showed West variations of slicers, pass shots, fisters, and ceiling shots the kid had never seen before. Barry spun like a blender and ran until his legs shivered with exhaustion. At the end, all color was gone from the younger man's face. The final tally was 21-1.

Coldiron shuffled over to the kid, stuck out his hand, and said, "Nice match."

West ignored him. He slammed out of the court and walked down the stairs to the locker room in angered and shocked silence. Coldiron hopped two steps behind. The kid owed him a yard and a quarter.

Barry slammed open his locker. "I got seventy-five dollars in cash. Will you take a check for the rest?"

"Is it a local check? You got identification?" Coldiron couldn't resist.

"What?" The kid was hot.

"Just kidding. Sure, I'll take a check. It'll spend."

Barry scribbled on the check and thrust it, along with the greenbacks, to Coldiron. Tate neatly tucked the money into the front of his jockstrap.

"You know, kid, you're not half bad. With a little coaching you might even be good."

"What the fuck are you talking about?" West was torn between collapsing and belting the guy in the mouth. One thing was for sure. He wanted out of there. He wished to avoid having anyone he knew finding out he had been humiliated by a jakey-legged old wino.

"Want to go for a drink and talk about it?"

Barry measured him. "Will you just fucking leave me alone?" He snatched off his wet outfit and stalked into the shower.

Afterward, Barry dressed and threw his overcoat over his shoulder. He walked by Crackers, who was still reading and eating, and down the stairs to the lobby. His hair was still wet, the color was seeping back into his face, and there was demoralization in his heart.

Back in his suit and horn-rimmed glasses, West looked less like the lean and perspiring gladiator who had just been given a lesson in handball. He pushed into a phone booth with a thud, dropped a dime into the slot, and dialed the number with such force his phone rang slightly with each digit.

"How much longer you gonna be there?"

Susan's voice licked at his ear. "Late. We're still a long way from going to press."

"Well, shit. Okay. I'll call you in the morning."

"What's wrong?"

"Nothing much. Just wanted to see you, that's all."

"Me, too. But I have to take care of business."

"I know. Catch you tomorrow. I'm going to get shit-faced drunk."

"Little radical, aren't you? We still going to the concert tomorrow night?"

"Yeh."

"Look, Barry, I don't want to mind read. And I don't have the time right now to play guessing games. You sound down. Are you?"

"Just a little depressed. I'd have to cheer up

to kill myself." He found himself laughing at his own comment.

"I know I'm terrific, but a canceled date with me can't be that serious."

"Naw. There's always self-abuse."

"That's true. Do I get to watch?" Now she was laughing. "Okay, out with it. What's going on?"

"Other than just being handed my ass by an old wino cripple, nothing."

"You mean Liccione?"

"No, I beat him. It was some guy I played after Liccione. No big thing." He was careful not to mention the money. Enough was enough.

"I thought Liccione was your big quarry. You can't beat everybody, Barry. Don't take it so seriously."

"You're right, babe. Look, I'll talk to you tomorrow. I'm dying in this phone booth. Thanks for listening." He sounded more placated than he was. Instead of hanging the phone up, he threw it at the cradle.

Barry pushed out of the glass box and began buttoning his coat when he noticed Coldiron leaning against the main desk, jawing at the room clerk. The kid had been feeling bad for yelling at Coldiron in the locker room after their match. He decided to apologize.

Coldiron was handing over two twenties and a ten to the clerk, and saying, "Here's what I owe you. My estate check arrived today."

The clerk was counting out his eight-dollars'

change when Coldiron spotted the approaching West. He quickly snatched the bills from the surprised clerk. Gambling, on a handball court or anywhere, was against the law in New York State. Tate didn't wish to chance the kid mentioning the match in front of the clerk. Coldiron was the stranger in town. Not the kid. The authorities had a way of detaining out-of-towners who hustled a local citizen.

"I trust you," Tate said and pocketed the bills.

"Be leaving us, Mr. Coldiron?"

"In a day or so," he answered to the day clerk. He started his shuffle toward the elevator.

"Hey. Wait a minute," came from behind him. Tate pretended not to hear, or that the voice was not calling him. He continued in his rapid two-step, trying to get out of the clerk's earshot.

"I want to talk to you," West called.

Tate turned, saw the clerk was paying attention to other matters, and waited for West.

"You still want to have that drink? My date for the night fell through."

"Been rough all the way around for you today, huh, kid?"

"How about that drink?"

"Sure, kid. Where to?"

"The Gates Bar is around the corner."

"I know it well. Lead the way."

Chapter Six

THE PLAN

The Gates was an historic mahogany and gilded-mirrored men's watering hole that had been the site of business and political deals for over a century. Its long bar was nearly always two deep with drinkers anytime between 6:00 P.M. and 3:00 A.M. Situated across the street from City Hall, three blocks from the Penn-Central Railroad marshaling yards, and surrounded by adult-movie theaters and porno shops, its clientele was mixed. The Monroe County District Attorney might be seen knocking back a drink next to an itinerant construction worker wanted for nonsupport in the next county. Or a millionaire real estate developer who owned one of the nearby office buildings could be buying a drink for a railroad fireman who had been a childhood friend.

The men's taproom featured a fifty-foot, belly-high bar. The white-and-black, ceramic-tile floor and the styled metal ceiling gave the place the acoustic rating of a cave. The room was loud and smoky. Johnny Antonelli, the city's favorite athletic son of the '50s, was pictured in his billowy Boston Braves uniform over the bar. Photos of visiting dignitaries and other local successes hung in less-revered locations along the wall.

There were no barstools at the Gates. Women needed stools to drink; men planted their feet on the ceramic tile floor and leaned their bellies against the brass bar railing. Joey Petroff was on duty behind the south end of the bar. Petroff, in his late fifties, was one of the area's better handball players. He had slicked-down straight black hair, a widow's peak wide as a shark's tooth, and a sarcastic tongue. He waved to West as the kid and Coldiron assumed the position at his station.

"Heard Liccione was easy today."

"No secrets in this town," West answered.

"The good dentist stopped by. What took you so long?"

"Played another match."

"Oh, yeh? Against who?"

"Meet him. Name's . . . what's your name again?"

"Coldiron."

"Mine's Petroff. What'll it be?"

"Draft of Utica Club for me. What about you, Coldiron?"

"Double of Jack Daniel's Green. Gimme a draft to clear the way."

"You live around here?" Petroff asked.

"No. Just passing through. As soon as I can."

"Play much four wall?" Petroff quizzed him,

as though he might be trying a drifting gun-fighter.

"Enough."

"Where do you live?"

"You might say my address is General Delivery, U.S.A. I sort of get around."

"How bad you beat him, kid?" The bartender had a big chest, wide shoulders, and the short, stumpy legs of a dwarf. The guy was all torso.

"The other way around. He put me away." West wished the subject hadn't come up.

"No shit. You gonna be around tomorrow, Coldiron? I'd like to see what you got."

"How much you got to lose?"

"Oh. Lookin' for a *pésce*, eh? He get into your wallet, Barry?"

"Never mind." West showed his irritation. "Just get us our drinks, huh, Joey?"

When the short man moved away, the wooden pallets on the floor behind the bar made a clapping sound.

Coldiron checked out the place. It was packed with business suits with enough booze in them so home wasn't where they wanted to be. The smell was old beer and stale cigarettes and cigars. Tate sucked in a big chestful and smiled. With a pocketful of money and another fish nibbling at the bait, things were obviously picking up. West's words cut through his thoughts.

"Okay, what's your secret? You put away

48

shots I've never seen anyone make. You some kind of world's champion I've never heard about?" The younger man slid his hands slowly up and down the perspiring glass of beer as he talked. They still stung from three straight hours of handball.

"If you mean like Jacobs or Haber, no. They're hot dogs. They beat out-of-shape businessmen all year for a chance to play each other for the National Handball Association title."

"Sounds like you got a hard-on for the NHA."

"The NHA is a bunch of ham-'n'-egg players or businessmen who get it up walking around the locker room with Haber or Jacobs. They like to see their names in the papers.

"Listen, kid, the best players in this country don't play in those faggy tournaments. You never hear about them."

"What's your trip, then?"

"You writing a book or something? If so, leave me out and make it a mystery."

"Just curious. Don't get so hot."

"If you gotta know, I hit the smaller tournaments. I also play stakes matches. Mostly small-time bets against old friends or an occasional doctor or lawyer who needs to donate to my retirement fund."

"You can add accountants to that list."

"That what you do?"

"Yeh."

"You sorta look like a book fruit."

"A book fruit who could slap you across that ugly puss with a barstool," Barry laughed.

" 'Cept you'd have to go down the street to get one. Calm down, kid. I was just kidding. Ready for a refill?"

"Jesus, you inhale the last one?"

"Just order another round. We have some things to talk about."

Barry looked for Petroff. The bartender was out of normal voice range.

"You like your job?"

"It's a job. Pays for my losses on the courts." Barry smiled and toasted Coldiron, then saw Petroff was nearby.

"Do it again, Joey." Petroff *kerplunked* into action.

With his juice-sized glass refilled with Green, Coldiron continued, "You were a fool to play me. You know that, don't you?"

"What are you talking about? When you first walked up the stairs, I felt guilty about taking your money."

"Listen to him, willya? Boy wonder with the magnum mouth and pellet-gun ass. Right now we both got our hand in our pocket. I got a fistful of money, your money, and you're choking your gopher. But you were feeling guilty. *Hee hee*."

Barry turned to his glass of beer.

"Look, kid, I may be cuttin' myself out of a steady meal ticket. I could hustle you every day of the week. But even I got ethics." He took a deep drag from his small, black cigar.

"Let me give you some information. Never accept a challenge from someone you've never seen play. Especially after burning yourself out in a previous match."

"What are you talking about? I was still fresh. I've played three matches in a row before."

"Maybe against the likes of the chimp you played before me. Or Dracula here, standing in the hole behind the bar. Neither of them could grab their ass with either hand.

"Listen, kid, you even let me on the court in blues. I must've shaded ten points from you, alone."

The younger man cringed. In his pitying the cripple, he had overlooked the fact that Coldiron had worn dark clothes.

If nothing that had gone before had impressed West, what followed truly did—even more than the trouncing that Coldiron had given him on the court. The Indian-Jew calmly ground his cigar out in the palm of his own hand. It was a paw that was so callused from millions of games of handball, Coldiron didn't even flinch when he did it. He absent-mindedly wiped the smudge on his pants and finished his drink.

Barry stared. Petroff had also been watching. They both had their mouths hanging open.

"Let's have another," Coldiron ordered. Petroff jumped like a trained dog.

"You sure drink a lot," West commented. He was still watching Coldiron's left hand, convinced the older man would scream any second.

"'I'd rather be a liver than have one, kid." Tate then threw back the freshly filled glass of bourbon, almost before Petroff had pulled the silver pour-spout from his glass. Coldiron tapped the bar lightly with the bottom of his glass for another.

"Look, kid, you got talent. Nothing spectacular, but knock the rough edges off, teach you a few things, and you might win a few bucks at the game."

"What do you have in mind?" West decided to play along. At least the guy was unusual and entertaining.

"I train you, work you like a mule until you're ready. Then we go on the road."

"How long does the training take?"

"At least a couple of months. Until I say you're ready."

"Could I make a living playing handball?"

"You kidding? Do you realize how many big, rich, and exclusive clubs there are out there? Just full of ham-'n'-egger fourwallers anxious to be parted with some of their money?"

"You're serious."

"Bet your ass. Handball scamming is a good life. We'd stay in the plushest clubs you've ever seen, so fine someone makes your bed when you get up in the night to piss.

"We'd eat in the best restaurants—creole places in New Orleans, fish grottoes in San Francisco, steak houses in Kansas City, lobster places in Boston. And there'd be all the booze you can drink. Nothing is too good. You'd have more walking-around money in your pocket than you got in the bank right now." Coldiron took a pull from his drink.

"I'm listening," West prodded.

"Then there's the broads. Do you have any idea how them ladies cream their silkies watching a muscular and handsome guy like you break a sweat and an opponent's back? Shit, you'd get so much tail, you'd need a splint for your dick."

"And you?" West's eyes were beginning to glaze from the beer and the excitement of it all. "What do you get out of all this? What's your stake in coaching me?"

"Fifty percent of what you win."

"How much is that? The square root of shit is still shit."

"Cute. Give you guys an education and you try to beat the piss out of everybody with it. With my training and coaching, we could clear fifty thousand each the first year. Easy. That is, if you did exactly what I told you. The bread is there; the living is good. But unless you learn the game, I mean really learn the game, you'd get your skinny ass kicked. Twenty-five years ago, I had my way on the slats. I made some big bucks."

"How'd you get hurt?"

"Auto accident in New Orleans." Coldiron hit his drink again. "Well, kid, what do you think?"

West laughed. "Right, Coldiron. I quit my job, leave everything for a trip around the country with a guy I don't know from a bag of assholes."

"If Columbus had been blessed with your courage, he'd still be cuffing his meat in Spain. The chance-takers make the bread, kid. The rest eat dirt. Shit, the way I look at it, you can play with your books anytime. There will always be a need for accountants, as long as everything is so fucking complicated."

"Maybe I can do your taxes for you sometime."

"Taxes? You kidding? I haven't filed one of those dumb forms in twenty years."

"You mean you haven't paid income taxes in that long?"

"Naw. They sent me one of those brown envelopes once, and I wrote *deceased* on it. They haven't bothered me since."

Barry almost choked on his beer.

"Look, kid, here's my number. Call me if you change your mind." Tate scribbled on a cocktail napkin. So large was his hand, the pencil looked like it was stuck in a good-sized rock when he wrote.

"This is the number of the Y."

"I don't waste money on fancy frills." He finished his drink, saluted the kid, and shuffled away from the bar. "Good night, kid. I'll be in town for a couple more days."

West watched Coldiron move across the tile floor. "Guy can really talk, can't he?" he said to Petroff.

"He can really drink, too. Nineteen dollars and ninety-five cents worth, to be exact."

Barry slapped his forehead and said, "That cheap son of a bitch." He dug out a credit card and slapped it hard on the bar.

"No cash tonight?" Petroff asked.

"The bastard beat me out of all that on the court."

West went straight home. Eight hours at Rochester Circuits, two rugged handball matches, and nine beers had done him in. He would see Susan the following night. They had tickets to Neil Diamond at the War Memorial and plans for dinner before.

He climbed wearily into bed, only to find he couldn't sleep. Coldiron's offer had excited him; his blood was rushing like crazy. In the darkness, the stranger's wild talk ran through Barry's mind like a passing train. However ludicrous, the plan offered him an exit from his secure semideath at Rochester Circuits; it was a mediocre flatness he had come to dislike more and more.

But how about Susan? some inner voice asked.

So what? another one challenged. *She won't marry you, anyway. What do you have to lose?*

Just your job, asshole, the first voice answered. *For sure she'd marry you if you couldn't even pay your rent. She'd love driving you to the unemployment office every two weeks.*

West ended the mental conversation with a shake of his head. "Christ, I could have a group portrait taken of myself."

He walked into the living room of his one-bedroom apartment, pausing to make imaginary handball shots. Out of boredom, he flipped on the TV, only to punch it back off when a fifteen-year-old Elvis Presley movie came into focus. He went back into the bedroom and got dressed.

Barry decided to take a walk to quiet his mind—anything to dim the pictures of him humiliating some opponent in front of a full gallery, while Coldiron collected big money and the phone numbers of Barry's gorgeous female admirers.

"Fuck. I don't need a TV. I've got a movie of my own," he said and walked out in the cold night. A half block from his apartment building, he wished he'd stayed indoors. The temperature clawed toward zero and the wind off Lake Ontario shoved him around the sidewalk.

Even in the dark, his neighborhood, a one-time elegant section of old Rochester, looked rundown and dirty. Old money and civic pride had somehow kept the transitional area from totally crumbling. Barry walked into the wind until it hurt his face. Then he went back.

The following evening at the Villa Italian restaurant, Susan noticed Barry's preoccupation immediately. Her attempts at conversation ended in one-word replies, then silence. She looked stunning in a floor-length, charcoal brown jersey dress that showed her ample breasts and erect nipples. Even that didn't rescue Barry from his thoughts. She chose to let his inattention slide.

At the concert, amid 12,000 Neil Diamond fans standing and clapping to the entertainer's burningly emotional performance, Barry was in another world. Several times Susan squeezed the inside of his thigh, way up top, always an attention-getter. She smiled to show radiant teeth. Her hair looked even richer and glossier in the dull light. But Barry was insulated from all of it, even passion. His return smile was weak.

She waited to confront him until they returned to her apartment. "Are you on something? You've been spaced out for five hours."

"No, nothing. Really." Something prevented him from telling her. As if keeping the secret made his fantasy more delicious, or that it might've sounded more ridiculous if exposed to reality.

"Bullshit. Either tell me, or quit acting like a

zombie. I'm beginning to feel like a necrophil-iac."

He gave her a big smile. "Okay, here it is. I played handball with an old-time hustler named Coldiron last night. The one I told you kicked my butt."

"Yeah? The match you were going to commit suicide over?"

"The same one. Well, he made me an offer." He ran it down to her, omitting the part about the women twelve inches on center.

"You mean you'd quit Rochester Circuits?" She was surprised. That was the real showstopper. "Wow. The most impulsive thing I've ever known you to do is go to a movie during the week. Or sleep without your pajamas on."

"Funny. Ha ha. You might like to know that I am seriously thinking about doing it." There was daring in his voice and stubbornness in his chin.

"Sounds exciting. Going to?"

"Don't know yet. What about us?"

"What *about* us? I'll still be here. So will Rochester Circuits."

"But I hardly know the guy. He could be a fraud."

"So what? Wouldn't hurt to look into it."

"I'll see." He backed off. She had called his hand. As usual.

"Ah. You're too cautious. You look at the negative side of everything. If Christ walked across Canandaigua Lake, you'd be the first to notice he had dirty feet." She was teasing him, trying to draw out his adventurous side. It was the thing Susan liked the most, but daring was the quality Barry showed her the least of.

He reddened. "What's that supposed to mean? Just because I'm responsible doesn't mean I'm afraid."

"Look, Barry. You're the dearest person I know. I love you. But you're too set and conservative. Responsibility is one thing. Walking death is another."

"Wait a minute. What's all this? I didn't tell you about Coldiron's offer so you could attack me over it."

"I'm not attacking you. Can't you see that? It's just that you're too locked in. I want to see you loosen up. Become less pink and unused."

He came off the sofa, slowly and deliberately, as if he was being squeezed out of himself. "Pink and unused? Bullshit. I can do anything I want. You're a lot of help. It sounds like you think I'm some kind of sniveling fool."

"No, I don't. I love you. I just want to see you live instead of exist. That's all."

Maybe things had been building up between them; or Barry's long hours at work, coupled with his lack of sleep the night before, had worn him down; possibly getting shellacked by Coldiron had started his fuse burning. But one thing was certain. Susan's nickings had set it off. Barry did something totally out of his character. He stormed out of her apartment, yelling and waving his arms, "I'll show you who's pink and unused."

He slammed the door so hard, the draperies shook on their traverse rods.

Susan sat stunned. She fished a cigarette from her purse, lit it, and let herself back on the couch. Her jaw loosened as she blew big smoke rings into the air. Then she smiled. Then she let out a deep, belly laugh.

"He actually got mad. Really pissed," she called into her empty apartment.

She loved it. Barry—conservative, starched Barry West—had actually hinted he might break his pattern of insisting life be ordered and guaranteed. She poured a glass of wine from the crystal decanter set on the carved, wooden Thai coffee table. She thought, *Maybe, just maybe, my boy is loosening up. Maybe Barry West will cut the chain.*

Susan turned off the lights. She sat, thinking into the darkness about the possibility of a new Barry hatched from his button-down cocoon of ledgers and cost projections. The idea thrilled her.

Across town, someone else was also hoping the plan would prove tantalizing enough to appeal to Barry's daring nature. Coldiron had decided to gamble. He'd give the kid a couple of days to think about it.

Tate had bought himself some time with his winnings. He had pocket money and a gallon of Green stashed in his suitcase. He had settled on a plan to deal with his car and the irate service station owner. He had told the guy that if he didn't come up with the $150 repair money in a week, he could keep the car and sell it.

Coldiron had a feeling about the big, blond accountant who could hit the black ball a ton.

Chapter Seven

THE BEGINNING

Coldiron went through all but ten dollars of his winnings in three days. He had concealed the sawbuck in his shoe. It was his fare to Providence.

The pressure began building on him again. Potato Nose on the desk was making the "lock-you-out-if-you-don't-pay-up" noises once more.

Even creaming West had worked against him. Word had gotten around. He couldn't buy a stakes match. The better players wanted on the court with him, all right, but only for the competition of it. Tate had devised a stock answer for that one: "I don't even choke my gopher for practice."

He was beginning to think he was soft in the head for waiting around Rochester. He hadn't heard a word from the kid, and for all he knew, West thought him to be a loony old drunk. But there was something that had kept him there; some feeling in his tired bones told him to hang around. The Providence tournament wasn't for another ten days, anyway. He had nowhere to go. And there was that feeling he had. Something told him it was to be his turn again.

Soon necessity would overshadow his intuition. If something didn't pop for Coldiron fast he would have to press his second plan of action into effect. That was jumping on a bus to Providence in the middle of the night.

Barry wasn't faring much better. His inner voices were having a field day. The accountant in him lectured about job security and career responsibility. That daring part of him, a force that was growing more powerful by the hour, implored him to step from the curb. It talked of the thrills and excitement that went with being a handball hustler; the joy of earning good money doing what he enjoyed best.

Nights he dreamed of matches with the great ones; he saw himself playing before big cheering crowds at the likes of the New York Athletic Club, Lakeshore Club in Chicago, and the Jonathan Club of Los Angeles—legendary places he had only read about that would be his private playgrounds. He envisioned beautiful girls by the dozen pushing at each other for a chance to get at the great Barry West. Coldiron was standing in the background with a grin on his face and their big winnings in his pocket. Susan begged him to marry her. They were dreams that matched his real-life fantasies.

Monday at work was a series of staff meetings. Barry's escape from the blue cloud of cigarette smoke and the bureaucratic babble were his mind movies. There were more scenes of rousing victories. He went in and out of his fantasies to realize how boring and suffocating the endless meetings were. He just wasn't up to taking part in the subtle corporate power plays and personality manipulations. Rochester Circuits may have had rights to Barry's body. Coldiron's proposal had totally captivated his thoughts.

West talked with Susan on the phone that evening. It was the first time they had spoken since Saturday night.

"Sorry about storming out the other night. Things had kind of built up."

"I understand. Sorry I was kind of rough on you."

"It's okay. Guess I needed to look at a few things."

"How'd it go at work today?"

"More of the same. Tomorrow's the big meeting on my proposal. My butt will be on the line. I'll be representing the entire accounting division."

"You'll do okay. You could do it standing on your head."

"Thanks. I'm still nervous about it. The heavies from marketing and corporate staff will be there."

"Look at it this way. The worst thing that could happen is you could get fired. Who knows, it might be the beginning of a pro handball career. Not many guys have alternatives like that."

"Yeh. Right. If that didn't work out, I could eat my gloves." He was laughing.

"The only thing you'd be losing by trying would be a gold watch. And about seven tons of boredom."

"Okay. Okay. I'll call you tomorrow."

"Yeh. Let me know how you do. And I want to see you. The batteries on my vibrator are wearing down."

A big laugh from Barry this time. "I'll see that you get some new ones."

"Byyye," she teased.

He laid the phone in place and stared into nowhere. He smiled. Susan's nicks were hitting home. She didn't know it, but her constant prods that he cash it all in and go with Cold-iron were falling on fertile ground. She was by-passing his logical and cautious mind and appealing to a growing spark within him. The intuitive call for freedom that was welling inside him was getting his attention. Completely. He was having difficulty concentrating on anything else.

But her loving jabs and his overactive mind were not enough to get him to cut the rope. His provocation had to be stronger and more dramatic. He was still being ruled by a lifetime of conditioning. He had been well drilled to take the safe route, go for the security, think of the future.

The following morning, Barry arrived forty minutes earlier than Rochester Circuits required its salaried employees to be at their desks. He wanted to prepare for the department meeting on his proposal. The report needed a going over for any last-minute changes. He wanted to be ready for his boss, Dick Kane.

Kane was overweight and had a bad complexion and a worse temperament. His eyes filmed over when he got nervous or mad, which meant most of the time.

Kane had never been fond of West. It was nothing particularly personal toward Barry, it was just that Kane liked to use his seniority with the company as a leverage against everyone.

He was a lifer at Rochester Circuits. With nineteen years and strong union backing under his straining belt, it would've taken an act comparable to raping a blind nun at the board of directors meeting to get him fired. And Kane knew it. He was a bully.

That the accounting department was large enough had prevented any solid confrontations between Kane and West. Barry knew that to get into it with Kane meant that his career might screech to a halt right there. A big blowup with his supervisor could be a life sentence to the same desk. Barry tolerated Kane's need to show his superiority, and got his work done.

Which is why he was there at twenty minutes after eight that Tuesday. Barry wanted everything in order for the meeting.

His first hint of trouble came when he didn't

find the typed proposal and ten copies on his desk. He stepped into the secretarial squad area only to find Margaret's desk locked.

"Damn," he said. There was nothing he could do but wait until nine, so she could give him the material. He'd just have less time to prepare for his 10:00 show.

He thought of the snack room full of wide-grinning vending machines and figured a cup of hot coffee would help get his heart started. He crossed the large open room. Occasional movements of other early arrivals could be spotted. Mostly they were secretaries putting the finishing touches on their faces.

At ten after nine, Margaret was still nowhere in sight. Barry was getting more nervous.

"Have you heard from Margaret?" he asked Denise. She was the quietly pleasant brunette who occupied the swivel chair and desk next to Barry's secretary.

"Not this morning, yet. She left early yesterday. Her son was sick." The look in Denise's eyes said she was unconvinced.

"Oh, Jesus." Barry turned in disappointment. Just in time to see Kane chugging over to him.

"Be ready at ten, West?"

"My secretary has the proposal. She's not in and her desk is locked."

"Dunphy has a key. I'll meet you in conference room six at ten bells. I hear the marketing boys are anxious to get this project off the ground. Bottom line is that we want to beat the

Japs to the punch." Kane's wide backside was hemmed in by chalk-stripe blue pants. It weaved neatly through the office furnishings on his way back to his office.

Dunphy was the minty supervisor of secretaries of the accounting squad. He had chicken eyes, a Victor Mature-style toupee that was too large for his head, and an ever-cheerful attitude. Dunphy had always tried extra hard to please West. The secretarial supervisor referred to Barry fondly as "Stallion Thighs" to the girls in his squad. Barry rounded Dunphy up and explained his dilemma.

"No sweat, tiger. We'll get her open for you."

Dunphy's optimism lifted Barry's spirits. The supervisor then tiptoed to Margaret's desk, pulling en route on the yo-yolike key container attached to his belt.

"You're saving my butt," Barry said and quickly bit his lip in regret.

Dunphy got a twinkle in his eye. "Oh, good. It's worth it." He rotated his hips a little as he talked.

"You know what you're looking for?" Dunphy unlocked the middle drawer and pulled it open. Then he rested his hand on West's shoulder.

"I ought to. I gave a week of my life to the fucking thing," Barry answered.

What Barry saw next took his mind from the

irritation of having Dunphy's small, pink, and hairless hand sitting on his shoulder.

"Oh, fuck me," Barry blew. Dunphy smirked. The report was still a rough draft. It was in the same condition as when he had handed it to Margaret three days earlier. "The fucking bitch hasn't done a thing to it. I'm sunk."

"If it's that important, Barry, I could have one of the girls jump on it." Dunphy was righteously concerned. But his leaky-radiator voice almost made him sound comical.

"Unless you've got someone that can type eighty pages of charts, graphs, and text in exactly seven minutes, it won't work. At this very instant the guys from headquarters are planting their asses in the conference room. And I'm supposed to be the star. Except that right now, I'll unanimously be voted the no-brainer-of-the-month award."

"Jesus, I'm sorry," Dunphy said.

"Thanks, Mike. Might as well get it over with." Barry sighed deeply, saluted the chief of secretaries, and started for Kane's office.

"You're telling me it isn't ready? After all the extra time?" His supervisor's eyes were already cloudy. His face was approaching scarlet.

Kane pushed away from the desk of his glass-walled office, got up and snatched hold of the door, then slammed it. The acoustic access panel in the ceiling jumped and landed loudly against its frame. Several dozen eyes sneaked looks at Kane waddling across his carpet, past the standing West. Supervisors got carpeting. Corporate executives got paneling, thicker carpets, and bigger checks.

Kane's caster-mounted chair nearly got away from him when he landed on it. Once safely roosted, Kane wiggled slightly to release his testicles from under the folds of his thighs. He rose high in his saddle. He was ready.

"At this very moment, there are twenty people in the conference room waiting for us. That's over six hundred dollars an hour worth of angry talent expecting to see a proposal our department has committed itself to present. And you're saying it's not done? Please. West. Tell me you're pretending. You're practicing your comedy routine for the office outing."

"I'm sorry. It just isn't finished." West kept his voice and chin low. He didn't want the scene to attract attention. He needn't have bothered. Kane's glass partition was being watched like a giant TV screen.

"My ass is on the line here, West. I've already made one excuse for you."

"That's not true. And you know it. I've only been on the thing part of the time."

"The point is that you have let this entire department down. You've made us look like fools, West."

"I said I was sorry. What more do you want? I'll take the entire blame at the meeting."

"Sorry? Sorry? Sympathy is in the dictionary, between shit and syphilis. I want the god-damned report. Why isn't it done? Will you tell me?" Kane was shouting. He loved seeing West cringe. He liked pushing people around, making them back down.

Barry wanted the heat off. He wanted out of the fishbowl office. "My secretary left early yesterday. She didn't let me know and she's not here this morning."

Kane sat up. His stomach inched over the edge of his wooden desk. Accountants and secretaries got fake wood. Supervisors got the real thing.

A smile belched through Kane's mean mouth. Now West was reverting to form. He was trying to lay the blame on someone else. Barry was blowing the whistle on his secretary. Kane had the accountant where he wanted him. In full retreat.

"You know that's no excuse. You are responsible for your secretary. Her job performance affects yours. Obviously." Kane's face was florid.

"How was I supposed to know she wouldn't have it typed? She didn't tell me she was leaving." Barry knew he was sniveling.

"With your ass on the line, West, I would think you'd make it your business to find out. Let me repeat. I don't give a monkey's ass about your secretary's attendance record. I want results. I want things done when they're supposed to be done." He was now at full yell.

To that point, Barry had acted as he always had when bullied by Kane. He'd cringed and tried to stand aside and let the shit hit someone else. What came next surprised even him.

West gripped the fabric arms of the chair, leaned forward, and began forming words. He talked slowly and quietly at first, but he was building.

"I've listened to enough of your shit, Kane." The words poured through the glass. The corporate voyeurs sat up and took notice. Two secretaries stood and craned their necks looking for the source of the screaming.

"You can take your report and cram it up your lard ass. You'll have to shit first to give yourself a hint!"

Kane blinked. He looked as though he'd just been hit in the nuts with a hockey puck. A look of angered surprise settled on West's face. Muffled cheers came from somewhere amid the metal office shrubbery.

"One second, West. Who the hell . . . ?" Kane was in reverse.

There was no stopping the kid. He sprang from the chair, shouting, *"Another word outta you, Kane, and I'll drop you like the sack of shit that you are!"*

Kane grew a mustache of sweat. He saw he was facing a madman. West had snapped. "Hold it. Don't do anything you'll regret. We can work something out. I'll tell the boys in Building A something. They'll understand. Don't worry."

It was Kane who was worried. The big boys would ask questions if someone of West's qualifications and longevity quit. If the word got out he had browbeaten him into walking out, it wouldn't look good for Kane. Employees had certain rights. At that moment, though, the supervisor was scared to death West was going to punch his lights out. Screw the record.

"Look, West, we can get the thing typed today. I'll call a meeting for tomorrow." Kane made sure to keep his desk between them.

He needn't have. Barry went the other way. To the door. Five years of frustration and stifling flatness had formed into a wave of rage. It had the kid on its crest. The intensity of his reaction to Kane's bullying him had more to do with the buckets of irritation West had submerged in the time he had worked at Rochester Circuits, possibly even over his entire life, than with the incident of the uncompleted proposal. Barry West had eaten a lot of words in twenty-six years.

Excitement charged him. Seeing Kane, the office despot, cringe felt so good to him; hearing Susan's pleadings for him to loosen up and take off with Coldiron played in his ears like a freedom waltz. The idea of becoming a handball hustler hung in front of his mind like a flag of liberation. He could do it! Coldiron said he could! Susan said he could! Now he was doing it!

His words of personal revolution were sweet on his lips. He was drunk with this, his moment. He had gone too far.

Barry pushed at the open door and politely screamed, loud enough so that he was heard clearly over the entire forty-thousand-square-foot accounting department, *"Shove my job up your shorts, fatso. I'm through!"*

Chapter Eight

THE SPECIFICATIONS

The strong smell of freedom marshaled Barry's will. It took him five minutes to clean out his desk. Kane was paralyzed with fright. He watched from the safety of his office.

West stuffed his personal things into the collapsible briefcase that had once belonged to his father. In it he packed his pocket calculator, an assortment of pens and mechanical pencils, his private telephone directory, and the two handball trophies. It was all that he could call his own from five years of sitting in the exact same spot.

No one made a move to talk with him. It was as if they were afraid of catching something. Larry, who occupied the stall next to his, called to him. "Hey, West. What are you doing? What's going on?"

"I'm getting out. Bailing. Have them mail my check to me at home, will you, Larry?"

"Yeh, sure."

Dunphy appeared at his elbow. "You sure, Barry? You know what you're doing?" He looked hurt.

"You betcha, Mike."

"What will you do?"

"For openers, live. Beyond that, I'm not sure."

"Good luck." Dunphy's voice trailed off. Everyone around West was stunned. He was the last one they had ever expected to lose it like that.

In fifteen minutes Barry was striding up the icy and slowly disintegrating front stairs of the YMCA. Two questions had nagged at him since he had pulled out of Rochester Circuits' big parking lot. They were two questions he had not been able to answer: *What if Coldiron has taken off, left town? And if so, where can he be found?*

Both questions were answered as he hurried into the cavernous lobby. There Coldiron was at the front desk, jawing with the day man. The old guy looked awfully good to West.

The place seemed unusually quiet. Until Barry realized that he had not been there at ten-thirty in the morning during the week in the five years he had been at the plant.

The Y appeared more massive and utilitarian during the day. Its Depression-era, WPA-styled architecture was more imposing in the sunlight. It could have been any of the mental hospitals, post offices, or other ponderous structures thrown together by out-of-work labor during Franklin D. Roosevelt's effort to get the economy going again in the 30s.

"Coldiron. Am I glad to see you!" West charged the desk.

"Hey, kid." Coldiron was also excited. He just didn't show it. "What's going on?" He was in his traditional blue sweatshirt, thrift-store, wide-wale corduroys, and blue, high-topped gym shoes.

"Is your offer still good? Still want to manage me?"

"Let's go talk about it. You eaten breakfast yet?" Tate talked as though the day hurt his face. His eyes narrowed with each word. He was hung over bad.

At a small and clean diner-restaurant two blocks from the Y, Coldiron and an agitated West talked over their breakfasts. The younger man was having eggs. Tate nursed a Green.

"Thought you wanted something to eat."

"Eggs are bad for the cholesterol count. Now, as you were saying about taking off with me."

"Yes. I'm interested."

"What about your job? They stop keeping books?" Tate felt better with each nip of Green.

"As of an hour ago, I'm a member of the one-hundred-ten-dollars club."

"What the hell's that?"

"Unemployment insurance. I quit my job. I'll be able to collect a hundred and ten dollars from the state, after a waiting period."

"Got your balls out of the company safe, eh?" Coldiron toasted the kid.

"Something like that."

"How about your old lady?"

77

"If you mean Susan, she's all for my going with you and trying it. How'd you know about her?"

"Christ, you slobbered all over me about her the other night at the Gates."

"Oh." Barry figured he must've been drunker than he remembered. He didn't recall talking about Susan.

"You sure you ain't gonna start bellowing for her ten miles out of town? I don't need any leg driving you love-crazed and me nuts, begging you to come home every twenty minutes. I'll have a lot invested in you."

"Susan's not like that. Me neither. She even said she'd lend some money to our venture, if we needed it."

Coldiron looked across the table through his bloodshot eyes. He was certain he had died and somehow got to heaven, in spite of his record of chronic irreverence and flagrant atheism.

Here was this strong and eager kid, potentially his meal ticket, with all the natural equipment to become a handball great, copping that money was there for the picking. The operation looked sweeter all the time.

"It ain't gonna be any cakewalk, kid. There's some hungry hustlers out there, just itching to get into my pants. They'd like nothing better than to nail old Coldiron's jock to a front wall."

"I know it's not going to be easy. The other stuff, I don't know."

"One thing for sure. You'll bust your ass 'til I say you're ready. That I want clearly understood, right from the beginning. There's only one captain of this ship. And you're looking at him."

"Understood, *mein capitan*." West threw him a salute.

"First thing I get is your word you'll do everything I say. Even if it's something you might think is dumb. There is no time for arguments. I know exactly what needs to be done. I don't want an original thinker. They don't win the big money. You can do your mental exercises on your own time. Agreed?"

"You drive a hard bargain, Coldiron."

"Agreed?"

"Okay, okay. Agreed." West thought the whole thing funny.

"Okay. I'll take you on. We start tomorrow. Be on the court by eight in the morning. Ready to go to work. If we're lucky, if you do exactly what I say, and if you hustle like an antelope getting his ass chewed by a lion, we'll be ready in three months." Coldiron watched the kid's eyes for an answer. He got it from somewhere else. West cocked his head in question.

"Three months? You serious?"

"Bet your ass. For ninety days, thirteen weeks, eight hours per day, handball will be your life. You'll be getting a lifetime cram course in three months. If you don't think you can take it, kid, let me know now. I'd rather

79

end it right here. I don't need any more hand jobs."

"You got it. I can handle anything you can dish out."

"About the woman . . ."

"Susan."

"Okay, Susan. You see her when I say so. I don't want you fucking away your brains and energy. Either you're a great fuck, or a great handballer. You decide."

"You'd better watch your mouth, old man." The stranger was on sacred turf. And West was beginning to feel like an unwilling volunteer for a suicide mission. If he hadn't poured so much gasoline on his bridges before lighting them, he might've had second thoughts. Coldiron represented the only game in town to West.

"Let's just call things by their right names. If you're up all night, laying pipe, you won't be worth a shit to me on the court. I've seen it happen to more than one guy.

"There's only one way. My way."

The younger man looked to the ceiling and expelled a deep breath. The waiter inserted another drink in front of Coldiron.

"I must be wacko. I quit my job, hang my lady out to dry, and turn my life over to some guy I know nothing about, except you drink like prohibition starts tomorrow. Shit, you might be a fraud, you could be on the run from the law, anything."

"Might be so. On the other hand, I might

not be. Which means you're in for more excitement, bread, and broads than you've ever seen. Order another round."

Coldiron guzzled two more Greens. Barry paid the check. As they got up to leave, Tate announced, "Oh, by the way. No sense blowing dough unnecessarily. I'll be moving in with you. That way I can give you my full attention and we'll be saving a few bucks."

"You mean so you can keep an eye on me. Right, Coldiron?" Barry laughed.

"I can see you're a quick learner, kid."

Barry shook his head. Three hours earlier he'd had a good job, a guaranteed salary, and control over his life. Now he had no job, no security, a roommate who doubled as his resident manager-of-morals and jakey-legged handball coach. West wondered whether something might have come unraveled in his head.

He even thought about what his friends would say if he tried to explain his recent decisions. Or worse, what his parents might think. They had always maintained that their only child had good sense. He was grateful they had moved to California three years before.

Chapter Nine

THE CLASSROOM

Coldiron and West had the locker room to themselves at quarter to eight the next morning. They donned their gym clothes and caught the elevator to the Y's top floor without a word. The place was cold and tomblike. The tired hall lights were all that was happening in and around the silent handball courts.

"We'll grab this one," Coldiron said, motioning to Court Two.

"Just like homecoming. This is where you got me for the hundred and twenty-five bucks."

"Good a place as any to start."

Barry pulled on a new pair of gloves and an unopened can of balls from his equipment bag. "Might as well begin my indentureship with new equipment."

"You can put that stuff away. You won't be needing it this morning."

"What?" West was puzzled. "We going to have a round-pound in there?"

"There you go runnin' your yap. Right off. Look, just do what I tell you to do. Leave that stuff out here for now."

"If you want my opinion . . ."

"When I want your opinion, kid, I'll give it to you."

Barry shook his head. He had already decided to see if the old guy made any sense. He had committed himself to playing along for a while, no matter how ridiculous the stranger's suggestions were. Coldiron could play handball as he had never seen the game played before. That's what it was all about.

He followed Coldiron into the court and closed the door behind them. The lights and exhaust fans woke up and snapped on. It was cold in there. A shiver raced across the kid's body, raising turkey flesh in its wake.

West noticed something at once about Coldiron. He was a different man on the court. He had seen it when they had played the Friday before. It was as if the churring of the fans and the bleached intensity of the court lights seeped life and confidence into that battered body.

Out on the street Tate looked old and broken. In the confines of his kingdom, in a handball arena, the Indian-Jew was a shark in water; Tate was a Mississippi gambler with a pocketful of aces.

"Today we study the court." His voice grew clipped. He was all business. Coldiron was a man with a carefully formulated plan of training.

The kid let out a long breath. "Study the court," he repeated.

"We begin here, at the door. Doors are

simple devices; they don't sound like a big deal."

"Agreed," the kid added sarcastically.

"But they can be the difference between winning and losing a match. In our case, everything we've got could depend on how well you know about doors." Coldiron moved his big palms along the wood surface. He felt carefully, as if he might be the final inspector in the Rolls-Royce plant.

"This one's slightly warped, see? It doesn't fit the frame right. The ball can't play true. Not enough for a replay or a hinder, but enough to change the flight of the ball." He picked at the door's protruding edge. The top joints of his bananalike fingers bent backward easily. They had been deformed by being broken numerous times scraping shots from the sidewall or floor.

"This door is oak and hollow-cored. They make 'em that way so they can breathe. It also makes 'em dead. The ball comes away slower than off the wall. Again, not enough to be noticeable to the untrained eye. Just enough to fuck up your timing. Or the other guy's, if you use it to your advantage." He winked at West.

"How about the other day when we played? Did you? . . ."

"You get an A on your first test."

Coldiron continued. "Watch for composite doors. They're wood core laminated with a thin piece of masonite. They play like concrete."

West started to understand just how well the

old guy knew his stuff. There was power flowing out of those gray eyes.

"Okay. Now the back wall. It's concrete. Bad stuff for spinners. Concrete straightens out a shot; English bites better on wood. On this type of a court, keep your garbage on the floor."

The old man massaged the back wall. He might've been a chiropractor feeling for the source of his patient's pain, so carefully did he rub. He made his way to one corner, waiting for his fingers to show him what Friday's match had already told him.

"Like I thought when we played. There's been water damage. The sidewall is wood. It warped while the concrete back wall stayed put. They've tried to fix it by sanding and filling the bad spots. The corners are dead. The ball gets a funeral here."

Coldiron spent a full two hours going over every inch of the court. West learned if the courts are above the second floor, chances are good their front and sidewalls will be wood or plaster composite. Coldiron explained how it was too expensive for clubs to put concrete courts above the second floor. The structure needed too much costly beefing up to handle their excessive weight. Below the third floor was a different story. They'd be concrete.

The old guy showed him how to check the slope of the floor, how to eyeball the walls for plumb, where to look for any small fact that could be used to steal a point or two in a game.

They walked every inch of the front wall. The wall, Coldiron explained, was the key to the game. "Everything plays off this surface. Study it."

Tate taught West what a "wow" in the wall was—the slight bulges caused by poor construction that could make the ball deflect slightly erratically.

The two men walked the floor. Coldiron spoke of different hardwood treatments. Varathane versus varnish, and how the ball reacted differently to each. He went over methods to counteract the ball's skidding. He explained how to detect whether the floor was tongue-and-groove or butt-joint construction. The latter leached moisture, a bleeding that could change the complexion of the game by altering the ball's spin.

The accountant learned when to call for a dry mopping, a move that helped prevent slips and possible injuries. Also, Tate pointed out, it was a ploy to slow down a game's pace. There were no timeouts during a stakes game, other than for an injury or an equipment change. A call for a mopping gave a player an all-important breather.

"I've seen the momentum of a game turned around because one guy called for a mopping."

"You mean there are no timeouts allowed? How come?"

"If you get hurt," Coldiron explained, "you

got fifteen minutes to continue. Otherwise, you forfeit the match. And your bet."

"Why is that?"

"Something had to be done. Guys would fake injuries when it was obvious they had no chance of winning. They'd get a postponement and then skip out on the bet. Or some players would lie down to break another's momentum. Christ, I've seen matches where a guy'd fall down three times a game, just to slow things down. Got to be ridiculous."

"Makes sense."

"If you ain't in good enough condition to play a full game, you got no business on the court."

Coldiron talked about the new, composition-type flooring systems experimented with by a few clubs on the Coast. "They're shit. If we happen to play on one of those surfaces, you'll need special shoes; you use tennis shoes with smooth bottoms. If you wear kicks like you got on, you'll be playing like you have four packs of gum stuck to the bottoms."

Then Tate pointed upward. "Now about ceilings . . ." They looked up while Tate spoke and until Barry's neck ached. Coldiron talked of various ceiling surfaces and the strategies called for by each. West learned about different light fixtures; he heard about types of wire used to cover them, and how various kinds of lights cast different shadows.

"Mercury vapor can screw you up at first.

Everything looks green. Always get in a few warmup games under mercury vapors. Get the feel of them."

"Jesus, I feel like I'm in a construction enginering class," West commented. He tried rubbing the soreness out of the back of his neck.

His teacher continued on about ceilings. "Older clubs and the rich new ones still use wood. Shots travel their true arch coming off an inch of hardwood. They're the best.

"You can always tell the kind of ceiling by throwing your ball at it and listening." He demonstrated by reaching into his pocket, fishing out a ball, and rifling it off the ceiling. "Hear it? That *thunk* means gypsum. Most clubs have gone to it, to save money. Wood sings. And plays faster. Remember, always check overhead before starting."

Tate finished with the ceiling. Barry was grateful. So was his neck.

"The very first thing when you walk into any court, is to go over the corners. Don't get on all fours, but walk around, bounce your ball, pretend to be warming up. *But goddammit, memorize the corners!*

"Look here." Coldiron got down on his hands and knees at the junction of the side and front walls. "You can see this floor has settled."

He pointed. West saw nothing. "See that space? It's small, but it tells you something; a fact that can buy you a win or cost you a match. With this kind of settling, corner shots tend to die. The smallest crack will eat the shot. Play these corners all day with soft shots. And bend. The lower you are when you shoot, the lower your ball comes out. Gives your opponent less of a chance to return. *Don't play corners like these hard.* Lay your ball in like you're putting money on a teller's counter. Which is exactly what we'll be doing a lot of, if you get down what I've been saying. Our biggest problem will be picking which bank we want to fill up."

West's mouth hung open. "Is that how you played it Friday?"

"Bet your skinny ass."

"No wonder I didn't have a prayer. You had this court cased. The fucking match was rigged before we started."

"Not quite, but you're getting the drift. The difference between a good handballer and a great one is up here." Coldiron cradled his temple between his two index fingers. "There's a bunch of ham-'n'-eggers with ability. The ones with the savvy you could fit in a small closet."

The old guy bristled with excitement. He was a coach with an abundance of raw material; he was the college professor with an enthusiasm for sharing what he knew; and he was an old handball scammer with big ideas. "Now, listen. This is important. If the front corners are tight as a thirteen-year-old girl's pussy, drive your shots. Get low and whistle 'em. The ball will come out low and hard, so the other guy'll scoop slivers trying for a return. And when the corners are like loose gash, lay it in soft. Remember that."

They spent two hours going over every surface, hidden and exposed. West was intrigued; Coldiron was playing into the kid's analytically trained mind. He was learning aspects of handball he had never considered.

"And I thought I was a student of this game."

"You were," Coldiron picked up. "Grade school level. You just moved into grad school under Dr. Coldiron. Kinda like the ring of that. Dr. Coldiron. *Hee hee.*"

Tate began reminiscing about some of the game's greats as they sat, backs against the rear wall. They were players, according to Coldiron, whose names rarely appeared in the sports section of newspapers, but who dominated the game. They were anonymous to all but the most serious followers of the sport; they carried towering reputations among the handball hustling circuit. They were guys like Spiderman Massey, who earned over $100,000 a year on the courts; Julius Lowenburg, alias Jungle-Jew, a competitor who would test another's endurance to the breaking point, then break him. And who Coldiron swore he'd seen "beat the piss out of Paul Haber," perennial national singles champion, nine games in a row for $10,000.

He talked of Jimmy Reddick, former free-safety for the Montreal Alouettes of the Canadian Football League, until he'd been discovered betting on his own games. According to Tate, Reddick was six feet, six inches of explosive speed and raw endurance.

"His shot is so strong, he could paralyze a man if he hit one of the guy's spots."

"What spots?" West was loving it.

"Forget that for now. That's only self-defense stuff."

"Will you show me?"

"Only after I know I can trust you."

"Trust me? I quit an eighteen-thousand-a-year job and just about swore to celibacy on little more than your word, and you don't trust me? What do you want? A little blood?"

"Let's just leave it at this. If you get hit in one of several places on the body, you drop like you been shot," the old guy said. Talking of the circuit and the great ones had given Coldiron a morphined, melancholy look. His hungry eyes looked quieter.

"Does that happen often? Somebody take a shot at you?" West asked.

"Naw. A hitter comes along only every once in a while."

"What's a hitter?"

"Somebody who deliberately tries to lame an opponent. It's generally a punk who wants to win so bad he'll hurt people."

"No shit. There are guys around like that?"

"Yeh. But they don't last long. A hitter is a

91

renegade. He's a dangerous player who gets frozen out of serious competition fast."

Barry was like a kid hearing yarns spun by a favorite uncle. "What kind of a person would hurt someone on purpose?"

"Could be an old fox who once had something but has lost it. Pride does funny things to men. Especially those that had their way on the slats and can't take getting passed up by the younger players.

"Then there is the comer. That's generally the young guy so eager to reach the top he goes bad. He's unwilling to pay his dues on the circuit, so he tries crippling players he can't otherwise whip.

"The real pros aren't hitters. They got too much pride in the way the game's supposed to be played to take a cheap shot. Hitters are guys gone bad, or those who never had it in the first place. Booze, broads, old age, greed, or whatever can be the reason.

"A hitter gets to like the taste of blood. Like a wild animal or something. Or maybe it's just that the hit gets the job done. I'm not quite sure.

"The good players are real sportsmen; they've got ethics, a lot of class, and honor."

"How do you know the guy you're playing is not a hitter?"

"You don't get hit."

"Thanks."

"Couldn't resist, kid. The circuit is a small

town. The word gets out fast. A player who goes bad can't get a match. Or, an agreement is made among the top players to take the hitter out."

"What do you mean, take the hitter out?"

"I'll give you an example. There was this kid from the Coast who had been hitting people. He was up against Lowenburg in Chicago. The hitter served up the first point of the second game, when someone in the gallery broke silence and called his name. Out of reaction the kid turned to look. It was the same instant Lowenburg rifled his return off the back wall. Jungle's got a comet. His shot caught the kid in the eye. The ball exploded the right looker like a grape thrown against a brick wall."

West felt the blood run from his face. He shuddered. The loss of an eye was the one injury every handballer feared most. Many wore protective wire rims over their eyes for insurance.

"It was a set up. Jungle had been chosen to take the kid out."

"You ever taken anyone out?"

"Only once. In Kansas City. I drove a guy's nuts into his belly."

"With the ball?" West could hardly believe what he had been hearing.

"No. My fist. When he was pinned against the sidewall I caught him on the upswing."

Barry was certain that if he had eaten anything that morning he would've lost it right then. "Why aren't hitters just reported to the authorities? Let the cops deal with them?"

"We police our own sport. We clean our own house. We don't need no authorities."

"You're talking about instant justice, Old West vigilante shit."

"You got it, kid."

"What if the guy who's been targeted tries to avoid the hit?"

"It's tough. The hitter never knows when it's coming, or from who. That alone can drive a guy nuts. Just the anticipation. The waiting."

There was a hint of warning in the old man's voice. Barry was certain he had heard a slight hardening of Tate's mood as he talked of retribution, like it was his duty to pass on the word.

"Have you heard of anyone who's had to take out a friend?"

"Yep."

"Would you?"

"Yep."

"What if you had refused to take that guy out in Kansas City?"

"You don't refuse," Tate said solemnly.

Coldiron groaned as he pushed himself to his feet. "That's enough for today. Let's grab a bite and head home."

"You mean grab a drink, don't you?"

"Took the words right out of my mouth, kid."

Home meant more work, but of a different

variety. Coldiron pulled a small book from his battered suitcase. Tate and suitcase had moved in the night before. The pages of the book were yellowed. Its cover was bloated from moisture and worn ragged with age. The book and suitcase could've been a matched set.

"You're looking at the authority, kid. This is one of the original versions, printed in 1815. There are probably less than fifty copies left in the world. This book was written by Sean O'Dwyer. He was one of the game's pioneers."

West had never seen Coldiron handle anything so carefully. Except maybe a quart of Green.

Tate continued: "Handball was born in Ireland. O'Dwyer worked out and set down in writing most of the rules. This book is the source. He printed it himself. Printing was his trade. Handball was his life.

"Everything written or spoken about the sport is someone's interpretation of an interpretation of this book. Handball logic has been watered down more times than whorehouse whiskey. In fact, you're one of the few people, ever, to get it straight from old Sean himself. Read this book. Memorize it. Implant it in your head or up your ass, if necessary. Whatever gets you to learn what's between these covers. This is more important to you than the Holy Bible. This is *your* Holy Bible."

West took the book. The gold-lettered title

was barely recognizable. It read *The Arte of Handball*, by S. O'Dwyer.

He held it carefully as if some delicate archaeological parchment that detailed the beginnings of a civilization was cradled in his hands.

To Coldiron it did. O'Dwyer's book was the original gospel of the sport he loved. The ragged text documented the beginnings of the handball culture; a civilization, a way of life that the Indian-Jew had been following for over forty years.

West spent the balance of the afternoon reading the book's 160 pages, while Coldiron occupied himself in front of the TV, and sipped water glasses full of Jack Daniel's.

O'Dwyer's book was basic. It explained why the court was the size it was, and how the rules had come into being. They were rules that had changed little since the game had first been played.

Barry was getting Coldiron's point. Handball was a pure sport; it had resisted changes by those who had wished to bend its rules to fit shifting sports styles, or those who had wanted to alter its basics to popularize the game. Handball was handball, in the beginning, now, and forever. It would remain so as long as the likes of Tate Coldiron were around to guard its integrity.

West studied the faded and soiled pages; they were sheets that had seen many hands and eyes over the years. There were diagrams, primitive cross-sections of the regulation-sized court. There were specifications for constructing tournament-approved arenas. O'Dwyer had been precise on which materials were acceptable for use in building a court and which were not.

Then there were O'Dwyer's recommendations and crude illustrations for making different shots. There was a how-to section on playing opponents of different skills and tactical maneuvers. West was reading about essentially the same shots and strategies Coldiron had used to demolish him the week before.

The more he read, the more Barry understood. Handball was as much religion as it was sport. The basics of good handball had remained constant for almost two centuries. They were the stress points and strategies that were there to be learned by the diligent and serious seekers of handball excellence.

It came into focus sooner for West—sooner, perhaps, than it would've for someone whose mind had not been as trained for precision, logic, and mathematical order. The game had a formula, a rhythm that had been hidden in part by the years and by most players' unwillingness to serve an apprenticeship in order to learn its bedrock principles. Barry imagined it was an indentureship that could easily last for decades.

He also saw where the formula might be grasped in a matter of weeks. At the outside, in a couple of months. But he had come to understand it was the body that had to be rigorously schooled to assimilate the data and mental instructions so it could react instantly and with exactness on the court.

Therein seemed the difference, to West, between the bush leaguer Coldiron constantly called him and the great ones. Handball superiority was not inherited. It was not something you bought, or even learned from another. It had to be acquired and earned on any one of the thousands of courts throughout the United States, working into the blackness, alone and totally disciplined.

It was a dedication like Jimmy Reddick's deep, burning desire to get out of Harlem, not become ensnared by heroin or the other chemical vacations necessary for the surrendering of the spirit to the ghetto. According to Coldiron, Reddick had played handball nearly every day of his childhood to keep from stumbling into impoverished obscurity and to keep his body perfectly tuned.

West had heard of such dedication in other sports. Like George Shuba's impeccable swing with a baseball bat. It had been rated as one of the smoothest, most perfect ever. They had called it a natural gift. Shuba had acquired his "natural gift" only after years of taking cuts at a piece of string hanging in his parents' cellar as a youngster.

Or the thousands of hours Johnny Unitas had tossed a football through a tire suspended from a tree in his front yard to develop his pinpoint passing ability.

It was Adolph Schayes shooting foul shots in the playground long after the others had left, to become one of the premier free-shooters the game of basketball had ever seen.

These athletes all had one common thread. Their individual gifts had been earned by years of practice. And their minds and bodies had been pointed toward one goal. To be the best in the sport of their choosing. If they had been specially endowed, it was with dedication, more than with natural ability.

"There's one hell of a lot more to this game than I ever thought," Barry said and closed the book. He had finished O'Dwyer's gospel.

"You're gettin' the idea, kid." Coldiron was fitting his mouth around his third multi-tiered sandwich since they had been home.

"Suppose that's the reason for the racquetball craze. They've invented a game using the best of handball and tennis."

"C'mon, kid. Spare me. Racquetball is like everything else today," Coldiron said, flipping the channel selector on the TV. "It's a shortcut. People don't want to work at anything. They won't develop their natural skills. Christ, grown men don't want to hurt their hands. So they hit the ball with sissy rackets and call it a sport."

"Speaking of work, I've had it. I'm going over to Susan's," Barry interjected.

"Okay with me. Just remember, we go at

eight in the morning. Your ass drags from doing the horizontal mambo all night, and I'm gonna chew on it." Coldiron was still lucid for having downed nearly a quart of Green.

"You've got a toilet tongue, Coldiron. Anyone ever tell you that before?"

"Just a couple of ex-wives and a judge here and there. You should see me when I'm mean. Which is what I'll be if I catch you doggin' it tomorrow. Just be home at a decent hour."

"Yes, mom."

The following morning Tate was off the couch by 6:30. Barry was slower to crawl out of bed.

"C'mon, kid. You're on my time now. I ain't got all day."

West groped his way into the shower. Coldiron put on the coffee. He threw a can of frozen orange juice into the blender, added water, and whipped up a quart of the stuff. He poured himself a big glass, gave it a dash of Green from the bottle in the cupboard, and gulped it down. He was feeling good.

For the first time in years, Coldiron actually found himself looking forward to the day. The kid in the shower trying for consciousness represented Tate's bus ticket out of obscurity. His protégé had raw talent to burn, natural gifts Coldiron wasn't about to acknowledge just yet. He'd ride the kid, drive the nice-guy accountant out of him until Barry became the invincible, indestructible handball machine Coldiron knew he could become.

Tate was going to satisfy a couple of dreams behind the machine he'd build. One had been with him almost his entire life. It had to do with money. The other had haunted him since New Orleans. That one had to do with revenge.

Chapter Ten

TRAINING

The second day Coldiron let his student put on the gloves. Tate also strapped his on. They were dressed and on the court by eight sharp.

"My first bit of advice, kid, is that you store everything you know about the game on the shelf. We start from scratch."

"What's that supposed to mean?" West was more groggy than indignant.

"What that means is that you've got more fucking bad habits than a tailor shop in a nunnery. The only way you're gonna get rid of them is to start from the start. Which is exactly what we're gonna do this morning."

"What's the start?"

"Today we learn the serve."

"I know *how* to serve. Show me something I can't do."

"Just listen and watch. And quit overloading your ass. You'll see what I mean."

Barry positioned himself next to Coldiron in the service zone.

"It all begins with the grip. Here, show me how you hold the ball when you serve."

"How do I know how I hold the fucking

ball? I just pick it up, that's all. Then I drop it."

"That's what I figured. You telegraph your serves all the way to California."

Barry learned that how he gripped the ball did make a difference. Tate showed him how to spin and slide it so the ball had something on it when it came back up off the floor. Coldiron demonstrated how to cup his hand, how he snapped his wrist on impact so the ball danced off the floor or walls at crazy angles.

By turning his hand inward at contact, Tate made the ball hop to West's left. It was a difficult service for the natural righthander to handle as the ball moved into his body and away from the normal arch of his swing.

The old guy had a bagful of tricky serves. There were slices, hooks, cuts, and spinners. He made the ball bounce crazily and unpredictably. Tate could lay it in either back corner, low and dead. Barry nearly gave himself a hernia trying for the return.

He showed the kid how to shadow his hand with his body so an opponent was not able to figure what he was serving up.

Coldiron had one delivery that nearly spun West into the floor like a drill bit. He came across side-armed with an open hand that made the ball change directions coming off the sidewall. Its initial flight was toward the rear of the court as it glanced from the sidewall; there the black dot reversed course and headed back to the server. It was as if Coldiron had an invisible string attached to the ball. All while West chased around the court after it, cursing and swinging at air.

Tate was like a wily knuckleballer. He showed West deliveries the kid had never seen. There was nothing real fast; each offering had enough garbage on it to fill a dumpster. After one serve, Barry accused his coach of throwing a spitter at him. The ball had actually wobbled and jumped. The kid was certain he was seeing stuff Coldiron had learned from Sean O'Dwyer himself.

Only two aspects of the game were covered in the first week. The serve and the pass shot. The latter, Coldiron had explained, was one of West's glaring weaknesses.

"You try to kill everything. You gotta learn the percentage points on the court. Go for the kill only on the sure things; put away the high-percentage shots."

They both worked like dogs every morning. An hour was spent on service drills and an hour of pass-shot exercises. Coldiron positioned West on different spots on the court. The kid was made to attempt to drive the ball past Coldiron; he tried to place it just beyond the old man's reach.

"If all you got is a killshot, a good player will never give you anything to put away. He'll drive everything by you and camp against the front wall. Then he'll kill all your returns."

He made West practice lob passes, high bouncers that would take Coldiron out of position and give West undisputed possession of the court's most vital position—the center court territory. This was an imaginary six-foot-diameter circle, just to the rear of the service area and equidistant from the sidewalls.

"This is where you want to be; get here, even if you have to fight through a man. Live here and you'll get the best percentage shots in the game. The center court territory is slightly closer to the back wall. That's 'cause it's easier to move forward than backward," Coldiron explained.

They worked on the ceiling pass until West thought his arm would fall off. Then Tate worked him some more. Barry practiced crosscourt lobs, where the ball played off three walls before striking the floor. He learned the alley pass—a shot that was probably responsible for more injuries than any other. The alley pass hugged the sidewall. An opponent was apt to bruise, or even break, his fingers in his return attempt.

There was a matter of their partnership that needed clearing up. Coldiron dealt with it at the end of the first week of training. He chose the empty sauna. An exhausted West was holding his head in his swollen hands. Coldiron glistened with high-octane perspiration.

"We're gonna need a stake when we're done training. We'll need enough money to carry us 'til we hit some purses. Coin to live on and bet with. That could take six months. How much you got stashed?"

"How much we going to need?" Barry never looked up.

"I figure about two grand. That's going excursion all the way."

"That's a big stroke. I've only got a little more than a thousand in the bank."

"A grand, eh? It's a beginning." Tate was trying to look embarrassed. "What about all that stuff in your apartment? Your TV, that fancy stereo, furniture, all that shit."

"What do you mean? What about it?" Barry grew more alert.

"What good is all that crap going to do you on the road? Kind of tough to fit it all in your gym bag. ."

"I was thinking more of putting it in storage. It's all I got."

"Look, kid. We gotta have enough coin to last until you get good enough to start winning. We might have to weather a loss or two. If you know what I mean."

"Yeh, I know. Your confidence in me is overwhelming." West was too tired to put up much of a fight.

"It's not a matter of confidence. Shit, you'll be able to replace that stuff with the loose change in your pocket when the money starts rolling in. It's all just wood, electric wires and cloth, anyway."

"It's easy for you to say. It's not yours."

"The point is, if you ain't willing to give it all up, every fucking bit of it, you ain't free. The material goods own you. We're talking about a big return here."

"What about you? How much are you contributing to my freedom?"

"For openers, my one and only car is on the line for your liberation."

"You got a car?"

"You bet. And she's a beauty. A classic. I'm in the process of restoring it. Why, right now, it's in the hands of an expert car man, here in this very town. I'm having some more work done on it. She's a real cherry, all right."

"I'm listening."

"Kid, I'm betting the rent on you. I put my valuable piece of precision machinery up for sale this morning. Every dime of the proceeds goes into our kitty. How's that for a commitment?"

"I'm deeply impressed. Especially since I haven't seen a dime of your money. The way I see it, you've got nothing to lose."

"How can you say that? I've told you about the car. Everything I've got in the way of material possessions is on your nose. I'm gambling all the way that you're a winner.

"Besides, I don't believe in owning a bunch of things. You end up spending more time taking care of them than enjoying life. I just like to check in and check out."

"So far, all I've heard about is some mystery car I don't even know for sure exists and some philosophical bullshit from a middle-aged hippie. What about some hard cash?" West enjoyed flushing the old guy out.

"Jesus. Listen to him. Your fucking head is going to be figuring financial statements two hours after the rest of you is dead.

"What luck. Of all the possibles in this world, I gotta end up with a moneychanging, lovesick, and, I might add, nearly impoverished kid. What'd you used to do before Rochester Circuits, evict old ladies from their apartments in January?"

"Doesn't sound bad. Probably good money."

"Look, kid, take it from me; the bean counters of the world, those who'd squeeze a nickel 'til Tom Jefferson snots on 'em, end up eating dirt every time. People with imagination get the angel food cake.

"Furthermore, there's one rather important detail you've conveniently forgotten to mention in your little game of 'mine-and-yours.' You happen to be getting the best possible handball education available on this planet. There ain't no one who knows as much about the game as me. And I ain't even charging you a dime. You know how many guys who'd give their left nut for the information you're getting?"

"Oh, oh. Now he's hitting me with his modesty."

"So quit trying to figure it all out. Leave that to me. Either you're committed or you're not."

"I have a feeling I ought to be. And not the type you're thinking about."

West ran his hands through his wet hair. "All right. All right. I've trusted you this far. I've been thinking about unloading the stuff, anyhow. I'd only have to pay to store it."

Tate said nothing. Letting a man save face was a basic law of his world. Besides, he was busy running a quick tally on the worth of West's household goods.

"How do you figure I get rid of it?"

"Have one of those apartment sales. You know, like a garage sale. People will buy chocolate-covered rabbit turds if they think they're screwing you to get 'em."

"Right. Then we can sleep on the floor and eat off the toilet."

"You have the sale the weekend before we leave, dildo. In the meantime, figure what it's all worth so we'll know what to ask for it. I'll see that my old chariot gets sold."

Coldiron's offer wouldn't have held up well on paper. The balance on his bill at the station was $130, plus the owner was going to be charging him $5 a day storage. He had offered Coldiron $200 for the Ford, making Tate's kick into the kitty $70.

Training continued for another two months. An impassioned and obsessed Coldiron drove the kid on. He demonstrated and redemonstrated every shot, move, and strategy in his ample trick bag—a satchel of skills Tate had been filling since he had started playing the game at nine in the St. Louis orphanage.

Tate was seeking to blend his savvy with the kid's aggressiveness and impressive physical equipment. The old man knew intuitively that the combination was synergistic; their total would be far greater than the sum of the two parts. He was correct. The chemistry was unbelievable. The kid was eating up the new information and improving daily.

Coldiron showed him the ultimate killshot. Known as the rollout kill, it was a shot that demanded such consummate skill and concentration it either ended a volley immediately or left the shooter highly vulnerable to be scored on. Once the kid had perfected the rollout kill, he would have an unmatched scoring arsenal.

"The rollout is the lowest percentage kill," Coldiron instructed. "Only try it when it's a sure thing."

He showed the kid what he meant. From various points inside the service area, Coldiron executed the rollout. His ball struck the front wall with such precision, it hit so close to the floor, and was driven at exactly the proper speed, that it came away without a bounce or a sound. The ball ran along the floor like a black mouse. Barry had no chance to return it. Further, Tate put away rollouts with either hand.

"Now watch what I mean about percentages." When he stepped three paces back, beyond the service area and tried a few, his accuracy was sharply reduced. The ball began bouncing high enough that Barry easily put it away himself.

"If you attempt the rollout from beyond the service area, your chances of making it are reduced by seventy-five percent. Near the back wall, even the best players will only rollout less than three percent of their shots. If they'd try it from there.

"You take yourself out of position going for the low-percentage rollout. Your opponent will see you posing and stake out against the front wall. He'll kill all your misses. Which will be over ninety percent of your shots.

"*Remember. Once you're beyond the center-court zone go for the pass shot.*"

To drive his point home to the kid, whenever West got too aggressive and went for the low-percentage rollout, Coldiron stopped the volley. He penalized West the point and fifty pushups. Barry got the message and sore shoulders, fast.

They capped off each session with a match. Coldiron tested the kid on the day's lessons. He also checked on what part of Barry's game needed work the next day. But mostly, he wanted to keep his student teachable. Tate buried him each time. He refused to let up. He pushed the kid to the limit each day, then slaughtered him, head to head.

Not all the pushing of West came from his coach. The kid drove himself. Culminating the four hours on the courts, West jogged 10 miles around the circular track above the gym, did 500 situps, 300 pushups, and 100 behind-the-neck chinups. When he finished, his muscles twitched and jumped in exhaustion. At the end of two months, Barry looked as though he were wearing an armor of twisted white steel.

It was emotionally, more than physically, that the rigor started to show on the kid. He was growing irritable and restless. He seethed when Tate beat him on the court. It became a scene of a supremely confident trainer taunting and educating a wildly beautiful and snarling beast to new heights. Coldiron was completing what he had set out to do. He was driving the accountant out of Barry West.

The kid's game grew more savage and deadly. He was becoming a silk-smooth amalgam of Coldiron's tactics and cunning and his own rifle-quick reflexes and indefatigable stamina. Barry was becoming a perfectly tuned handball machine that could run constantly for hours without letting up.

Nine weeks into the training a cloud developed on Coldiron's horizon of big reputation and swollen bank accounts. With only his unemployment benefits coming in, Barry was running out of money fast. Which also meant that Coldiron was, too.

Moving into the kid's apartment hadn't depleted Barry's resources. Tate was a sparse eater. The rent was the same whether one or two people lived there. It was the liquor store bill that was sinking them. Tate's tab exceeded $100 a week. He guzzled Jack Daniel's Green like Kool-Aid; he drank the stuff in his coffee in the morning and with meals. At the end of a workout, Coldiron poured staggering amounts over ice until he passed out in front of the TV.

Barry waited for the night they had dinner at Susan's to lay his cards on the table. Being with her gave him the courage to share his fears. They would be flat broke before they ever got out of Rochester—something that terrified West. The past couple of nights he had dreamed about begging a gloating Kane for his old job back, while the people in accounting laughed at him.

Coldiron was, as a rule, indifferently hostile toward women, but he saw Susan as not fitting the traditional female mold. From the first, Susan had been anxious for her lover to accept Tate's offer, even if it meant she and Barry would be separated for extended lengths of time while they were on the road. She had even agreed with Coldiron's wishes that West stay away from her during the week. The old hustler saw Susan Burnett as a rare woman; she was neither a meddler or a ball-cutter.

Coldiron had paid her the highest compliment he knew of for a woman. He had told Barry, "She ain't no sniveling cunt. You got a good one there." The kid had trouble accepting the comment as praise for his lady.

"We'll have to shorten training," Barry reported over dinner. "My bank account is just about dry."

"Dry? I thought you had a chunk saved," Coldiron said. He was wearing his cleanest gray sweatshirt and had laundered his cords and tennis shoes for the occasion. His hair was matted back.

"I did. But we're going through it like a marine on a one-day furlough."

"We're gonna have to figure something out then," Tate countered.

"No more figuring things out. Let's just get going."

"You ain't ready yet. Every son of a bitch you come up against will put your ass through the wall."

Susan listened. Her chin was cradled in her hands. She was wearing Levi's that fit her like wallpaper, and a plaid, open-collared shirt. Her hair was tied back.

She also had a stake in the venture. Though different than Coldiron's material interest, hers was equally intense. The devilish old handball hustler sitting across from her, looking coy and schoolboy-scrubbed clean, was accomplishing something she had been unable to do. He was building her a man. Barry was becoming the independent, volatile, and daring person she had always believed he could be. Susan wasn't sure what the old and wily drunk was doing to her man, but she wanted more.

She looked at West. Certainly he still had a nagging, persistent fear of not making a living at handball, but he had also become infinitely more free since Coldiron had started tutoring him; he had shed many of his stifling and boring inhibitions. He had some confidence, not in the swaggering, macho sense, but more of a quiet strength of knowing he had something going for himself. He had become sensitive that the world was larger than Rochester Circuits. It was larger than Rochester, New York. His "who's-going-to-wheel-me-out-into-the-sun-at-sixty, profit-sharing" overcoats were dropping away. He was feeling better about himself. He had become more willing to let it all go, to step off the curb, into a life of total mystery. He also had more to offer to Susan as a lover. And a friend.

"How much will you need?" she asked. "Until he's ready, Mr. Coldiron?"

"Susan! You're starting to sound like Field Marshall Coldiron, like I'm a piece of meat or something."

She gave him her best knowing smile. It parted her full, wet lips and showed teeth that weren't perfect. Just good. Coldiron let out a *"Hee hee."*

"Look, I don't want you sinking your money into this. Bad enough I've blown all mine." Barry looked mournful.

"What I do with my money is my business. And you're not a bad-looking piece of meat at that."

"Glad you cleaned that up. *Hee hee.*" Coldiron pulled a deep one from the water glass full of iodine-colored liquid in front of him.

"Well, Mr. Coldiron, how much?"

"At the rate we're going," Barry cut in, "and judging by Coldiron's consumption of booze, we'll need another five hundred dollars just to survive the month." He looked embarrassed.

"Add to that another fifteen hundred bucks for walking-around money and front bucks," Coldiron added without flinching. Neither did Susan. Barry groaned and put his napkin over his eyes.

Coldiron stuffed his napkin into the neck of his sweatshirt and went back to dismantling the half chicken in front of him.

"Let me give it some thought," Susan said. "Two thousand is a lot of money for me."

"It'd be a smart move, lady, a good bet. The kid's a sure money winner."

"How much a pound am I going for tonight? Jesus," Barry said through his napkin.

"There'd be one condition." Susan ignored Barry's moans. "You'd have to guarantee me that there'd be something left." She wasn't smiling.

"Oh, don't worry, there'll be enough left," Coldiron smiled.

With that Barry threw down his napkin and rocked his head in his hands, palms deeply callused from slapping a hard rubber ball around a handball court thousands of times in the previous nine weeks.

It was three days later, with Barry off to Rochester Circuits to sign the necessary forms that would release to him his pension and profit-sharing account accrued from five years with the company (a process that would take several months before he would see the money, and therefore wouldn't offer any immediate financial relief), that Susan chose to make contact with Coldiron.

Tate was relaxing in front of the TV at Barry's apartment after a rigorous morning of practice. He wasn't surprised when her voice answered his growl into the phone, or when Susan asked him to meet her in Delaney's, an Irish eatery two blocks from Barry's apartment, for a drink. He had been expecting her to contact him since the night at her apartment when they had discussed financing Barry's handball hustling career over dinner.

He was slightly surprised to find her waiting at a table in the dark restaurant when he shuffled in. What Tate didn't know was that Susan had made the call from Delaney's.

"How's it going?" he asked, sliding into the straight-backed, wooden booth, across from her. He glanced up with interest at the stuffed head of some animal he didn't recognize that was mounted over their tobacco-colored and thick wooden table.

"Going," she said back.

"They ought to clean this place up a little," Coldiron said, motioning toward the peanut shells spread over the hardwood floor.

"Atmosphere, Coldiron, atmosphere. I figured you'd want a drink and ordered you a glass of Jack Daniel's Green."

"You're a saint," he smiled.

Susan looked alive and mysterious, the calm dusk of the restaurant setting off her dark eyes and hair. She was wearing a black turtleneck sweater and a deep-brown, well-worn, suede jacket.

"Let's get to it," she said, following the waiter's retreating hand as it moved away from delivering the double shot of Green and water chaser.

"What did you have in mind? *Hee hee*," he said, raising his glass in toast. "Here's looking up your kilt."

"Thank you," she answered, giving him just enough smile so her teeth showed.

"Look, Mr. Coldiron, I don't know what you've been doing to Barry. I want to tell you that I've never seen him this way. He's healthier, happier, and, well, I like what I see, *when I get the chance to see him*." Now it was her turn to offer the toast.

"He's in training, you know." Coldiron's tongue pressed against the inside of his cheek. He liked this woman.

"That's the good news," she continued.

"Would the bad news be that I'm only getting one drink?"

"No, Jesus, have another."

"You can call me Tate in here."

Susan motioned to the waiter, who danced over in tight pants that came up to his rib cage.

After Coldiron's drink was revived, Susan, staying with her initial Scotch and water, continued, her face drawn up in seriousness. "The bad news, Mr. Coldiron, is that I really don't trust you. Don't take it personally, but there's something inside me that says that if I give you the two thousand dollars, you'd take it and run, leave town in the middle of the night like the Holy Ghost." She leaned into her words, with no fear of saying what she did.

"You really believe I'd burn you for the coin?"

"Exactly," she said, fingering her glass. Her hands were strong-looking, a length that made them more sensuous than imposing. "Or rather, a part of me thinks you'd split. Another part says that your stake in seeing Barry make it as a hustler runs far deeper than the money."

"I'll let you see my parts, if you let me see yours," Tate replied casually, hoping to cover the fact that Susan's intuitive powers were surprisingly accurate.

"What guarantee do I have that you won't rip me off for the money?"

"Absolutely none." It was time. Coldiron liked offense more than defense. "But, lady, I gotta tell you, I ain't going for it. This Mother Cabrini act leaves me cold. Not for an instant do I think that you hesitating with the money has anything to do with me."

"Coldiron, what are you talking about?"

"You know exactly what I mean." Tate pushed himself forward, his wide forehead and protruding cheekbones glinting in the bar light. "Let me ask you, have you ever been married?"

"What does that have to do with lending you the money?"

"Plenty. Well, have you?" he asked between pulls on the Green.

"If you have to know, yes."

"What happened?"

"What do you mean, what happened? We got divorced. It was a case of mistaken identity."

"Sounds cute, but I ain't buying."

"And I ain't selling," she said, mimicking him. "We lived in New York and, in four years, grew in different directions. That's all. No big deal. Just a statistic."

"You mean he started laying pipe in some strange ditches."

"He what? . . . Oh, Christ," she said and looked up at the ceiling while digging a cigarette out of her purse.

"Well?"

"That, Mr. Coldiron, is none of your business."

"Look, I really don't give a rat's. But let's call things by their right names here, okay?

You're afraid to see Barry go, really. Aren't you?"

Susan dragged on her cigarette.

"Under all that liberated, feminist bullshit, there's a scared little girl who got fucked over by one guy, and who is very nervous that it might happen again. *That's why you don't want to part with the money. You don't want to look like a fool a second time.*"

"All right. All right. So what if a part of me doesn't want Barry to leave? That's a natural reaction."

"Christ, you got more parts than a Broadway musical."

"I'm listening," she said, feigning lack of interest with a flashing roll of her eyes.

Only Coldiron knew he had her hooked good. He had a sense about such things. It was called the con. "I don't even think you love him; the kid's too lame for you. You got him around instead of a poodle. Barry's too much of a lightweight for you. What you'd really like, the kind of man you dream and cream about, is just like me." He jabbed himself in the chest with his own thumb.

"I can't believe this," she moaned and laughed at the same time.

"I've been watching you operate; you ain't kidding me with all that release and freedom shit. You want Barry to loosen up and become independent and adventuresome, all right, but not too much, at least not so's you'd lose control over him." There was a gleam in those gray eyes.

"Where it's really at, Ms. Independent Woman, is that you don't have the balls to dance with the likes of me, someone who knows that the door opens both ways, a man who won't let you on his jugular vein. Shit, I could probably describe your ex-husband without ever having met him. Knowing you is enough."

"Please do. This is more fun than charades." This time it was Susan who signaled for the next round, a drink for each of them.

"The hair and build might be different, your ex might not look anything like Barry, but I'd be willing to bet the rent that he was about as independent as a wingless parakeet in a room full of hungry cats. And you ate it up."

Susan stared at him through the gathering smoke from her cigarette. Her face showed control. Her eyes said anger and pain. Coldiron had hit the mark about all of it, even down to Todd Shepherd, her ex-husband, and how the guy was always so meek and passive. Which was the main reason Susan had been so devastated when she had found out that Shepherd had been screwing one of the secretaries in the ad agency where he worked.

About the only things she had salvaged from the marriage were her maiden name and her career. Susan had made a small but certain mark for herself in publishing. When the opportunity had arisen for her to move to Rochester, and take over the editorial post of the weekly magazine, she had jumped at the chance to get out of Manhattan and turn her back on her agonizing memories.

"You son of a bitch," she said.

"Not as far as I know. But I could be wrong," Coldiron flipped. There was a gentleness in his voice now; he saw no sense in doing any more damage than he had; he didn't want to go too far. He'd flushed her out, and, besides, there was something very attractive about Susan and her controlled vulnerability. For a long moment, they watched each other, he with the look of knowing satisfaction, she with more anger than sorrow. And for that fleeting instant, each of them, Susan and the old fox, knew; it registered with two very different people, brought together by dominolike circumstances and coincidences, that if it were another time, another year for Coldiron, if he hadn't been so tangled in his private obsessions, and if she could ever truly let herself become more open and receptive to the whims of an adventurous and zanily crazy man, they might have tried it together.

But Coldiron's plan for the road had to supersede any stirrings of that kind. And Susan's need for a bridge between order and freedom, that slender junction linking security and abandonment, and her feelings for Barry would never allow it.

She broke their interlude of fantasy with,

"Let me show you how much I'm afraid to let Barry go." Susan slowly removed an envelope from her slender, leather purse and handed it toward Coldiron's wide mitt. Only she didn't let go when he tried to take it.

"There's just one catch to your windfall, Mr. Coldiron."

"Yeh?"

"Barry is never to know where the money came from."

"You got a deal," Tate said, bringing the fat envelope toward him. He could smell the money inside of it, the coin felt sweet and good and powerful in his big hands. "No problem."

"You can tell him anything you like, convince him you got the money from an old friend, anywhere but from me. I'll cover my end by explaining to Barry that I would like to kick in, but my parents in Bronxville have suddenly run into some financial troubles and I want to send them whatever I have. It'll work; my father doesn't manage money well."

"Okay by me. He knows I've been beating the bushes for bucks."

Coldiron looked over at Susan and felt his lust melt into respect. He saw a lady who was sincerely trying to break a habit. He'd tried to quit a few in his life himself.

It did go smoothly. Barry bought the story about the money, what with getting it from both Susan and Coldiron. As far as he was concerned, Tate had somehow dug up an angel, a

124

friend from the old days who fronted Coldiron the coin they needed. West also breathed better, knowing Susan hadn't cleaned out her savings to help them.

Financial pressures lifted, Coldiron settled into what Barry believed to be his last month of training. But Tate wouldn't commit to a definite departure date, he only kept repeating the same litany: the kid wasn't ready yet.

He picked up the tempo. He drove the kid even harder in practice and West's response was defiance.

Barry was convinced he had been ready weeks before. He sensed he should've already been playing stakes matches, save his coach's need to punish him into following authority. He even suspected Coldiron's hesitation to leave Rochester had more to do with the old guy's persistence to put the touch on Susan for money than a measure of the kid's ability.

Their relationship deteriorated into one of rebelling student and autocratic professor. The athlete had grown restless under the restraints of the coach that West was suspecting might know less than he did. The two rarely talked around the apartment.

It came to a head midway through the third month. Coldiron was in the balcony charting West's moves; he was checking that the kid was taking the best percentage shots. Barry was playing a game called suicide. He was standing himself.

It was a grueling exercise. Barry was doing something barely possible for two well-conditioned men. He covered the entire court, returning his own shots. It was a drill designed by Coldiron to tax the kid's endurance and reflexes to the limit. It was an exercise that also extended those limits; Barry was being pushed beyond pain and his own reason. The lesson was for the kid to see that there would always be something left, even after the body and mind screamed a different message. Beyond agony there was a well of strength—a sweet reserve that could be called upon once it had been discovered to exist.

The kid's chest heaved like a surgical oxygen mask. His legs burned. Despite the band around his head, he was nearly blind from his own sweat. He had been at it for thirty minutes, roughly equivalent to playing six full games of singles, without intermission and back-to-back.

"C'mon, kid. You're dogging it," Coldiron called down after Barry blew an easy return. It was the wrong time for the wrong words.

"*That's it,*" Barry yelled and rifled the ball, nearly taking Coldiron's head off. "*No more of this chicken-shit stuff. When the fuck are we going to stop jacking off? I want to play handball!*" His gray jersey and shorts looked as though someone had turned a hose on them.

"When I say so. Not until."

"When *you* say so? I'm getting sick of this drill sergeant shit. Who the fuck died and left

126

you in command?" Barry stood at the foot of the back wall.

"Pardon me. I think you must have me confused with someone who gives a shit."

"Yeh. Go ahead. Be cute. I'm the one down here sweating my ass off."

"Not right now you're not. You're shooting your mouth off."

On the couch that night, Coldiron knew he had run out of time. The kid was a good month away from being ready. But Tate worried that Barry might throw in the towel; he was that close to the breaking point. Stretching out on the couch in the darkness, arm draped over his forehead, Coldiron knew he had to do something. He didn't want the kid to cut bait and quit; Tate couldn't bear to have it slip through his gnarled fingers. Not when he was so close.

The kid was good. Not just good; he was great. Tate had secretly given him that. It was taking everything the old guy had to stay with West in their practice matches.

But there were flaws in the kid's game. Little things, defects an expert would pick up immediately, as a wolf smells blood, and demolish West. If Barry went down in flames, so did Coldiron. Along with losing the money, Tate's plan would get kicked all over the hardwood. He didn't know if he could take that. Not again.

Between swigs from the pint of Green he kept under the couch as a sleeping tonic, Coldiron searched every corner of his tired brain for a plan. He needed desperately to keep West a student and work the kid until the defects were remedied, but still get them out of Rochester.

Across town, in Susan's apartment, Barry was also concerned with his dilemma. Only he was ranting to Susan about it. She let him go on.

"The bastard is a sadist. He wants to drive me into the ground," West said, stalking around her living room in a fury.

"Now, that doesn't even make any sense. He's got as much to lose as you do."

"You mean the seventy bucks for the sale of his car? Shit, he's working on other people's money all the way."

Susan laughed. "I should rephrase that. He's got as much to *gain* as you do."

"You know what I think? He's a fucking fraud. There's probably no circuit. It's a joke, or his sick fantasy. He's just bullshitting so he can scam a place to live, get free food and booze. I'm beginning to doubt that he even got the loan, the two thousand dollars. I haven't seen any of it," he cried. Susan smiled to herself on that one.

"Son of a bitch drinks like he owns stock in Jack Daniel's. And he charges every drop of it to me. I'm waiting for the man at the liquor store to send over a couple of guys from Alcoholics Anonymous to talk with me. The goddamned guy is a fraud. I tell you."

"Ah. I don't believe it. Just trust him."

128

"Trust him, she says. *I am trusting him. Right into the fucking welfare office.* Which is where I'll be going to pick up my food stamps."

"I'll feed you. I'll get it back in trade."

"Funny."

She caught him from behind and began rubbing his neck. She made small circles with her strong thumbs.

"*Ooooh.* Yeh," he cooed and stopped pacing.

"You're tight." She pressed harder.

"Really."

Susan worked her way to his sore shoulders.

"Ouch." He jumped.

"Wow. Feel those knots."

"We had another ceiling shot drill today. I looked up so much I thought my eyelids would lock open. *Ooh.* Easy."

"I am. I really like to inflict pain. Coldiron taught me."

"Don't even joke about that."

She worked out the tightness in his shoulders. He relaxed under her fingers. Susan then turned him slowly around and worked his shoulders from the front. He got a long look at her white satin shirt that showed clearly the dark circles that were her nipples.

"Now that you've had your shoulders, you get your head," Susan said. Slowly she lowered herself to her knees, kissing his neck, chest, and stomach softly as she descended. She eased out his erect penis and took him with her mouth.

The following morning Barry brewed the coffee. Tate was able to keep a slug of Green down after ceremoniously sitting and watching the glass for nearly five minutes. Then he said to the kid, "Have your apartment sale this weekend. We're taking off next week."

West was so astonished he wasn't sure he had heard right. "Next week? You mean I was right? I am ready?"

"Yeh, kid, you were right. You're ready." Coldiron chased the Green with coffee.

It was a furiously busy week during which Coldiron didn't relent an inch. Barry had to sell his goods, clean up his affairs in Rochester, and see Susan on his own time—after the grinding workouts at the Y. At its end, Friday morning, West's blue Pinto was packed with his clothes and gym equipment. A case of Green sat on Coldiron's suitcase.

The proceeds from the apartment sale, Susan's loan, and what remained of Barry's savings left them with a $3,000 stake. Coldiron insisted on managing and holding the money. Susan had agreed, figuring if the old guy hadn't skipped with the stake by now, he wasn't likely to do it at all.

"I told Susan we'd swing by her office before we left," Barry announced as they pulled away from the curb in front of his apartment building. Coldiron nodded.

Tate stood outside the car, leaning against the passenger door, while Barry vaulted the granite

130

steps and melted into the lobby of the black Xerox Corporation Tower. Susan's magazine, *Women's Weekly*, was located on the thirty-first floor of the building.

He reached her small office in minutes. She was peering through horn-rimmed glasses at the paste-up boards leaning against the wall of her office. She looked lean and tight in a denim jump suit that zipped up the front. She moved to meet him.

"Set to do it, eh?"

"On our way. Coldiron's waiting downstairs. He said to say good-bye. And that he can't handle tearful scenes."

"Tell him good-bye for me. He's a good-hearted old guy. And I consider myself a pretty fair judge of men."

"Yeh. You know you're the one, Susan. I'll wait for you."

"Hey. No promises. No strings. Okay. Do what you have to do. I love you. But we're not joined at the hip."

"I love you, too. I'll call and write. Let you know where we are."

"For sure. Who knows? I might show up at one of your stops and surprise you."

Barry pulled her close and kissed her hard. Then he left. He had felt it coming; there was a choking sensation that moved up his chest and into his throat like pressing fingers. He didn't want to lose it in front of her. He wasn't that free.

She watched him walk out, knowing that if she ran after him, begged him to stay, he probably would have, Barry was that unsure of himself and the plan. But Susan knew it would never be any good that way, it would be the same as before; she had to break the pattern. No more recycled love affairs or marriages of her pitting her need to control another laid-back, easy-going man. She wanted something better this time, and no matter how bad the hurt hit her, and it was hard, she knew if she could let him go, and he came back when he was done, it would be better than it had ever been before for her.

Coldiron saw it as soon as Barry lowered himself into the car and released the emergency brake. "She's just a broad, kid. I'll admit, she's better than most of the run; nevertheless, she's still a broad."

"Just a broad? Life's pretty simple for you, isn't it, Coldiron?" Barry stared straight ahead. He didn't want Tate to see the dampness around his eyes.

"Yeh, pretty simple. The world's made up of two kinds of people. Those that jerk off too much and those that don't jerk off enough."

"Where do you fit in?"

"Depends on what time of the day you catch me. Now let's go and win us some coin, kid."

They headed into the cool sun. It was mid-April and there was still snow on the ground.

They were quiet, their minds fixed on different realities.

Barry thought of the woman he had left behind, how she was the one for him, how he doubted he could make it very long without seeing her. He had come to depend on her for reassurance and advice that he was doing the right thing.

There was a picture in Coldiron's head. It was their schedule. It was in the form of a triangle, one that was divided into small squares. Inside each space there was a name. It was the handball ladder of the top players in the country. Above the triangle, seemingly safe and protected by those below it, was a name that he knew well. It was a name that had been burned into his brain many years before.

The picture represented a road map to wealth and fame for the two men. And it was the realization of a dream that a tired, crippled man had been carrying with him for a long time, that had kept that man going when there had been nothing else.

Chapter Eleven

THE ROAD

They made it to Cleveland in eight hours. The ride was mostly boring and uneventful, except for one incident. Just outside Erie, Pa., they were nearly run into a guard rail by a tan Dodge van with an I FOUND IT bumper sticker. Barry swerved the Pinto sharply to miss both van and guard rail. Coldiron had been shaken out of a nap. He had rolled down his window and yelled at a shocked, young woman driver. "I don't want to lose mine, either. So watch where you're going, cunt. *Hee hee.*"

Tate directed Barry to downtown Cleveland and to an ancient but sophisticated-looking old building. The polished brass plaque read CLEVELAND ATHLETIC CLUB. MEMBERS ONLY.

"Get used to those plates, kid. You'll be seeing a lot of them all over this country."

"Okay with me," from the driver.

"We play in the morning," Coldiron announced. They unloaded their gear in the underground garage. The place was cold and damp.

"Who am I playing?"

"Does it matter? Even if I told you, the

name wouldn't mean anything. For the record, you're up against Jack Kritzer."

"You're right. The name doesn't mean anything to me. He any good?"

"Fair. I want to break you in easy. No sense losing everything right out of the gate."

"Thanks for the vote of confidence."

"Anytime, kid."

They took the elevator to the lobby area. It was a large room of dark wood and high ceilings, cluttered with too much leather furniture, the type where the red hide was fastened to the wood with dime-sized brass tacks.

The two were met at the chest-high registration desk by a short and thin man wearing a red blazer. Over his heart was a blue crest with gold letters spelling CAC. The coat fit him like a bag. He looked like he had pawned his ribs.

From under a generous shock of gray hair the man asked, "You gentlemen members?"

"No. We're guests of Mr. Kritzer," Coldiron answered. "We have a room reserved for the night."

The place smelled old, historic, and antiseptic. There were shadows of the past in the room. Barry felt excitement warm his stomach.

They chose to stay inside that evening. Coldiron had offered a review of Cleveland's night life. "Nothing going on out there except crime. It's so bad, the muggers are mugging each other. I ain't stepping foot out of this place." So they didn't.

After a good dinner that Tate signed the check for, Barry announced, "I think I'll go upstairs. See if I can get Susan on the phone. Then I think I'll turn in."

"Okay, kid. I'm going into the other room and take the Ohio bar exam."

In the room, Barry called Rochester. He already missed her. He was also having second thoughts about kicking around the country playing handball for a living. It was all so strange to him. Nothing felt familiar. He was glad he caught Susan home. She picked up the phone on the second ring.

"How's it going?" she asked.

"I don't know about this whole thing. It seems so crazy right about now."

"Hey, give it a chance. You can always come back. This place'll be here for a while. So will I."

"Damn, I miss you. Nuts, huh?"

"Not really. I miss you, too. But it's always rough the first few days. Especially for the one that leaves. You'll be okay. Look at it as a vacation, if you want. One from which you can come home anytime."

Silence from Barry's end.

"Try doing it a day at a time. You can change your mind without giving notice. You're a free man."

More silence from his end.

"C'mon. We'd like to eventually do a thing together, right?"

"If you mean get married, yes."

"Right. Well, if we can't be apart for awhile, how could we live together? Neither one of us is looking to be adopted. Correct?"

"Yeh. You're right."

"I know how you feel, though. The thought of not running by your place and hopping into bed with you is kind of tough to take."

"There's always self-abuse."

"I threw away the vibrator. Either the natural you or nothing. No additives, chemicals, or preservatives."

"I play tomorrow. Coldiron says I'll be losing my cherry."

"You're lucky to have one to lose. Know anything about the guy you're playing?"

"Not much. Supposed to be a veteran who's won some big tournaments."

"You'll do fine. Got butterflies?"

"Pigeons."

"Try to get some sleep. Call me after the match. Love you."

"You, too."

He hung up, thought about going downstairs for a beer, then decided to call it a night. The excitement of leaving Rochester, the drive to Cleveland, and the relief of talking with Susan all had served to wear him out. He wanted as much rest as he could get for the next day. He had no idea what to expect, what he was up against. Barry wanted to be ready.

Coldiron stumbled into the room at midnight. Barry had been tossing under the sheet and blanket for two hours, trying to fall asleep. His thoughts had been moving through his head like a violent river. He had finally succeeded in dropping off; he'd been out for about ten minutes when Tate's acrobatics began.

The first crash, the one that woke him, was Coldiron's ass-over-ankles trip. It was brought on by a coffee table catching him across the shins.

"You cocksucker," was his midair song.

"Who the fuck put curbs in the carpet," was the half moan that came after he had landed.

The second somersault came as a result of Coldiron trying to get his pants off over his gym shoes. The corduroy seized the rubber like it was sewn to his feet. He fought wildly in the darkness to free himself from their grip. Barry lay in bed cringing. Coldiron lost his footing and fell with a clatter through an end table and lamp. He finally gave it up and dropped into bed, half clothed, pants pulled down over his sneakers. He was snoring before he had stopped bouncing.

West got up for the third time to relieve himself. He was convinced his bladder and heart had to be connected. They were both overactive. So was Coldiron's sphincter. He began passing foul-smelling, pickled-egg-and-whiskey farts. They were to continue to seep into the room all night.

"Good Lord," Barry muttered. He yanked his covers over his head.

The following morning the kid took a bye on breakfast. That his stomach was doing a dance and that he had been treated to Coldiron's anthem of dry heaves prompted him to order orange juice, a cup of coffee, and the morning paper in the club's deli.

Coldiron's morning sickness was nothing new to West. The older guy spent the first half hour of every morning bent over the porcelain pony. The kid had gotten used to it, but he was nervous this morning.

He finished his second cup of coffee, folded up the paper, and got up to leave. It was eight-thirty and his match was scheduled for ten. Barry didn't even know where the courts were. He wanted to go to the locker room, get dressed, and leave himself plenty of time to warm up. Anything would've been better than sitting around while his head attacked him with what might happen in his first go at hustling.

"Where the hell is he, anyway?" he said aloud to himself. "Some manager, coach, or whatever the son of a bitch calls himself." He paid for his coffee and juice at the cash desk, hardly acknowledging the middle-aged woman who took his money. His thoughts were on his upcoming first test.

West was getting more nervous. He hadn't as yet been given the book on Kritzer. He had no idea the type of player he would be facing. The kid wanted some advance notice on Kritzer's strengths and weaknesses.

"Christ, for all I know I'm playing a one-armed, transsexual midget," he said aloud.

There was Coldiron across the smoking room. His coach was laughing and joking with a black porter. The guy's bald head shone as radiantly as the table he was polishing. Barry skated through the sea of plush burgundy carpeting and maze of highbacked leather chairs. The room smelled like a tobacco humidor.

"Jesus, Coldiron. I've been looking all over for you. Don't you think we should talk?" West asked.

"Sure. But first say hello to Uriah. He's an old friend of mine. We go back a long time. Uriah's a goddamned good fourwaller."

The black man's eyes glowed like buffed anthracite. "Aw, Tate, that was centuries ago." He reached out to West. His wrinkled fingers crawled around the younger man's palm as though they were ancient snakes. "Pleased to meetcha. Your coach here is saying you're a good one."

"At least he tells somebody how I'm doing. Thanks. Nice to meet you, too."

"Old Uriah put the best of them through the wall." Coldiron's eyes were narrowed from the previous night's drinking and his morning gagups.

"Playing Kritzer, I hear. Don't let him get you running."

140

"Somebody's got some information on the guy." West glared at his coach, and whispered, "What the fuck you doing? This is no reunion party. We gotta talk."

Coldiron ignored him and turned back to the porter. "Shit, you're over seventy and you could still put Kritzer away."

When Uriah let his ears lead him to Coldiron's direction, West realized the old porter was blind.

"C'mon, man, I haven't been on the slats for twenty-five years. Since before you had the trouble in New Orleans." The blind man's comment seemed to let the energy out of the room. Joy seeped from Coldiron's smile. West was too obsessed with his own dilemma to notice.

"Yeh, sure, Uriah. We got to make it. I'll catch you later."

"See you, Tate." The porter caught the paradox of his own remark and smiled through teeth that looked like ivory baby fingers. "Good luck, kid."

"Let's go, Barry. You've been choking the gopher long enough. Time you started earning some coin to pay your way." Coldiron did his shuffle to the elevator waiting area and punched the button that pointed down. Barry was right behind him.

The building was 1930s vintage. It had been revamped several times to keep up with the latest fashions in architecture. The elevator was one of the few holdovers from the old days. Its frame consisted of ornate brass extrusions. The inside of the car was velvet and wood. A round neon light hummed on the ceiling. Coldiron jabbed B and the elevator jerked into motion. A finely polished seat was folded against the car. A name plate mounted over the control panel read H. BORSKY. Under it someone had penciled SUCKS."

The elevator stopped gracefully and noiselessly at the basement, as a rock might settle on the ocean floor.

"This is the place," Coldiron announced.

"I gotta take a piss."

"You should get that thing fixed. You're in the john all the time."

They walked directly into a brightly lit locker room. The floor was green indoor-outdoor carpeting. Cream-colored walls sparkled. Where the Rochester Y locker room smelled like marinated sweat socks, this place had the aroma of a barber shop. Barry gawked. Jacuzzis, Whirlpools, and rubdown tables rimmed the outside walls. A color TV was on and surrounded by overstuffed fabric chairs filled with overstuffed men with white towels wrapped around their white bodies. The room was plush.

"We're on in a half hour," Coldiron advised the attendant dressed in all white behind the desk. "Kritzer-West. What court we got?"

The attendant was well muscled and he had an off-season tan. Employees enjoyed unlimited club privileges. The weight and sunlamp rooms were evidently two of his favorites. He looked down at the reservation sheet in front of him. "Let's see. Yeh. Court Four at ten. Kritzer's already signed in."

Barry felt a wave of anxiety curl through his stomach.

"Use locker fifty-three," the attendant continued. "Here's your key and towel. Enjoy yourselves." Tate took the towel and key. They both had the same blue and gold crest design as was on the desk clerk's blazer.

"Fifty-three, eh? Let's hope it's your lucky number, kid." Tate led West into a row of tangerine-colored lockers.

Barry's nervousness came out as false bravado. They both knew it. "Let me at this guy, Kritzer."

"Don't get too cocky. He's good. Kritzer's been in there with the best of them."

"You set 'em up, Coldiron. I'll knock 'em down."

"Okay, hero. We'll see."

West was dressed in ten minutes. He ran his hands under hot water for as long as he could stand it. A bone bruise would send them back to Rochester that same night; a bad spur could make his hand swell like a grapefruit and lay him up for three weeks. Not to mention the agony of finishing out a match with a bad hand. Everytime the ball struck a bone spur, it was like having a nail driven into your palm.

143

"I'm ready." White gym clothes wrapped around his lean and taut muscles, Barry was set for combat.

"Those new gloves?" Coldiron asked, packing his rumpled cardigan into the kid's locker.

"Yeh. Why?"

"Jesus. I teach you everything I know. . . . don't you realize trying to hit the ball with those will be like playing with a layer of snot on your hands?"

West examined his unused gloves.

Coldiron dug a piece of sandpaper out of his pants pocket. "Hit 'em with this a few times. It'll rough 'em up."

Tate shook his head and continued, "That's right. 'I set 'em up and you knock 'em down.' Fucking know-it-all kids."

The courts were one flight up from the locker room. They were serviced by two hallways—a narrow one provided access into the courts themselves; the other, wider and more brightly lit, opened into the gallery area. Each court could seat around one hundred. The galleries were deserted. There were six courts in all. Court Four was the only one with its lights on.

Upon reaching the lower hall, the sound of a hard rubber ball striking concrete cracked through the stillness like a horsewhip.

"What's that sound tell you?" Coldiron quizzed.

"That someone is playing handball."

"Smart fucker. A regular Rhodesian scholar.

I mean what does the noise tell you about the courts?"

"Walls are concrete. Ceiling not known until . . . there, a ceiling shot. The ball played 'White Christmas' coming off. They're hardwood."

"Okay, you've shown me you can hear. Now let's see how well you can play." Coldiron peeked through the vision slit in the thick wooden door labeled "4." The lights inside burned brightly. Jack Kritzer was throwing his ball, underhanded like a softball pitcher, against the front wall.

"Just play your game and you'll be okay," Coldiron said, turning to West. "Like Uriah said. Don't let him get you running. Kritzer plays a basic game. No frills. He's a percentage shooter all the way. He's probably too smart to let you get him running. If you happen to make him move, you'll wear him out."

"Any weaknesses he's got I should concentrate on?"

"Just play your game. Force him into mistakes. He'll make them eventually."

"Okay, Tate." The kid nervously shifted his weight from foot to foot.

"Go get him, kid. He's waiting for you. I'll be watching from upstairs. Good luck." There was paternal sincerity in his voice.

"I'll handle him okay." More false bravado. He had to urinate again.

"You'd better. It's all riding on this one."

145

"What?" The kid's head snapped around. "You bet our entire stake on this one match?"

"You got it, kid. No sense fucking the dog. We came to gamble, remember?"

Before he could protest, Coldiron had opened the door and eased him through the opening. The heavy door closed with a thud behind the kid. All he was conscious of were the lights snapping off and on quickly and the air conditioner's loud humming.

For a brief instant, Barry was blinded by the brilliance. Of course that sensation of stepping from dawnlike grayness of the corridor into the operating room glare was not new to him. But this time he had difficulty. He felt like he had jumped up too soon. He was dizzy. That everything rested on his shoulders was a reality he suddenly found frightening.

He made like he was adjusting the door so it closed properly. He was faking. He was trying to clear his head. Everything was fuzzy. He had spots in front of his eyes. In between his ears sounded like a TV after the network had signed off. He heard a noise like the sound of wind rushing through trees with newspaper leaves.

In seconds it was gone. He was thankful. He was okay. Barry turned to face his challenger. What he saw shocked him, so he thought his eyes were still unfocused to the light.

They weren't. It was just that his opponent looked nothing like he had expected. Jack Kritzer was bald and pudgy and on the slide side of fifty. The guy would've looked more at home bowling-on-the-green at a retirement village than playing stakes handball.

"You must be West." Kritzer pulled his glove off and knifed his hand toward Barry. It was small and soft.

"Nice to meet you," Barry responded. Then wondered why he said such a stupid thing. Here was this guy trying to separate him from his money and he's telling Kritzer how happy he is to make his acquaintance. *Hey, asshole*, he thought, *this ain't no fucking Junior Chamber of Commerce luncheon.*

"Go ahead and warm up," Kritzer said. "Take your time."

Barry began bouncing the ball off the front wall in "patty-cake" fashion. He immediately noticed the dust that had collected in each corner. The floor had settled slightly, though not enough so the maintenance man's mop could slide under the wall. These corners called for a soft kill.

He had picked up another fact while pretending to adjust the door. The steel jamb and concrete had not been ground perfectly flush. The metal overhung the concrete by a fraction; there was enough lip to change the flight of the ball. Maybe not enough for a hinder-call, but enough so the ball might hang a split second longer in the air and throw off a shooter's timing. A hinder replayed the point. Missed timing meant a loss of service or of a point. A big difference.

Barry took some shots off the back wall; he whistled several against the ceiling and made a couple of alley passes, just to get the feel of the place. Everything was concrete, except the floor and ceiling. His ears had told the truth in the hallway.

"Anytime you are," West said.

"Throw for serve?"

"Okay." West backed up against the wall.

"Go ahead," the older man said.

Barry whipped side-armed. His ball struck the front wall about two inches from the floor.

Kritzer let his fly. It caught the joint between the wall and floor perfectly—so neatly, if he had been throwing putty, he would've sealed the crack.

"Yours," Barry understated, staring at the wall.

"We go the best of three. First service alternates each game."

"Sounds good." Barry took his place near the back wall. He gave a silent order to his knees to quit trembling.

"How's your ball?" Kritzer asked. His toes pointed away from his body when he walked.

"Just came out of a can." West tossed it to him.

"Mine, too. You'd be surprised how some of the new ones are dead."

He watched Kritzer hold both balls shoulder

height. His opponent's feet were nearly parallel to his shoulders. West's ball responded best. Kritzer tossed his into the balcony. A hand reached over and snatched it out of midair.

"Thanks, Coldiron," Kritzer said.

Tate's familiar grunt of acknowledgment came from the shadowed seats. In his concern to study the condition of the court, Barry had forgotten all about his coach. He never thought he'd see the day when he would welcome Coldiron's growl. He did at that moment.

Kritzer walked slowly to the server's box. He dribbled the ball as he went. West took the few seconds to get his strategy down. He planned to get the old guy right out of the server's box, then get him running and wear the old duffer out early. Then he'd put him away.

Barry lined up one step to the left of center. Kritzer looked back. West nodded his readiness. Barry's career as a handball hustler was about to begin.

Kritzer's initial offering surprised him, causing a split-second hesitation. The serve died in the back left corner before Barry could reach it. What had made the kid balk was that Kritzer was lefthanded. He had been caught completely off guard. He had never faced a southpaw.

Not only was Kritzer a lefty, he was also a damned cunning handball player.

The match's outcome was never in doubt. Kritzer discovered the kid's weaknesses right off. West had a lethal right; he killed everything the older man showed him to his strong side. Two shots in two games. To his portside, the kid from Rochester was a piece of cake.

Kritzer picked him apart with reverse spins and slices. Everything the older man dealt up moved exactly the opposite way from what Barry was used to seeing. It was all one-eighty. Barry almost threw his arm into the seats trying to dig out Kritzer's garbage. When he managed a return shot, it was weak and poorly placed. Kritzer had an exclusive lease on the center court zone. He let West have the back portion of the court. He didn't need it.

When Barry got off a ceiling shot, it was too feeble. Kritzer was there to kill it. If the kid tried charging the front wall, he helplessly watched an alley pass scream by him. Kritzer got *him* running. He slaughtered the kid down the alleys. He nailed the cocky accountant's jock strap to the front wall. He put the kid through the wall.

When West shook Kritzer's hand before leaving the court, he had to choke back tears of disappointment and rage. This was a different man than the one who had walked into Court Four ninety minutes earlier. He was sullen and bitterly dejected. He had been handed his ass, 21-6 and 21-9. His and Coldiron's dreams of an odyssey of victory and adventure were over. Practically before it had begun. Berry hated the thought of facing his coach.

Tate was nowhere in sight. It figured. Barry knew he was probably drinking his brains out in the nearest gin mill. Or hanging by the neck in their room. The kid really couldn't blame him if he did either.

He made his way back to the locker room. He showered and dressed in silent despair. His future as a handball hustler had been jumped all over by a lefthanded man he had never heard of, and probably would never see again.

The yellow-haired, tanned attendant in the ice cream suit flagged West down on the way out of the locker room. "Your partner said he would meet you upstairs in the men's bar."

"Thanks." Barry dreaded it. Even seeing the attendant had embarrassed him. For all he knew, the entire Cleveland Athletic Club was snickering at him behind neatly manicured fingers.

He found his coach leaning over the bar. Coldiron was sipping out of a glass as big as a flower vase. The men's bar dripped coin. Well-dressed businessmen in dark and proper suits and with well-groomed vocabularies sat around cherry gaming tables. Coldiron looked more like he belonged in the janitor's office.

"Thirsty, kid?"

"Yeh. Give me a Carlings Black Label. And a .45." Barry could've sworn he saw Coldiron smile.

"Don't take it so hard. Even the best of us have dropped a few." Coldiron turned his big glass as he spoke.

"Yeh. Sure. Let's celebrate." Ten years earlier West would've sobbed. Standing at the bar, he felt like there was a lump of peanut butter caught in his throat.

"Let's get the fuck out of here. I want to get back to Rochester while we have enough money for tolls and gas," West spat. He rolled the cool beer glass in his palms. His left one was red and swollen. His right practically unused.

"We got some matches to win. You're not giving up on me, are you, kid?"

"What do we use for traveling? What do you bet? Credit?"

Coldiron propped himself against the rail so he faced the kid. It was quickly evident to Barry that the drink his coach was nursing wasn't the first he'd had while West had showered and dressed.

"It's like this, kid. You got the left hand of a faggot hairdresser waving good-bye. I knew you weren't ready in Rochester. But you had hot pants."

"You thought I was going to lose?"

"Thought? I fucking knew it. Shit, I been standing here drinking these buckets of Green since Kritzer threw out his ball."

"What are you talking about?"

"What I'm talking about is a free handball lesson. Did you actually think I'd be dumb enough to bet *any* of our money on you? It was a setup, kid. Kritzer was doing us both a favor.

The only difference was, I knew it before you did."

"Are you fucking shitting me? You mean we were just jacking off down there?"

"You're half right. Kritzer was playing handball. You were jacking off."

"It was for *fun*? There was no money bet?" West's voice had gone from dejection to violence.

"You got it, Einstein. I'll set 'em up and you'll knock 'em down, remember?"

If they had been in a down-the-street corner bar, someone might've stepped in between them. Or their argument may even have been ignored.

They were in the Cleveland Athletic Club's men's bar. Proper gentlemen who pay $1,500 a year for the privacy aren't often faced with shouting and hurled obscenities in their sanctuary. The patrons got confused; they began craning their necks like turkeys in a thunderstorm.

"You motherfucker! I ought to jam your ugly head up your ass." The kid lunged for Coldiron. "I'm going to knock that nose off your face."

Coldiron was ready for him. Careful to shield his drink with his body, he took one giant step back.

Bridge players and lunch patrons began inching toward the door. Their quiet muttering underscored the shouts from the bar. The club members automatically left the silliness for the hired help to handle. These were oil company executives, insurance magnates, and financial wizards; they were not common, roll-in-the-beer-and-mud barfighters. The doorway became a crush of the retreaters and those who had rushed from other areas to see about the source of the yelling.

"Settle down, you moron," Coldiron said as he backed away. "Somebody do something. The son of a bitch has gone crackers."

The only one around to help was the bartender. He was a swarthy, short, bald guy who should've been riding thoroughbreds instead of being a bar shaker.

Coldiron held his big palms up in front of him. West put one right between them. It was a chopping left that clipped Tate over the ear. The punch had caught him flush, but didn't hurt much. The older guy had enough Green in him to anesthetize an entire hospital ward.

To the bartender's credit, he tried to stop it. He stood on the sink behind the bar, reached over, and grabbed West in a headlock. The kid tried shaking him off. The little guy held on for everything he was worth. His enraged mount grabbed at the bar. He found an abandoned, burning dollar cigar in one of the big glass ashtrays. The guy was probably fortunate that West didn't come up with the heavy ashtray. He probably would've torn the top of the bartender's head with it. As it was, he put the cigar out in the guy's bald spot. The little guy let out a yelp and released his grip on West's neck. Holding his smoldering head, he wiggled past a pile of dirty dishes and through the pass window that connected the kitchen to the tap room.

It subsided as quickly as it had started. That they still had money, and the comedy routine of the bartender extinguishing his head as he pushed through the window, which was smaller than his shoulders, had slaked Barry's rage.

"You mean we didn't lose anything?" he asked.

"Not a dime. Now take it easy." Coldiron's big hands still faced the kid.

"Well, I'll be go to hell. Let's have a drink." West turned to the empty back bar. Through the pass window the bartender could be seen throwing water on his blistered head.

Coldiron calmly walked around the bar and set the bottle of Jack Daniel's in front of his spot. The club members began inching back into the room. One of them braved a remark, "This isn't a boxing ring. If you want to fight, go up to the freakin' gym."

Coldiron extended his middle finger downward and said, "Can you read upside down, asshole? *Hee hee*." With the other he massaged the egg-sized knot that had sprouted over his ear.

Chapter Twelve

POSTGRADUATE WORK

"You sly old fucker. You almost did a rollout on my heart." Barry laughed loudly. "I was even thinking of jumping into my car and heading for Rochester, instead of facing your ugly ass."

Coldiron nodded.

"What happens now? Where do we go from here?"

"Nowhere. At least not until you develop a left hand and can play a southpaw. If you learn to hit the fucking ball half as hard as you punch, we'll be okay." Tate continued rubbing the side of his head. It was beginning to throb.

The bartender pushed through the stainless-steel back-bar door. A wet rag was perched on the top of his head. His eyes never left Barry.

Coldiron continued, "Kritzer has agreed to work with you. We start tomorrow morning. Now let me drink in peace, willya? You embarrass me." He turned to the bar and his tight lips formed a faint smile. The student was once again teachable. The only thing it had cost the coach was a knot on the side of his head. In view of the kid's potential, Coldiron would've

156

gladly let him beat on his noggin for an hour with a two-by-four. Pain was nothing new to him. He and hurt had walked together for over twenty-five years.

Barry's attention went to the bartender and his head. "Sorry about the cigar business. Let me have a look." He reached across the bar.

"Stay away from me," the little guy snarled. He recoiled and grabbed a quart of gin by the neck. "I'll bury this in your face."

For reasons of economy they grabbed a hotel room two blocks from the CAC. It was a clean place, and it wouldn't be a drain on their money while they stayed in town for West's continuing education.

The two men were standing in the club's lobby at nine the next morning. Coldiron looked especially terrible. His hand had appeared ready to leave his arm when he had attempted to drink coffee earlier. The whites of his eyes weren't.

"Kritzer's waiting. Let's go build you a left hand, kid." Coldiron winced with each word. His head throbbed from Barry's left hook and from a vicious hangover. Even the well-filtered air of the CAC brushing against his face pained him.

The scene was like the day before. Kritzer was bouncing his ball off the floor, patiently waiting for the kid to push open the door.

Only this time, instead of hobbling upstairs to watch, Coldiron followed Barry into the court. From his gym bag he brought out what appeared to be an oversized truss. It was a leather harness sewn to a wide belt.

"Hmmm," Barry said, "what's planned for today? Maybe a little S and M action? You bring the Mazola oil, Tate?"

"Come over here and I'll show you what's planned for today."

West was even more certain that this time Coldiron had burned out his clutch with booze. "That's the dumbest contraption I've ever seen."

Kritzer kept bouncing his ball, without saying a word, like it was no big deal; it appeared to be a ritual he'd been through before.

"Hold it a second," West said, playfully backing away from Coldiron and the truss.

"Oh, come on. We don't have all day." Coldiron looped the belt around the kid's waist. "You're not my type, anyway." He snapped the buckle tight and adjusted the harness around Barry's right arm.

"You gotta be kidding. I feel like I'm in psycho."

"Whatever," Coldiron said and walked to the door. "I'm going upstairs. I gotta get well." With the quick off and on of the lights he was gone.

Barry stood there, feeling very stupid.

"Go ahead and loosen up, kid," Kritzer said.

Warming up wasn't so bad. Barry took his time and adjusted to being one-armed. His trouble began when they started their volleys. He was not only playing against Kritzer, a very good handballer, he was battling against his own instincts.

West lined up in his natural righthanded stance. Then he nearly tore his arm from his shoulder trying to rip his hand from the harness to hit shots that came to his right side. Twice his feet got tangled with the effort and he fell to the floor in a squirming, cursing heap. He spent the entire morning off balance. He felt and looked like a heavyweight boxer wearing a straitjacket at his first ballet lesson.

He stood Kritzer for twenty-five games a day, one-armed. Barry played everything the guy threw at him—lefthanded. Kritzer tried to lay every shot down the left alley.

In the beginning, West missed everything by a mile; he didn't even come close to returning the older guy's tricky, southpaw stuff. Barry was getting crazy with frustration.

Then he started connecting. Which provided him with a different form of frustration. His working hand began resembling a piece of raw liver. Each morning he gritted his teeth with the pain of the first few shots striking his inflamed left paw.

Coldiron was merciless. He was riding the crest of West's crushing defeat while the kid was still hungry and humble. The blond accountant's ego had been laid to rest for the time being. Tate knew to take full advantage of his pupil's surrender in order to correct the fatal flaw in his game. He also knew the task would never be any easier than in Cleveland. Especially after the kid had a few victories under his belt.

Kritzer maintained his low profile during the sessions. He tossed an occasional word of encouragement to Barry when it appeared the kid was ready to break from the frustration. And at the end of the two-week training, the surrogate instructor knew he was on the court with a complete and awesome specimen. Barry was a formidable handball competitor with unmatched natural ability and stamina; the kid was clearly gifted.

At the conclusion of the two-week schedule, he reported, "You got yourself a horse, Coldiron. The kid's a winner."

"Can he handle your lefthanded junk?"

"The kid's whipping me."

Coldiron smiled. West was doing something onehanded that few men in the country could do with both hands. He was beating Jack Kritzer. The kid was handling the guy who had twice been national champion in the '40s and still was one of the premier players in the Buckeye State. At fifty-four years old the lefty could still put most of the players in the country through the wall.

The old fox had also defied a lifetime of conditioning. He had turned Barry into a completely ambidextrous player. Better than ambidextrous. The kid now had a lethal left. Just how strong, was summed up by Kritzer: "He can put it away from anywhere on the court. His left is so powerful, he could kill a man with it."

Chapter Thirteen

RESTART

When they checked into the Illini Athletic Club, the kid was feeling good. He had his confidence back. It was of a different quality than the humming-in-the-dentist's-office stuff he had put out in Cleveland. He knew his game was in excellent shape.

Coldiron had even let up on the kid. By doing so, he was silently telling West that he was satisfied with his progress.

Tate had good reason to back off. The old fox knew Barry's game was without a weakness. The kid was holding a full house. He had a complete arsenal. He could shut down anything any opponent could deal up. The only ingredient he lacked was experience. A few hundred hours on the court, head-to-head with the best in the game, would remedy that. Finding the top players, lining them up so as not to bring the kid along too fast, was Coldiron's job. It was one he relished.

Though untested, West also knew he was on the way to big things. He had a hidden and strong basis for his self-trust. And Coldiron had told him so, in as fervent terms as the coach was able. Tate wasn't one to hand out daisies.

"If you get beat, kid, it'll be because you'll beat yourself. You'll do it with mistakes. That's the difference between the good and the great. The great make fewer mistakes and know how to jump on an opponent's miscues. There's little difference in ability between the great and the good.

"The best players have total concentration. They could read a book laying on the runway at O'Hare Field. A great player will always use his focus to force a good one into beating himself. One move, one look, a couple of unorthodox shots, a sudden burst of energy can turn a match around. The great ones are masters of the psyche. Remember that, kid. The only person who can kick your ass is attached to it."

It was for real now. The money was on the table. Coldiron wanted the kid to have everything going for him, including a belief in himself. West was holding the winning hand; he could afford a little faith. Tate's dream of big bucks was draped over the blond kid's strong shoulders like an invisible garland. And what's more, he had come to like Barry. The kid had hung in there. That was a quality that Coldiron respected in a man.

"Who we up against?"

"His name is Hugh Ballantine. He's vice-chancellor of the University of Illinois." Tate's voice had lost some of its harshness. He was businesslike, but gentle.

"Another old man?"

"If my wet brain serves me well, you've been getting put through the wall by old men a lot lately."

"True."

"Ballantine is about forty-one. He came up fast. Something about saving the big boss's ass from a bunch of hippies. Used to be an English prof when I knew him."

Fate, more than ability, had vaulted Ballantine into the second-highest office of the second-largest university in the country. The English professor had been chosen by the group of terrorists who were holding the administration building during the '68 riots, to negotiate the release of the chancellor, Dr. Trolley. Ballantine had earned the respect of the student population by his passionate and articulate antiwar stand. That closeness to the kids had endeared him to the State Board of Regents, which had been terrified its institution would be leveled by riots. He was the youngest man ever to hold the position of vice-chancellor.

A lean, rangy, and deceptively strong man, Ballantine lived alone and modestly in a two-bedroom apartment in professor row. He banked much of his $55,000-a-year salary and used the rest to satisfy his passions in life. They were handball, mountain climbing, and young women. In that order.

Ballantine played handball four times a week to unwind from his swivelchair life. For one month a year he disappeared into Colorado's high country to clear his mind of city grime and job stresses. The handsome academician was also frequently seen squiring exquisite-looking ladies around Champaign. He was prized material for marriage. And if not marriage, many women sought a night of his pleasure.

Barry watched the vice-chancellor warming up, through the slit in the door of Court One. Coldiron rubbed the back of the kid's neck. He was ready to let his prizefighter answer the opening bell.

"Do your job, kid, and you shouldn't have any trouble with this guy. Just play your game. Kill your percentage shots. Force him into mistakes. Don't try to run with him." Coldiron swung open the door and let his charge into the arena.

While pumping Ballantine's hand, the first thing West noticed was his opponent's legs. They tightened like steel coils with each step he took. The girth of his thighs appeared larger than his finely tapered waist. No wonder Coldiron had warned him against trying to run with Ballantine. The guy was in perfect condition. From the crotch up he was built like a marathon runner. His chest was expansive, stomach flat, and arms long muscled. And those legs looked like they could carry him at full speed all day. In a running game, West knew, it would probably be him, not Ballantine, who would succumb first.

Barry mentally set his game plan while he walked the court. "Anything I can't kill goes to the ceiling or down the alley. This fucker is a gazelle."

Warming up, Barry thought of the bet Coldiron had made. Tate had said he'd start small; he'd let Barry get used to playing for money. "No sense in scaring you," his coach had said. His match with Ballantine was going for $250 per game and $500 to the winner of the best of three contests.

West thought, *A grand isn't exactly leftovers.*

Ballantine spoke first. "I'm ready anytime you are."

"Throw for serve?" Barry responded.

"Let's go." The vice-chancellor wasted no words. He used enough of those in his job. On the court he was pure sportsman; he was all business. He played out of love of competition and the thrill of wagering on himself. He was there to demonstrate his game. Not to talk about it.

Barry earned the right to first service with a throw that landed so squarely in the front wall crotch that when it came away his ball made the sound of a stick being pulled from mud.

Walking to the server's box, Barry tried not to think about how nervous he was. He glanced toward the gallery. It was empty except for the solitary figure sitting in the top row. Coldiron was the sole spectator. He would watch for any flaws in his pupil's game, things that could be worked out and improved upon for the next match.

Barry smiled to himself, thinking of one lonely man sitting in the upstairs shadows. *Big screaming crowds, eh? That fucker would con a polio victim out of his iron lung.*

There were few flaws in West's game for his coach to record. The kid played a masterful match. He refused to allow the academician to get him running. He kept his concentration. Ballantine was good. West was great.

Whenever it looked like Ballantine might drive him out of the center-court zone, Barry drove a fister off the front wall and forced the other man to the rear-court area. West's ceiling shot was working well. Ballantine could barely get under it. He nearly tore out the end of his fingers trying to pick West's perfectly placed high bouncers off the back wall. His returns were weak. Barry killed them with ease.

He found no defects in the accountant's game; so strong was West's left, so many shots did the kid kill from his portside, Ballantine never did determine which was his natural hand.

It was all West. Time and again, Ballantine gamely charged the front court, hoping to flush Barry out by driving alley passes by him. But the kid cut off his low screamers with light-ning-fast reflexes. It was Ballantine who got to

167

watch the ball drive past him. He had to change direction with a slamming of his feet against the floor, so violently he appeared to shear himself off at the ankles dozens of times.

Barry continually played him against the grain. When Ballantine moved right, West placed the ball to his left. If he tried to adjust by overcompensating to his left, he was shown a right slicer that found him hopelessly out of position. The stranger from Rochester tied him in knots.

Barry took the first two games, and thus the match, 21-3 and 21-6. For an hour's work, he and Coldiron had added $1,000 to their kitty.

Ballantine had said very little during the two games. Other than announcing his score, "your point," "my serve," or "hinder," he had played in silence. It had been evident to him that he had no chance. A part of him had been, of course, disappointed. But he was also an admirer of greatness. He had been in awe of the completeness of his blond opponent's game.

That evening Barry talked long-distance to Susan for an hour. He joyously ran down every detail of his victory. Coldiron got drunker than West had ever seen him. Both men were flying high. They were just burning different fuel.

Chapter Fourteen

FAT TIMES

"Kid, tonight you get your first taste of victory cream, so to speak," Coldiron said, leaning back in the passenger seat of the Pinto, chewing an unlit Parodi Italian stogie. That Tate was munching instead of smoking it was a point of gratitude for West. The nasty-smelling little things made him sick.

"What are you talking about?"

"According to my calculations, with our stops in Champaign, Chicago, Springfield, and Evanston, we've depleted the cash reserves in the State of Illinois by six thousand skins."

"That much, huh?"

"Correct. That's the good news."

"I have a feeling I'm going to hear the bad, whether I want to or not."

"You've probably poured half that much into payphones talking to your 'chioocc' in Rochester."

"My who?"

"Your girl."

"C'mon, it isn't that bad."

"Almost. Look, kid, I like the broad. I really do. But you need some diversion, something

169

to round you out, a little dessert to go with your main course. You could use an activity unrelated to handball so you don't go stale on me. Either that, or I'm gonna invest our winnings in Ma Bell stock.

"Besides, my blond warrior, I've been watching you, the way you look at the lovelies, lately. You might be laying it on thick with Susan how much you miss her, but you can't fool ol' Tater, here. You ain't quite as love-nuts for her as you once were."

"What do you mean? That's horseshit," Barry said. "And what kind of diversion are you talking about, anyway?"

"We're gonna get you laid, kid. We're gonna get our gophers milked. Detroit's got the best hooors in the country. You're gonna get a divorce from your own hand. At least for a day. *Hee hee.*"

"That's what I like best. A guy who's his own best audience. Come to think of it, you'd better be. Your material sucks."

Coldiron adjusted his bite so the Parodi pointed at his nose. "*Hee hee.* Yeh, you can't fool ol' Tater."

"In addition to being a piss-poor comedian, and a lousy judge of my relationship with Susan, you're full-on wacko. You know that?" Barry was now chuckling. "I don't suppose it ever occurred to you that I wouldn't want to get laid?"

"Of course. If you were still doing what was

170

good for you, kid, you'd be at Rochester Circuits jacking off at your handball trophies and playing with your books."

"Oh, Jesus. Now I got a live-in counselor. You want to hear about how my mother kicked my cat when I was three and that's why I'm fucked up now?"

"Who's running this show? Have I steered you wrong yet, kid?

"Be sure to use new gloves when you cuff your dick. Leaves fewer blisters. More counselor talk. *Hee hee*."

"I'll remember that."

"We got us a two-day layoff, pardon the choice of words, and you're gonna loosen up a little."

They had barely hit town and located an inexpensive hotel near the site of their next encounter, when Coldiron ordered, "Let's go, kid. We're gonna find us some gash."

"How do you plan to do that? Call room service? Never mind. In this place we'd get Quasimodo in drag."

"You don't like my travel arrangements?"

"Not really. Just so the cockroaches get to bed before I do. What happened to those ritzy places you talked to me about when you were convincing me to drive around the country with you? Or is this the way it is in every marriage? Promise 'em the Hilton, then bring 'em to Flea Bag Inn."

"Now, kid. We'll only be laying low for a

while. We don't want to make Connie Hilton any richer, do we? I'd rather have the coin to bet. That way we make more coin."

"You sound like the fucking U.S. Mint."

"Back to the business at hand. Sorry about that. Back to getting us laid. I know this town, so just follow me."

Coldiron wasn't exaggerating. Within fifteen minutes he had the Pinto in front of a multi-tiered brown colonial house.

"If I remember right, kid, there's every shape and color in there."

"You been here before?"

"About ten years ago. They used to have a sit-down bar on the first floor where you sip and eye the lovelies. All the plumbing is done upstairs. Let's check it out."

"Ten years? Wait a second. Whorehouses aren't like department stores. They don't stay in business for long. How do you know it's still what we're looking for?"

"Just c'mon. There's only one way to find out."

The place was as Tate remembered. The first floor of the old house was a lounge. Several women, in various stages of undress and make-up, attempted to attract one of the three men in attendance.

The cocktail waitress, a bored-looking gum chewer attired in what looked like a taffeta Bo-Peep outfit, took their order.

"A pint of Jack Daniel's Green for me and a Coors for my horny friend."

Barry looked away. The waitress yawned.

"Do you ever *not* drink Green, Coldiron?"

"Kid, this is an insane world, one big outpatient clinic, if you will. They lock up those people who know how to live on this planet. The really crazy people got the keys. For me, I'd rather have a bottle of Green in front of me, than a frontal lobotomy."

They found seats in a lounge that resembled a waiting room in a doctor's office. West eyed the merchandise.

"Yeh, right," Coldiron teased, "you don't want to get laid. You look like a blind dog in a meat market."

Their drinks were delivered. Coldiron flipped the waitress a ten. "Keep it, honey."

"Whattya think? Is it the life or isn't it?" Coldiron talked through the Parodi and a grin that would get him arrested around a schoolyard.

"Yeh." The kid's attention was already locked in on a sepia-skinned woman. She couldn't have been over eighteen. She had a full Afro and the high cheekbones and the almond-shaped eyes of a Eurasian. She was wearing a white muslin robe-dress. Her skin glowed against the garment.

"Got yours picked out already, eh? Go for it."

"She sure is fine."

Coldiron motioned to an older woman who turned out to be the madam. Her age and fashion set her apart from the others. She was a dignified-looking fortyish and wore an expensive two-piece knit suit.

"Hey, mama. My friend would like her." Coldiron pointed to the dark girl.

"Oh, yes, Blossom. She's one of our most attractive girls. Born in Jakarta." The madam motioned to the younger woman. "Room Twelve, dear."

Coldiron made a move for his wallet.

"Please, not here. Blossom will settle up in the room. We like to be discreet. Makes us look less like that butcher shop you were referring to a moment ago."

"Meat market, you mean. *Hee hee.*"

"I've got money," West said. He waved Coldiron off. Blossom threw Barry a smile, and he followed her upstairs like he had been hypnotized by it.

"Be sure to show her your gopher shot, kid," Coldiron called after them.

He turned to the mildly irritated madam. "You're doing the guv a favor. Consider your work here a mercy fuck. The poor bastard's in love."

"Nothing wrong with being in love, is there? Isn't then when you never have to say you're sorry?"

"Lady, when you fuck your Irish Setter is when you don't have to say you're sorry."

174

The woman blushed.

"Getting you to turn red is like teaching the Pope the rosary. *Hee hee.*" Coldiron was out of control.

She wanted to head him off. He had the whole place laughing. "See anything here that raises your temperature gauge?"

"How about you? I'd like to bounce you around the room a few times." He tweaked her breast.

"Sorry," she smiled. "My warranty has expired."

Coldiron finished his drink, chomped down on his Parodi. "By the way, you put any more water in this booze, you'll have to serve life jackets with your drinks."

"Look, Mr. Whatever-Your-Name-Is . . ."

"Coldiron."

"Mr. Coldiron, we aren't looking for a stand-up comic this week. If you wish to avail yourself of one of our girls, fine. If not, would you please quiet down? Or you'll have to wait for your friend somewhere else."

"How about that one?"

He had selected the hungriest-looking one of the lot: the auburn-haired white woman who had licked at her lips whenever Coldiron glanced in her direction. Next to the madam, his designee was probably the oldest one of the flock.

"That's Jasmine. She'll do you right, mister."

"Jasmine? Blossom? What the fuck you runnin' here? A florist? Your name's gotta be Tulip. Right?"

He walked up to Jasmine. "C'mon, honey. I'll show you my stinger."

"Number Sixteen, Jasmine. Go easy on the old man," the madam said.

Tate bowed and waved his nose at her. He hobbled up the stairs after his choice. Her round bottom delightfully filled her high-waisted gabardine slacks. He took a big bite of it. She jumped, started to yell, then turned and smiled. Business hadn't been so hot for her.

"*Hee hee*," from Tate.

They stopped in a room that looked like the sitting room of the original house. The woman began undressing next to the big bed. She pulled her burgundy shirt over her head. Her breasts shimmied free.

"Wow. They yours? Or transplanted cannon shells?" Coldiron croaked from the other side of the room. His pants hit the floor.

"It's fifty dollars for the hour. I do whatever you want. Just no kinky shit." Her tone was that of asking for the salt at a diner.

"Sounds like a deal." He had his sweatshirt up over his head. The cigar was still clenched in his teeth.

In one motion, Jasmine wiggled out of her tight-fitting slacks. Her cream-colored bikini panties came off with the effort. She had a tight and good body. No sagging was visible in the quiet light.

Prostitutes aren't easily startled or shocked. They see the best and worst of life each day. When Jasmine turned to collect from Coldiron—it's always pay before passion in brothels—she shrieked, "What the fuck? . . . What the Christ are you doing?"

Tate was standing next to the bed. He had his erect wang in his big hand and was pumping wildly on it.

"For that kind of money, lady, you ain't gettin' the easy one. *Hee hee.*"

Chapter Fifteen

BACK TO BUSINESS

The Automotive Executives Athletic Club building looked modest from the street. There was little style to its brick, limestone, and window exterior. The place could've easily passed for an office building. The finely polished door hardware and the red-coated doorman were tip-offs that something other than middle-level business was going on inside. Members being delivered in sleek limousines was another.

Inside the twelve-foot oak doors of the club, all mediocrity ended. The AEAC was the relaxation palace for the *crème de la crème* of Ford, Chrysler, General Motors, and American Motors. Any economic rivalries were left outside the AEAC. The place breathed wealth, power, and aristocratic commonality.

So finely managed was the AEAC, three of the five top-rated restaurants in all of Detroit were located within its walls.

It was strictly a men's club. Other than female employees, women were not allowed above the first floor and could dine only in the restaurant located just off the club's lobby. And only as an invited guest of a member.

Several feminists' groups had attempted to break the all-male code of the AEAC over the years. Without exception, those efforts had been unsuccessful. Economic pressure and unfavorable media exposure were favorite tools of women's liberation. The club had all the money and members that it needed; members who wanted the place left like it was. Nor did the AEAC particularly care about public image. It didn't cater to the public.

Its rooms were reserved on a permanent basis. Members simply bought them outright, for the purpose of entertaining government officials, union bosses, or foreign colleagues and dignitaries. Or the suite might be used for a discreet dalliance by the member himself. The club had a secret list of numbers for a stable of girls from nearby Michigan State University.

The AEAC catered to every bodily need or pleasure of the men who controlled America's highways. The club's physical conditioning personnel and athletic facilities were the best that money could buy.

Its initiation fee was $10,000; annual dues totaled $2,500. The club's membership screening procedure was a page out of the CIA covert investigation manual. Applicants needed to be at least second-generation millionaires to be considered. The AEAC was old money and, politically, just to the right of Genghis Khan.

With this as a backdrop stood Coldiron and the kid. They had been invited to compete in a club where more money was gambled at cards, backgammon, chess, squash, and handball than in some of the midsized Las Vegas casinos.

A formally dressed desk manager motioned for the two men. Barry followed his mentor through the quietly elegant lobby. Giant oil portraits of Henry Ford, Walter Chrysler, Lynn Townsend, and other club founders hung on the wall, scowling at all who passed. West was intimidated by the scene.

The men they passed were all dressed nearly the same in three-piece, dark blue suits, white shirts, conservatively colored ties, and hair that looked like it was trimmed every other day and set with an epoxy spray.

"We in church or something?" Barry whispered as they walked. "Christ, it's quiet in here."

"No. People here have more money than God does."

"Names, please." The desk manager had a thick British accent and condescension in his chin.

"Coldiron and West. Mr. Fresina is expecting us." Tate's mention of Fresina's name cut through the Britisher's haughtiness.

He checked the leather-bound book in front of him, then nodded in recognition. "Yes, sirs. If you'll take the elevator that's located under the clock, to the seventh floor, you'll find the locker rooms and courts. Please enjoy your stay with us."

"Gotcha," was Coldiron's reply.

They turned for the elevator. The clerk did a second take on Coldiron's baggy sweatshirt and cords and high-topped gym shoes.

Barry leaned to his coach. He tried to talk without being overheard. "Fresina? The accountant who came up with the idea for the hot new sports car a few years back?"

"One and the same."

"He had his picture on the cover of both *Time* and *Newsweek* last year?"

"That's him."

"He's the executive VP of the biggest car manufacturer in the world."

"Look, kid. Before you get star-struck and swoon out on me, what did the guy at the desk tell you?"

"That I'll be playing someone famous?"

"Forget the automotive maggot for a second. You book fruits sure get impressed with each other."

"That the courts are located on the seventh floor?"

"You're getting warm. What about the courts? What did the guy at the desk tell you about the courts?"

"Oh, that."

"Yeh, that. We're here to play handball. Remember? Forget the fucking cosmetics. You and me couldn't even get a job making the beds here."

"The courts being on the seventh floor means

the walls are probably wood or plaster. Concrete would be too heavy for the seventh floor."

"Like I've said all the time. I'm in the company of a genius."

Not only did Barry get to play handball with Sal Fresina, thirty-year-old boy wonder of the auto industry, he dismantled him. The kid from Rochester went through Fresina and three other men in two days. In total, he left three auto executives and the president of an international labor union lighter in the wallet by more than $8,000.

They had been tromped by an unknown, a stranger on whom there existed no book, one who was handled by a cripple with little patience and a big thirst.

Barry West was playing the game the way Sean O'Dwyer had designed it to be played. He performed without fault, with a purity of rhythm that was a joy for Coldiron to watch.

Tate was in heaven. He had a suitcase full of money and a horse that could run away from the best of them. They had scaled nearly a quarter of the way up that invisible triangle. It didn't look like anyone could stop the kid.

Chapter Sixteen

THE LURE IS SEEN

It was mid-May and Overland Park, Kansas, looked like it had been hosed down with mud. The sun had just set behind the clouds that had hung over western Missouri for a week. On the outskirts of Overland Park, near where Kansas City bridged the Kansas line, a two-story, handsome brick-and precast-concrete office building sat alongside the expressway. Though nearly six o'clock, the parking lot was almost full. The cars had tan sidewashes from the week's worth of rain. The scene looked like a faded sepia-colored photo.

The tall man in the gray raincoat and white silk scarf pushed himself from his white-on-white Cadillac Seville. He walked to the front door of the building. Two names were spelled out in anodized aluminum letters over the double glass doors. The name on top was twice as large as the one below it. It read: MID-CONTINENT CONSTRUCTION CORPORATION; the smaller sign read: NATIONAL HANDBALL ASSOCIATION.

The rangy man let himself into the warmly lit reception area. He removed his toe rubbers and left them on the rack near the door, then nodded to the receptionist over his gold-rimmed glasses.

"Jake in?"

"Yes, Mr. Gleason. Mr. Bradford is in his office. He's expecting you." She was lean, conservatively dressed, and wore glasses that seemed too large for her narrow head and close-cropped hair style.

The reception area was semicircular. Hallways led away from it as streams flow from a pond. The man removed his green felt hat and laid his raincoat across his arm.

In his midfifties, Dutch Gleason walked with the grace of someone in good physical condition. He made his way to a big wood door bearing the black porcelain sign that read: J.A. BRADFORD, PRESIDENT AND CHAIRMAN OF THE BOARD.

The man rapped softly on the closed door and called, "Jake. Dutch, here."

"Come on in," was the muffled reply.

Gleason, blond-gray hair matted slightly from his hat, turned the silent door latch and let himself in. It was an office he'd visited almost daily in the thirty years he had worked for the man behind the big desk. Dutch still eyed the place curiously. It was habit.

Bradford's private sanctuary was an expansive room with one wall of windows that opened onto the atrium of plants and fountains. The charcoal brown carpet was deep and thick.

When Dutch stepped across the room, it was quiet—like he might be walking on the floor of a pine forest. Pictures and awards certificates covered nearly every square foot of the honey-colored paneled walls.

One side of the office was dedicated to the construction business. Colored photos of hotels, shopping centers, apartment complexes, housing tracts, oceanfront condominiums, and industrial buildings covered the walls. They were shots of some of Bradford's landholdings. Construction was Jake Bradford's bread and butter.

On the opposite wall, thirty feet away, were mementos of Bradford's obsession: handball.

Many of the greats were pictured. There were the old-timers: "Murderball" Ranft, first national champion in 1919; "Blond Panther" Platak, winner of seven consecutive singles titles before World War II; and the legendary Vic Hershkowitz, rated one of the best ever to strap on the gloves. Some of the more recent champions were shown in action shots: Jimmy Jacobs, six times singles and six times doubles champion; Paul Haber, the irascible and personable perennial singles star; and Fred Lewis, first winner of sanctioned professional play.

The wall behind Bradford's desk was a floor-to-ceiling trophy case. Exhibited were brilliantly polished plaques and figure trophies. Bradford's name was engraved on every one of them. They said they had all been won in doubles competition.

Dutch Gleason smiled to himself. Seeing the awards always tickled him. Not so much a tribute to Bradford's skill on the courts, the trophies and plaques were more a measure of the absoluteness of his power. Jake was a good handballer, but not a great one. As president and czar of the National Handball Association, he always had his pick of the litter in choosing a tournament doubles partner.

It had become customary for the national singles champion to pair with Bradford. Turning down Jake's invitation to compete at his side could mean being passed over for lucrative NHA-sanctioned tournaments. Dutch Gleason couldn't remember one player who had ever refused Jake's request. His boss could see that even the most popular player in the country got blackballed.

"Still wet out there?" Jake asked, taking Gleason's hand. At fifty-five, Bradford weighed what he did as a kid carrying golf bags for the wealthy at the Shawnee Country Club. Now he was many times a millionaire. Someone carried his bag at that same country club.

He also owned the National Handball Association and Dutch Gleason, its commissioner.

"Still wet out there, Jake."

"Looks like we get no spring this year. From winter right into summer." Bradford combed his gray hair so as to cover the small bald spot at the top of his head. He had short, stubby legs

186

that had served him well in his over forty years on the handball courts.

"What's up?" His intense blue eyes followed Dutch into the chair that faced his desk. Jake was tanned from his long winter weekends in St. Croix. Having had bad teeth as a kid, he had the habit of smiling without parting his lips. He had retained the habit but not the teeth. A California dentist who had provided many movie stars with their bright smiles had provided Bradford with his.

"Just wanted to talk," Dutch answered.

"Forms. Jesus Christ. It's getting so the paper weighs more than the buildings we put up." Jake shuffled documents from one pile to another on the kidney-shaped desk. Gleason watched. "Wait just a second, Dutch. Let me finish with this requisition."

Gleason looked at the guy he both admired and stood in awe of; his boss had accomplished miracles for the sport which they both loved. Thirty years before, when the American Handball Association had refused Bradford's requests for changes in tournament rules—changes that promised to popularize the game, Jake had simply started his own association.

Having provided the country's top players jobs with Mid-Continent Construction, in return for their exclusive participation in Jake's NHA-sponsored tournaments, his association had quickly grown more powerful than the

AHA. Bradford had then legitimized the game, by bringing to it the glamor that he had promised. He had interested television networks in covering the top matches. Bradford had constructed posh handball-racquetball clubs from coast to coast. The NHA came to completely dominate the sport. The AHA had shriveled and died.

"Okay. Finished. What do you have?" Bradford asked. He removed his reading glasses.

"Thought you'd like to know. Coldiron's got a horse. It's some kid who's been whipping everybody he meets. He's supposed to be a good one." Dutch watched for some reaction from his boss.

"His name is Barry West. They say he's got the heart of a thoroughbred. Nobody had ever heard of him until Coldiron got ahold of him. Coldiron's passed his savvy to the kid. So far nobody has even come close to touching him." It was then Dutch saw the change in his boss's eyes. They grew more vivid like that when he was angry. Or afraid. He had come to know Jake well over the years. They had shared a lot.

"Coldiron, huh? He would have a good one. He'd have a hell of a horse."

Thirty years working for Bradford had taught him the cues. The conversation was finished. Gleason got up.

"See you later, Jake."

"Right, Dutch. Keep me posted, will you?"

"For sure."

Bradford returned to signing the papers on his desk. "Whew. Paperwork," were the last words Dutch heard as he closed the heavy door behind him.

Chapter Seventeen

FLYING HIGH

By the time they hit Ann Arbor, Coldiron was up to his ass in cotton. In little more than two months the kid had earned $27,000. This didn't include Tate's private side bets that were helping to put the bulge in the old man's well-worn pockets.

Tate had also begun a ritual in each city they played. He threw a celebrate-the-good-times party. At these gatherings would appear men in their fifties and sixties—friends of Coldiron's from handball's old days.

Coldiron arranged one such gathering after Barry had performed some delicate athletic surgery on two prominent University of Michigan Medical Hospital physicians. It was a victory that was particularly sweet to Tate. He still held that medical incompetence was largely responsible for his walking like he had fouled his pants. The butcher in New Orleans who had set his legs had done a poor job.

The party in Ann Arbor was staged at Paglio's Italian restaurant. Tate and the kid were joined by Tony Grasso, Mike Zaleski, and Bobby Petta. It was at this gathering that

Coldiron was to learn for sure that West was no longer committed to Susan Burnett.

The kid's phonecalls to Rochester had grown less frequent and less lengthy. Barry's eye for pretty ladies had become readier. Which was okay with Coldiron, who had never understood why anyone would pass up a piece of tail over a woman who didn't happen to be there. Tate had summed up what he had thought of the kid's self-imposed chastity earlier in their swing. "For you to stay faithful to some broad on this trip is like bringing the game warden on a hunting trip."

The five got a big table in the backroom of Paglio's. It was a family restaurant and the food was excellent.

"Saw you play today, kid. I like what you got," Tony Grasso said. He had a full beard. It was dark and fierce with brushings of gray around the chin, and so thick it appeared Grasso was pushing bites of ravioli into a moving bush.

Grasso was a name the kid had heard Coldiron mention numerous times when his coach talked of the great ones from the old days.

"Thanks. Been lucky," West replied.

"Luck, shit. This old river pirate don't bet anything but sure things." It was Zaleski, the one that looked like an ex-fighter rather than a handballer. His nose was flat against his face, his cheekbones shined like white plums, and his flat forehead reached for straw-colored hair that had long since gone south.

It was Petta's turn. "Yeh, but even Coldiron don't work magic. The best jockey ain't nothing without a good horse." He and Grasso were a vaunted doubles partnership on the court.

As the evening moved on, Barry's attention was drawn away from their table. He only half listened to the foursome, who were getting drunker and louder with each round. Coldiron looked mournful and Zaleski's face resembled a stop sign.

The object of West's glances was their apple-assed waitress. Not much beyond twenty, she was the kind of woman who was naturally sexy. She didn't have to work at it.

The name tag hanging from her left breast read "Rose." Her skin tone, black unruly hair, and flashing dark eyes pegged her as having Latin ancestry. Her white uniform fit her well-put-together body like it was part of her; its buttons were being tested from her neck to her thighs. When she had first appeared at the table, Barry had felt the stir.

The beast had arisen in West weeks before. It rattled its cage when Rose gave Barry that wild look.

Except for the Detroit escapade, it had been three months since Barry had been with a woman. So much had he dedicated himself to thinking, eating, and sleeping handball, he had pushed all thought of other ladies out of his mind. Until lately, when he had found himself looking longer and fantasizing more.

He hadn't encouraged his lustful imaginings. But they were there. They were real. He was finding it more and more difficult to sit on his rising sexual appetite.

The group at the table was in a heckling mood. The more they drank, the harder they got on each other's cases. Barry was spared as a target of their barbs. It was an in thing between Grasso, Petta, Zaleski, and Coldiron. While they nicked at each other, Barry made a trip to the men's room.

Rose was leaning against the service bar as he passed. He asked, "What's going on?"

"Doing it by the numbers. Slinging the old lasagne around. Nothing but pure excitement."

"How about after Paglio's? What do you do when you leave here?"

"Not much. I sit around watching game show reruns and listening to my hair grow." She looked bored. Barry hung in.

"How about getting together tonight after you finish? We can both listen to your hair grow and play our own games. Who needs 'Hollywood Squares'?"

"You slick devil, you. Listen, at three o'clock in the morning my curls go into remission. Along with the rest of me. About the only games I'm into then go on in my dreams." She sorted through a tray of drinks, checking them out against her order card.

"Name's Barry."

"Don't remember requesting." She gave him that wild smile. Excitement beat in his temples. She seemed more amused than irritated by his persistence.

"You didn't. I thought I'd volunteer it. You look like the shy type."

"Didn't know it showed. Excuse me while I adjust my dress."

"What about it? Getting together later?"

"Give me a chance to think. Now's too busy. We'll talk later. That is if you still can. You and your friends drink like priests the day after Lent."

"In my case it's peer pressure."

"Peer pressure? Dig him. You some kind of college professor?"

"Naw. I read that somewhere. I've got just about enough intelligence to hurt myself."

She laughed. He walked away with the feeling they would be talking again. He let himself into the men's room.

"I'm not buying that wine, just leasing it," he said to an empty bathroom. He had a hard-on. He was also getting high. A piss shiver hit him and he put one hand against the wall to steady himself. He finished and went back to the dining room.

Petta, Grasso, and Zaleski had evidently decided it was Coldiron's turn in the barrel. He was at the receiving end, now. In doing so, the group also provided West with his first real knowledge about his mentor's past. Together nearly seven months, West knew little more about Coldiron than he had when they had first met at the Rochester Y. The kid's only information had come from Tate's old handball buddies they had met in their travels. Otherwise, the old guy's past was a mystery.

"Good to see you're not pushing a cab any longer," Grasso jabbed.

Coldiron flinched. Then his head went back to tilting in every direction like it was on ball bearings. "Ah, get off that shit," he croaked.

"You mean you haven't told the kid about your K.C. cab-driving career?" Zaleski asked.

The trio looked at each other and cackled. They knew they had him.

Coldiron tried to take the offensive. "Heard there was a Polack gangland slaying here last week." He had leaned across the table until his face was inches from the laughing Zaleski's.

In doing so, he continued to impress Barry with his recuperative powers. He could be on the verge of passing out, be facedown drunk, but somehow rally his senses and become lucid. He had done it once again there at Paglio's.

"Really?" from Zaleski.

"Yeh. They found two guys with their heads tied together, shot in the hands. *Hee hee.*"

Petta moved in like a Kamikaze. There was to be no letting up. "Didn't that fag try to hold you up first?"

"Something like that." Coldiron's face got redder. He was getting mad.

Barry was loving it. He was actually seeing Old Steelface blush. He wanted them to continue. He wanted to hear it all, but was afraid to prod them on.

He didn't have to. They were having too much fun winding their old friend up like a cheap toy.

Petta continued, "If you hadn't blown all your fares on Green, he might've left you alone. He had to get something for his troubles. Isn't that the way it worked, Tate?"

"It was my first ride of the night, numbnuts."

"What'd he tell you?" Now Grasso was on him. "How'd it go? 'Since you ain't got no money I ain't leaving empty-handed.'" He was trying to sound very swishy.

"Then he made you lean through the side window of your cab while he rolled you up in it. That's how it worked, right, Tate?"

"You cocksuckers. That's a bunch of horseshit and you know it." Each man got glowered at by Tate.

"Rolled him up in the window?" Barry asked. "Why?"

"Why? Well, the guy peeled off Tate's pants and punked him," Zaleski said. He was doubling up with laughter.

"Punked him?" It was West again. "What are you guys talking about?" The comment earned him a second or two of Coldiron's homicidal glare.

"The guy fucked him in the old bunghole," Zaleski answered. Loud enough so the surrounding patrons heard.

"Are you kidding?" Barry asked.

"Of course they're bullshitting. You don't believe that crock, do you?" from Coldiron.

"Christ, they printed it in the *Kansas City Star*. It was a lead story," Grasso chimed. "They all but said the guy left stretch marks on Coldiron's ass."

"You tell him you loved him, Tate?" Petta asked. "Did he hurt your neck when he pulled your head around to kiss you?"

"Did you get his phone number?" Grasso jabbed.

It was at that instant Tate kicked away from the table. He was going to go after all three of them. At once. Barry tried to get between his coach and the others. Coldiron was clawing mad. The others stayed put. They couldn't move from the laughing.

"Lousy, low-life motherfuckers," Tate screamed.

"Watch your mouth," from a surrounding table. People were on their feet. Coldiron didn't notice. His eyes never left the howling trio.

Out of the kitchen came a bear of a man. It was John Paglio, owner of the restaurant and casual friend of both Petta and Grasso.

"Hey, Tony. If you and your friends can't act like humans, get out," he called.

Coldiron held his ground. Fury burned in his face. Paglio saw it and kept his distance. No one around their table moved. West stood there, with a stupid look on his face. Petta, Zaleski, and Grasso were still laughing their brains out.

"Petta. You remember that overhanded shot you used when we won the state doubles?" Grasso asked.

"Oh, yeh. I recall," Petta answered.

With that Grasso flipped a piece of food in the air. Petta swung like he was throwing a rabbit punch and picked the bite of ravioli out of midair. He laid it neatly on Paglio's forehead. It stayed there.

"I'll have your nuts for that. I'll have them in the minestrone soup," the big guy bellowed and charged Petta.

"You'll have them in your ass." Petta side-stepped Paglio's rush.

"Naw, that wasn't the shot. It was more like this, man," Zaleski called and side-armed the hunk of sausage. It caught Paglio flush in the ear and stunned him.

Coldiron then killed a piece of lasagna against Zaleski's wide forehead. The Polish guy looked like he had been shot. The massacre was on. Food started flying in every direction.

The restaurant owner retaliated by rubbing an antipasto from a neighboring table in Petta's twenty-dollar haircut. Coldiron found the back of Grasso's neck with a hunk of linguini. It was raining food. The fight was contagious. Others in the back room started throwing bits of their dinner at random targets. It became a game. There was debris everywhere.

In five minutes it was over. The foursome who had started it had become allies against the rest of the back room and the restaurant's owner. They were friends once again. Their faces, hair, and clothes were stained with sauce. They looked like medical students after performing their first surgeries. It had been a sauce bath. Barry and Rose had cut out in the middle of it. They went to spend the night in the kid's hotel room.

Chapter Eighteen

THE CHANGE

By the time Coldiron and the kid worked their way into the South, they had been on the road for a little over five months. They were also more than $60,000 to the good. And it looked like they had only dipped into the till. The road promised them much more. Everywhere they went, the best handballers wanted a crack at Barry West. His growing reputation was attracting them in flocks.

Barry had been beaten only once since Cleveland. That lone loss of their Eastern and Midwestern campaign had come in Indianapolis. West had developed a harsh case of the chest flu, which had severely hampered his breathing. He was disoriented from fever and medication. His rhythm and coordination had been seriously affected. The defeat had set them back $2,500.

The kid got his first taste of Southern graciousness and wealth in Virginia. In a club whose origin dated back before the Civil War, with style and service commensurate to the social conditions of the nineteenth century, West played on courts that received dust moppings at five-point intervals during his games. Finely

dressed, quietly dignified, and polite black attendants saw to the athletes' every need. Theirs
were locker-room-attendant jobs that, according
to Coldiron, had been handed down from generation to generation. As had the right to belong
to the Fredericksburg Club.

The kid had been winning more handily
than ever. Though his competition had grown
keener as they went, and, in spite of the grueling schedule Coldiron had been arranging for
him, West seemed to be improving weekly. His
victories were coming easier.

It had also become evident to Barry that the
old man was in some kind of a hurry, as if they
had to do it all in a certain period of time. The
kid was pulling on his gloves at least three times
every week. Sometimes as many as five times.
His coach seemed obsessed with tearing the
country apart behind the abundant talent of
Barry West.

If Coldiron hadn't been so driven with
arranging the kid's schedule of matches, if he
hadn't spent so much time and thought glorying
in their growing pile of money, if he hadn't
been so intent on moving up that triangle his
mind showed him every night before he passed
out from Green, he might've noticed earlier.

Sure, the kid was unbeatable. He was winning big. He was demolishing everyone whom
Coldiron put him up against. But it was how he
had been winning that was to finally become

evident to his coach. Barry West had begun hitting people.

At first Tate hadn't noticed. Once he did, he was sure it was coincidence. Handball was a game in which the ball travels in excess of one hundred miles an hour. It was a sport in which the players moved rapidly around the court—a contest in which each player's hands sweated so profusely the ball could easily get away from someone. Accidents could and did happen in handball. Players often got hit with the bullet-like shots. It was considered part of the risk of playing the game—regrettable when it did happen, and the man who accidentally hit his opponent felt bad. It just happened sometimes. *Sometimes.*

Not until Fredericksburg was Coldiron's attention drawn to what was happening—when he realized that what he saw might not have been an accident.

It was in a match against Mike Montague—who was, like West, a real comer in handball but, unlike Barry, was backed by a group of prominent and wealthy sportsmen—that the change in the kid began to come into focus to Coldiron's bleary eyes.

Montague was a year older than West and was equally as aggressive on the court. He had just driven an alley pass along the left sidewall in an attempt to move Barry out of the center-court zone. The shot had gotten away from the Southerner; it was too high—above the shoulders and two feet off the sidewall. To be effective, an alley pass needed to be as close to both the floor and sidewall as possible. As it was, West was left with an excellent opportunity for a roll-out kill. He was in good position and the ball hung in the air like a ripe apple. The dozen or so people in the gallery, Coldiron, and even Montague himself figured West would easily put it away.

Only the kid didn't go for the rollout. He exploded out of the rear corner, catching his opponent's hard drive in its full momentum, and proceeded to drop Montague with a vicious shot to the back of the neck.

Montague was unconscious on the floor. Coldiron stood in shocked concern with the others in the gallery. He wondered if the others had seen what he had. Montague hadn't even been in the kid's shotline to the front wall. It appeared that West had deliberately hit his opponent, like he had lined the guy up in a rifle scope. Tate hoped his eyes had lied.

The place was quiet as Montague's second held a vial of smelling salts to the fallen man's face. The player's head jerked. His neck spasmed around the area where he had been struck by the ball. He came out of it, but not before his stomach had its say. Montague vomited on the man bent over him; it was the involuntary reflex that sometimes accompanies a deadening blow to the base of the skull.

He was helped to his feet. The stricken man

walked unsteadily, holding onto his attendant. Then Montague got sick again.

Coldiron shifted his attention to West. What he saw sent a chill through him. He was looking at a face without remorse. It was the face of a man without shock. It was the look of someone who had just completed a mission.

Montague was done. He had been hit in such a way that the energy had left him like the air being let out of a balloon. West had nailed him in one of the spots. Mike Montague was unable to continue within the fifteen-minute forfeiture-time allowed. West had won the match in the first game. He had barely broken a sweat.

Montague was led from the court. West politely offered his hand in sportsmanship. His injured opponent hesitated, but accepted. Coldiron, watching from above, wondered. It looked like there was something missing from West's well-wishes, as if it were an act that was more expected of him than voluntarily offered.

Coldiron waited until they were packing their car to leave to talk with West.

"You got off easy today. Too bad about that kid getting hit."

"Yeh. I felt real bad. He's okay, though. Lucky he was only shaken up."

"Yeh. Real lucky. What happened down there? Didn't you see him when you teed off?"

"No. The guy jumped in front of me after I had already pulled the trigger. There was nothing I could do. I really hated to see it happen."

"Right, kid. Those things are a bitch. Sometimes a guy just seems to jump in front of your shot. I know how it goes."

"That's what happened. Montague seemed to just jump in front of me at the last second.

"Where to next, Tate?"

"South. Way south," Coldiron said and climbed into the passenger side of the car. He'd try to forget what happened in Fredericksburg. He really wanted to believe the kid.

Later that same week, Barry was scheduled to play a wealthy Alabama industrialist in Mobile. The guy reputedly had inherited about three million dollars, a ship-building firm, two manufacturing concerns, and a love of gambling. His name was Corley Stinson and he was addicted to handball. He also absolutely hated to lose at anything.

While Coldiron and West were getting checked into their Mobile hotel, they were approached in the lobby by a magnificently structured honey-blonde woman. She knew exactly who she was looking for.

"Hi there, Mr. West." The words rolled through her full lips.

"Tell her I'm busy," Coldiron said. "Maybe I'll be able to fit her in three months from next Tuesday."

She ignored Tate. "Mr. Corley Stinson asked me to show you around our little town."

"Somebody turn on the music? Could've sworn I heard music," Tate smiled. She did sound like she was singing her words.

"Mr. Stinson asked me to spare no effort making you feel at home."

"Okay. This is the sort of welcoming committee I like. Right, Tate?"

"Sure, kid, sure."

The woman's khaki slacks looked as though they had been sprayed on her. "How 'bout starting off with a little dinner?"

West was warming up. "Sounds like a good program to me. Count me in."

Coldiron put his hand on the kid's shoulder. "Come over here a second, will you? We need to talk about something."

"Sure, Tate."

"We'll be right back, miss," Coldiron said.

They got out of her earshot.

"What is it? What's the problem?" West asked.

"If your hard-on hadn't sucked all the blood from your brain, kid, you'd figure it out for yourself."

"What do you mean?"

"Let me spell it out to you. You're playing Stinson tomorrow at nine in the morning, right?"

"Right."

"Miss Pneumatic Hips over there has been sent by none other than Corley himself, right?"

"Again you baffle me with your perception."

"She's gonna show you the town, correct?"

"Right, again."

"So you go. She fucks you until your legs are like noodles and Stinson picks my pocket. The cunt probably cost him two-hundred-bucks rental for the night. Which is what he most likely spends a day on cigars. Which is also not a bad investment when you consider there's ten grand riding on your match with him tomorrow."

"It doesn't make sense. I thought Stinson was loaded. Why would ten thousand be so important to him?"

"It has nothing to do with the coin, kid. It's his ego, not his wallet, that couldn't handle the bruising. Stinson fashions himself as a champion on the slats. He'll probably have his mother and the rest of his family there to see him kick your butt. These Southerners have funny pride. Most of 'em are still fighting the fucking Civil War."

"I'll be okay. I'll handle him."

"I'm asking you to think about not going out with the woman. It's a setup."

"Look, Coldiron, I told you I can take care of myself. You just set 'em up and I knock 'em down. Remember? How much sleep I need to win my matches is my business. Okay?"

"Sure, kid. You *knock* 'em down." Coldiron's thin lips bit each word. He looked at the kid for a long moment. Each was aware the other knew that Fredericksburg had been no accident.

That night Coldiron tried to shut off his mind with Green. His thoughts made it through the alcoholic haze. He lay in bed and tried to answer the questions that sliced at him. The same ones came at him. Over and over.

Why is Barry doing it? The kid has more talent than seven guys. Maybe Fredericksburg was an accident. Maybe the way Montague got hit, looking like he was set up, was your imagination.

As the questions were the same, so were his answers to them. Barry had started hitting people on purpose. There was no mistaking that. Fredericksburg had only turned his mind to it, allowed Coldiron to add it all up.

An occasional hit could easily be an accident. Even a couple of them. But Barry had picked off several people in the last month. That was more than coincidence. Especially with a player of West's caliber. The kid could put an egg in a china cup at fifty feet without breaking either. Barry West could put that hard rubber ball anywhere he wanted.

Which is what Coldiron knew he had been doing. West was sticking people in the spots. He was hitting them in the right places to slow them down, force them into losing their concentration, or, as in Montague's case, into forfeiting the match to him. What was especially frightening to Tate was that the kid had the skill and power to cripple a man. Even kill him. Coldiron had showed him how.

Tate was wracked with indecision. It was making him crazy. Should he confront the kid? Lay his cards on the table? Let West know he was heading for big danger? Then what? What if he did? What if West told him to shove it and walked? What if he ended the partnership and went on without Coldiron? The kid could make it without Tate. But Coldiron knew he sure as hell couldn't make it without the kid. And he was so damn close. They were three quarters of the way up the triangle. And the cash was building. Coldiron could almost stand on it and reach his dream.

The following morning he ran into Barry in the lobby. Coldiron was on his way to breakfast. The kid was just coming home.

"You go on in an hour. Meet you at the club. It's two blocks from here, on Canal Street." Tate made no attempt to hide his irritation.

"Can you wait for me? I'll just be a couple of minutes."

"I've got some things to do. I'll see you there."

"Hold it a second, Tate. You pissed at me?"

"You know the agreement. No partying the night before a match. You look like you got a lot left. Hope she was worth it."

"Lighten up. I'm winning, aren't I? I don't

hear you complaining about the money you're collecting."

"I'm not."

"Besides, from what I hear, Stinson is a piece of cake."

"How would she know? She play handball? He'll have to be, kid." Coldiron walked by him.

Barry's match destroyed any doubts Coldiron might've had that the kid was hitting people on purpose.

It happened in the third and match-deciding game. West had his hands full with Corley. His dark-skinned and handsome opponent was playing an extremely skillful game of handball. Plus West was exhausted. The rugged tour and his being out all night was showing on him.

Midway through the third game he hit Stinson. West was trailing 10-11 at the time. He was running out of gas when he paralyzed Corley with a bullet to the groin. The Southerner's scream had barely stopped rebounding from the stark walls when it was discovered that his left genital had been shattered. He was still writhing on the floor when the ambulance attendants wheeled the gurney into the court. The match was over.

Tate walked back to the hotel. His legs were killing him. The pain in his heart was even greater. He had to have time to think. Coldiron had a killer on his hands. The kid would stop at nothing to win.

Even winning was no longer enough. The

kid was addicted to the thought of becoming the best in the game. He had tasted the sweetness of fame. He was a top gun. They were lining up to take a crack at him. Lining up to play a hitter who liked the taste of blood.

One part of Coldiron knew clearly what he must do. The kid had to be dealt with before he killed somebody. He had to be taken out.

Another part of the old fox refused to accept the obvious. Tate had been a loser for twenty-five years, clawing for crumbs. That made it easy to deny, not that the kid was a hitter, but that West had to be dealt with. A very convincing voice in him said the kid would turn it around before it got too far.

Fear helped Tate consider that Barry would stop hitting people. Maybe if he lightened up on the kid's schedule, so West could get more rest, more time to let off steam. Maybe if Barry were less pressured and frantic, he would go back to playing honest four wall. Maybe it wasn't too late. Maybe the obsession to be the best wasn't too great. Maybe the taste of blood wasn't too strong in the kid's mouth. Maybe those who voted to take out the hitters hadn't yet noticed. Maybe he could forget the whole thing. Maybe.

There was the triangle. And the appointment Tate had promised himself he'd keep, that night in the alley in New Orleans. Coldiron was gripped with his own obsession. It was every bit as strong as Barry's compulsion to win.

In the final analysis he knew it was only a matter of time. He could only push it down so far with Green. The inevitable could be postponed for only so long. Coldiron's prayer was that his own compulsion and the Green could dull his conscience long enough until he could hobble up what was left of that triangle. He had to keep that appointment.

Chapter Nineteen

CONFRONTATION

"I flew down this morning," Susan said over the phone.

"Howdy," Coldiron answered. "Barry's not here right now." Her call had caught him off guard. He had been napping poolside, under a sun umbrella, at the Doral Country Club in Hollywood, Florida, when the waiter had stuck the phone on the table. He was attired in a brightly colored shirt, seersucker walking shorts, and the regulars, his high-topped gym shoes and the unlit Parodi.

"How'd you locate us? The kid tell you we'd be staying here?" His mind worked as he talked. Coldiron didn't like the unexpected.

"Coldiron, I haven't heard anything from Barry in over two weeks. The last word I received was a postcard from New Orleans saying he'd be playing in Fort Lauderdale this week. I'm down for an editors' conference, so I thought I'd try and track you down. I called the Bayshore Handball Club in Lauderdale. They told me where you were staying.

Coldiron picked up the concern in her voice. He liked Susan. He didn't want to see her get hurt. If she hadn't guessed by now, he didn't want to be the one to tell her.

"We've really been on the run. The kid has hardly had a chance to eat and sleep. You know me, I've been playing him regularly. You want to get your money's worth, don't you?"

She chuckled on the phone. "Of course. How is he? Is he okay?"

"Doing great, miss. The past few months the road has been our life. And life seems to be agreeing with him."

"I'm at the Fountainbleau in Miami Beach. I'll grab a car and drive up to see you. I'd like to surprise him."

"Oh, he'll be surprised, all right." Coldiron looked across to the other side of the pool. His protégé was talking quietly with the Jewish princess from the Bronx that he had spent the previous night with. "He'll sure be shocked to see you. I'm sure he'll love it."

"Great, I'm on my way."

"Listen, Susan, on second thought," he blurted, "that won't be necessary. Why don't we just meet you at the Bayshore Club for lunch? Lauderdale is between here and there. It'd be a lot closer for you. And we have to be there anyway to take care of some business."

"Sounds fine. My treat, okay? My magazine is paying for this trip."

"That include drinks? *Hee hee.*"

"That includes drinks, Mr. Coldiron," she laughed, too.

"You got it. Is twelve-thirty okay?"

"See you there."

The Bayshore Club was a meeting place for international sportsmen from all over the hemisphere. Its membership rolls and guest list boasted many of society's glitter names. Hemingway had boxed in the downstairs gym and had sipped cocktails with two of his wives at the clam bar that overlooked the channel with its slips filled with luxurious yachts. Jackie Gleason had often been seen in the billiard room adjacent to the color-splashed flower gardens that had been tilled with black soil imported from the Red River Valley of North Dakota. Inside the whitewashed walls of the club had strutted international playboys, millionaire expatriates from Cuba, Mafia chieftains, and industrialists. In addition, some of the best handball players in the country plied their skills on the courts located in the Bayshore Club's basement.

Susan's milky complexion pegged her as a recently arrived Northerner as she walked across the oakboard floors of the club's main restaurant. Big yachts gliding along the waterway made a changing portrait of floor-to-ceiling windows. Barry and Coldiron stood as she approached their table. Coldiron shook her hand. West hugged her and planted a kiss on Susan's cheek, much in the manner that he would greet a favorite aunt.

"Hi," she said.

"Really nice to see you. When did you get into town?" West asked.

"This morning. Thought I'd check in on all my ex-lovers before the workshop started tonight." She was wearing a vested off-white suit with an open-collared navy blue shirt. Her dark hair was tied back. She looked stunning.

"Glad you chose to see me first," Barry answered.

"I never said that," she jabbed. "It's already noon. How are you two, anyway? Still burning up the handball world?"

"My slavedriver-housemother plays me almost every day. Not much time for anything else. Just win, win, win."

"By the lack of phonecalls and letters, old Coldiron must keep you hopping."

"You know how it is." Barry averted her eyes.

"Sorry. Just a little anger, mixed with joking. So you're doing well, eh? Still want to be an accountant?"

"I'm afraid you'll never get him back on the farm," Coldiron added. "He's hooked on the good life."

"It looks like it agrees with him. You too, Mr. Coldiron. How are you holding up?"

"As long as Lynchburg, Tennessee keeps turning out Green, I'll be fine."

"I didn't imagine you went on the wagon."

"Speaking of that . . ." Coldiron looked around for a waiter.

"When do you play here, Barry?"

"Tonight at seven. Care to come?"

"I'd love to. Okay with you, Mr. Coldiron?"

"Okay with me," Coldiron lied.

Lunch was consumed amid more than forced humor. If it had been just that, Susan would've only been bothered. West's arrogance and poor manners disgusted her. When she had last seen him, he was shy and pleasingly innocent. Less than seven months later, she sat across the table from a stranger. His attention was splintered. He openly eyed other women. He was generally insolent and evasive toward her.

Susan kept looking to Coldiron for some sign. The older guy kept his eyes away from her. By two o'clock she decided she'd had enough. "I have to run." There was polite hurt in her voice. An hour and a half of being uncomfortable was starting to show on her.

Hearing from Barry only once every two weeks or so, over the past couple of months, had told her that he had cooled on their relationship. He had offered the excuse of his schedule, but his voice had told her differently. Though it hurt, she could understand that. His treating her as a nonperson was shattering to her.

"I need to get back to my hotel and do some preparation. I have a meeting later this afternoon."

"You have to go already?" Barry was more embarrassed than concerned.

"That's right." She didn't like the feelings

that ran through her. Her stomach was clenched. She didn't see herself as a jealous person, but those poisons were there, also. And she was angry.

"When you come back tonight, maybe we can have a drink after the match," Barry offered. He was throwing her a bone. All three of them knew it.

"I think I'd like that." She signaled the waiter and paid their check. "As I said, my treat."

Coldiron had stayed quiet through much of it. Susan seeing the kid play was not his idea of fun. Beneath her attempts at dignity in the face of hurt were questions. They were questions Coldiron wanted no part of. They were the questions he had even stopped asking himself.

The first thing that surprised Susan that night when she stepped into the gallery of the Bayshore Club's Court Three was how few people there were. Counting Coldiron, there were eleven men in attendance.

He was in his usual spot, in the first row, leaning against the sidewall with one foot on top of the glass wall that protected the spectators from a high and wild shot.

"You always play to such large crowds?" she asked him.

"Stakes handball ain't a spectator sport. Usually it's only the bettors and handlers who watch. Or those with an interest in the match, such as someone scouting one of the players."

She gazed downward, into the brightly lit

big box. Barry's blond hair flashed in the fluorescence. It was then, more than at lunch, that she noticed it was considerably longer than when he had left Rochester.

"Who's he playing?"

"Name's Alan Rich. He's from New Jersey. That's his coach over there." Coldiron pointed across his chest to the other side of the gallery.

When Susan caught sight of the swarthy guy with the wide nose, wild eyebrows, and curly hair that looked as though he had it done in a gas station grease pit, she said, "Jesus. What's his other hobby? Breaking fingers?"

Coldiron smiled. Barry spotted her from below and threw her a wave. She acknowledged it with one of her own.

"*Whooo*. This is exciting," she exclaimed.

"Your first time at a match?"

"First one. Is this Rich guy any good?"

West's opponent was warming up. He was young, about Barry's age, but shorter, with more body hair. He wore a beard that grew into the hair peeking out of the top of his white shirt.

"Yeh. Barry will have his hands full. He should handle Rich if he plays his game."

The combatants signaled to the match official that they were ready. He sat in the same spot as Coldiron, only on the opposite end of the gallery. He called to the players, "Throw for serve."

"Shouldn't we sit down?" Susan asked.

"Go ahead. I'll stay here. I want to see it all." From his perch, Tate could look down the back wall as well as see the rest of the court clearly. The spectators moved to the glass wall. Most took seats in the front row and propped their feet against the protective wall.

Rich's coach looked over at Coldiron and asked, "Another fin?"

"You got it, Rocco."

A man in the front row called, "Cover seven yards, Coldiron?"

"You're on."

"What the hell does all that mean? Was that English?" Susan asked.

"Side bets. A fin is five hundred bucks. Seven yards is seven hundred bucks."

"Just like that? Twelve hundred dollars? How much is riding on this one?"

"Three thousand for the match. Another twenty-five hundred in side bets."

"Coldiron! That's fifty-five hundred dollars!" Now she sat down.

"I thought he was the accountant." Coldiron pointed the well-chewed end of his stogie at the court.

"No wonder you don't charge admission to these things. You don't need spectators."

"Just like choking the gopher."

"Choking the what? Is that a bet, too?"

"Jacking off. That ain't a spectator sport, either."

"Oh, Coldiron. You're such a ladies' man," Susan laughed into her hand.

"Comes naturally. Oh, sorry." He fixed his small, gray eyes on the proceedings below. He wished she weren't there.

Tate watched Barry win first service. As the kid walked into the server's zone and Rich lined up in the rear court, Coldiron said softly to himself, "Not here. Please, not in front of her."

The match was a tight one. Rich had all the moves and he was in good condition. He challenged every aspect of West's game. He kept trying to grab the offensive.

Barry hung in. He met each of his opponent's charges with one of his own. The ball moved around the court with a whistle. Going into the third game the duel was even, one apiece.

As the match had progressed, Susan saw beyond the excitement to realize that the man she was watching below her was not the man she had said good-bye to in Rochester. She was looking at a cold, arrogant, and ruthless machine. Barry played the match without enjoyment. He treated his opponent as if he were some inferior being.

He scowled at Rich; he taunted him with obscenities that were drowned in the exhaust fan's noise before reaching the gallery. They didn't need to. Susan read Barry's lips. She translated his facial expressions. She felt the cold radiation of his eyes. There was no trace of sportsman in

Barry West. He played and acted like a hired assassin.

When it came, it rocketed Susan from disillusionment into paralyzed horror. At the second of impact, an involuntary scream rushed from somewhere deep within her. It was in perfect time with everyone in the gallery who jumped to their feet and Rich's coach who vaulted over the glass wall. He dropped the fifteen feet to the floor and raced to his fallen athlete. Rich was stretched out in agony from being hit in the ear.

"*Aaaaagh,*" the player moaned. He pressed his hand to the side of his head. Blood oozed through the sweat-stained fingers of his gloves. Barry retreated to the back corner and leaned against the wall. He made no attempt to check on the condition of the fallen player. He crossed one foot over the other and waited, as though he were expecting a bus.

Susan was on her feet. The back of her hand covered her mouth. She was biting her knuckle in revulsion. Coldiron's head was lowered as if in prayer.

The game was forfeited. The Coldiron-West express was richer by $5,500. Rich's eardrum had been burst by a vicious shot while he had been pinned against the front wall. It had been like shooting ducks for West. His opponent had made the fatal mistake of rushing the front wall to feign a soft kill, while trying for a pass. West had anticipated the shot perfectly. He had read the move, caught the ball full force, and driven it back at the helpless Rich. There had been the sickening, hollow, smashing sound of small bones and cartilage exploding at impact. Rich had had no chance to avoid the hit.

Susan rushed from the gallery. She met Rich's coach, Rocco, who was returning to the gallery.

"That was no accident, Coldiron." His mouth was twisted in fury.

"You're crazy. Your kid was posing against the front wall. West couldn't help it. He was going for a rollout."

"Six feet off the ground?" Rocco spat. He threw a fistfull of bills at Coldiron's feet. "You'll get yours, you fucker. That kid of yours is as good as dead." Then he stormed out of the gallery, back past a shocked Susan who had heard him.

Coldiron bent to scoop up the money. He slowly climbed down over the seats to the glass. West was readying to leave the court. He was mopping at his forehead with the sleeve of his shirt. The two men stared at one another. Coldiron gave the kid a look he would've given to a mad dog, a look of frightened respect. Then he turned and scaled the high concrete seats.

Susan was waiting for him. Anger washed from her dark eyes. "I want to talk to you. Alone." Her face was tear-stained.

"This way." Coldiron led her down the hall. He found a deserted racquetball court and let them both into the darkened gallery. He closed the door. Only a cube of gold from the light in the hall shining through the small window of the gallery door fell over them.

"I want to know what is going on," she demanded. Coldiron could feel more than see the contempt and disgust in her face.

"I don't know what you're talking about."

"Bullshit. You saw what happened down there. Don't give me that."

"That? An accident. It happens all the time."

"That was no *accident*. I know Barry. I saw the look in his eyes. The way he acted. He's mean. He's sick."

"What look in his eyes? You've been watching too freakin' many late movies." Coldiron dug in. He was defending himself as well as the kid.

"Please, Mr. Coldiron. Don't make me out to be a fool. I'm not one."

Coldiron let her continue.

"I wanted him to leave with you, to get out of Rochester, to become more of a man. But he's turned into an animal. I wanted something in between what he was and what he's become."

"Now fucking hold it! I don't think it has anything to do with a handball accident. Are you sure you aren't a little bit pissed 'cause he eyed a few women in the restaurant today? Or maybe it's because he's cut those apron strings you've had around his neck for two years?"

"You son of a bitch. You know that's got nothing to do with it. Even if it were true. I can accept bad manners. A cold, heartless killer I can't." Tears mixed with her anger.

"You're overdoing it, aren't you?"

"You've turned him into something very ugly. Something dangerous."

"Now look. I ain't a babysitter. Yours or anybody else's. And I ain't building you some 'Ozzie and Harriet' husband. I want a championship handball player."

"Is that what you call him? A championship handball player? He *deliberately* hit that other man! Barry *destroyed* that man's ear! Can't you *see* that?"

"Goddammit, I didn't get into this to have some lovesick cunt screaming in my ear. If you don't like . . ." He was nearly blowing her out of the gallery.

What Susan did next surprised both of them. She turned on him. She ripped into Coldiron with everything she had. She slapped, scratched, and punched at him. Tate just stood there and took it. He made no attempt to protect himself. She was finished in seconds. The attack had filled some need in both of them.

"If you don't like the game, stay away," he finished. She had torn his face open near his nose. Blood appeared in the scratch line.

"I won't be back. Don't worry. He's *your* problem." She turned and pulled the heavy door open.

"You gonna see him before you go?" Coldiron asked from the shadows.

"I don't know. I don't know. He's a stranger," she said, fighting back more hysteria. Then Susan left.

She knew she had to try, at least once, to turn West around, attempt to pluck him from his hurtling train of terror. Susan was waiting for Barry as he walked under the heavy-timbered archway that was the entrance to the club's grounds. His hair had been carefully blown dry so it swayed silkily in the warm wind. His tan looked deeper against his white tennis shirt and white shorts.

"Oh, hi," Barry said, doing a double take when he saw her.

Susan froze with anger and a new feeling she had not before experienced with him—fear. She tasted his arrogance, his smugness in the face of permanently maiming another man, as he walked to her. She hoped he couldn't tell she had been crying.

"Barry, what happened in there? Why?"

"Why? What do you mean, why? It was an accident. Happens all the time."

"Don't hand me that, we both know it was no accident hitting that other man. Even Coldiron admitted it."

"Look. I don't need this from you, Susan. You don't know what you're talking about." He reached for her and said, "Now, c'mon. Settle down. Let's go have a drink."

She turned out of his grasp with such determination that it startled him. Susan was wearing heels; her fierce eyes were level with his.

"Barry, please, I'm asking you to stop. Quit this now, before it's too late, before you hurt someone else." She paused, remembering the horror of how fast his ball had traveled before it had struck the other man, "Even kill someone."

"Oh, knock off that shit, willya?"

For the third time that day her tears came, and for the second time they welled up against her will. "Can't you see, you're poisoned with it? You've become a stranger to me. I don't know you. Please. Come home with me. Come back to Rochester. Stop this thing, now. While you still can."

"You don't own me. Lay off. I don't owe you anything. We're not joined at the hip, remember?"" His voice carried into the parking lot and into the flowered courtyard of the Bayshore Club, where an occasional face looked toward their argument.

"Who the fuck do you think gave Coldiron the two thousand dollars to get you here? It was *my* money. And now I feel partly responsible for creating this insanity in you, for hurting people." Her rage shook her. Barry made no movement to help quiet her sobs, though, at that moment, it was what she wanted more than anything.

"Your money?" he asked. It quickly added up; he had doubted at the time that Coldiron had anyone who would lend him that kind of money.

"That's right." Not caring any longer that he knew, she was losing him to something she didn't understand, let alone accept. Susan was nearly desperate. "We can do the things we have talked about."

"You mean get married? Hah. It was different when I wanted to, wasn't it?" Barry could've hit Susan with a brick, and it would've pained her less than the sneer that hung on his face. "So you can jerk me around by the ear whenever I'm a bad boy? No thanks, honey."

"That's right. It'd never work. You're an *animal*." Her voice sounded each word, rhythmically and caustically, "An arrogant, self-obsessed, self-seeking asshole, who will stop at nothing to get what you want!"

What West did next, more than anything he had said or done up to that point, with the possible exception of hitting Rich on the court, measured for Susan how far apart she and Barry had grown. Barry calmly reached into the back pocket of his tennis shorts, extracted a wallet that opened like a small book, and counted out some money, his share of his winnings in his match against Rich. Then he tossed the handful of bills into her tear-etched and flinching face. "Here's your two thousand, with interest," he snapped.

She stood there, as if West's gesture had momentarily turned her to stone, while $2,750 fluttered to the ground, a few of the greenbacks turning over slightly in the Florida breeze.

It was as if she were leaving someone she had never known; Susan turned and left, abandoning the money on the ground and the arrogant outlaw who had once been her gentle and sensitive lover.

That night Coldiron dragged his legs around the hotel room. His face burned where Susan had laid it open with her long fingernails. The pain below his waist was even more unbearable. Even the Green didn't touch it anymore. Tate knew he'd need another operation soon, but that night, alone in his room, he really didn't care whether the doctors took his legs off at the throat.

His real pain was in his head; his inner voices had grown relentless. Even poring through the bankbooks, a trick he had used in the past, that showed he and the kid were over $100,000 to the good, didn't shut them up anymore. Barry was bringing the coin in by the bucketfuls. And Coldiron felt cheaper than he ever had in his life.

Even most of the triangle stood below him now. He was at the top. He could reach out and grab the name that stood over the point. It had all been going so sweet. Now it had turned bad on him.

His head kept mauling him with one burning thought. That he was a leftover man, after all. Coldiron would always come close, but he'd never make it. Some men were like that. His mind chanted it in rhythm to the throbbing in his legs, "*Loser, loser.*" Over and over. "*Loser, loser. Killer, killer.*" He was getting nuts with it.

"*I ain't no fucking loser!*" he screamed into the night.

He knew it would be another sleepless night. Another night of sipping the bottle, hoping to slip into unconsciousness before dawn. He needed rest from his own head. Desperately.

Sleep had always been a luxury for Coldiron. Lately it had become almost a nonexistent one. Each night he would beg for that sedated stillness that would melt the image of what he had created. And what he had become.

But it was still early. He had to pay interest on his winnings. He paid in horror.

The triangle. The bankbooks. Coldiron could almost feel them disintegrating along with his legs.

He fell into bed and closed his eyes. Maybe he'd get lucky. Maybe he'd fall asleep before that face made its visit. But it was there. It always was. That face from twenty-five years before.

He reached under the bed and choked open his bottle of Green. He grabbed the sweat from his brow. He tried closing his eyes again. It was there again. The face. Then the triangle. It dripped blood. He was jolted upright by a recording of Susan's scream and the vision of

230

Alan Rich's head snapping with the concussion of the ball shattering his ear. Coldiron felt it. It was like a long, hot needle being inserted into his ear. All the way to his brain.

Coldiron sat up. He was dripping wet. He downed another mouthful of Green. He felt its burn. He felt the burn of the scratch of his face. Then he saw the Buick. The crushing, silver bumper was moving at him. He heard Susan's scream. Then the face came back, with its satisfied half smile. Then there was the triangle. It ran blood now. Then another face. A new one. One that hadn't visited him in the night for a long time. It was a woman. She was tired, but kind-looking. She spoke to him softly. She told him that his mother had been killed in a car wreck. Then the voices: *"Loser, loser."*

It went on like that all night.

Chapter Twenty

CLOSING IN

If Coldiron had a home, Boston was it. He had lived there, off and on, for thirty years. But if the road should be considered where Coldiron had spent most of his life, then certainly Beantown was his handball home. The Four Wall Lounge was his living room.

The Four Wall Lounge was devoted to the legend of handball. It catered to the greats of the sport, both past and present. On any given night, the small bar could be counted on to play host to the best of the Boston-New York-Philadelphia corridor. The greatest handballers in the world came out of the ghettos of the big Eastern cities.

Handball's cradle was the inner city. The sport had been born amid the squalor of eighteenth-century Dublin. It was in the cities where kids began playing handball before they were old enough to start school. While their suburban, middle-class cousins learned to ski or ice skate in the winter, or play baseball in the summer, inner-city kids taught themselves to beat a hard black ball off the brick walls of gray buildings.

The Four Wall Lounge was steeped in such tradition. It had catered to generations of handballers. The place had seen poor neighborhood kids become lawyers, doctors, teachers, or businessmen and move to the more affluent suburbs around Boston. But the little bar near Boston Commons always had its doors opened to its sons in sport.

When a winner walked into the joint, whose walls were decorated with handball memorabilia dating back to the turn of the century, he was paid the respect an award-winning writer, playwright, or actor might receive from certain off-Broadway watering holes. That was the treatment Coldiron and West received when they arrived in the Four Wall Lounge.

Coldiron knew almost everyone in the place. He was one of their favorite sons. He was accorded the welcome of a returning war hero. West was unimpressed. The two men sidled up to the bar, next to a slightly balding, perpetually smiling redheaded guy.

"Red, how the hell are you?" Coldiron beat the guy on the back.

"Squeezing by. And you, you old pirate? Hear you got yourself a horse."

"Yeh. This is him. Barry, I'd like you to meet Red Waterbary."

Waterbary was in his forties and a dedicated handballer. He stuck out his hand. "Hi, Barry. Heard a lot about you."

"Yeh, thanks." West gave Waterbary his

hand, but not his attention. His eyes went over the guy's shoulder to the spot where another redhead stood. This one was about five-foot-six, built more to his liking than Waterbary, and wasn't balding. Her hair was curly and wild. She looked right back, staring West down.

"Look, catch you later, Tate. You too, Red," he said and pushed through the twosome.

"Hold on, kid. I want Red to have a chance to talk with you. You guys have a lot in common," Coldiron said, and motioned for the bartender.

"You talk to this redhead. I'll make it with that one. *We* got something in common," he said and pulled away from Coldiron's lightly restraining paw.

It had been more the way Barry had said it, rather than what he had said, that irritated Waterbary. The old-timer felt he had been dismissed by the upstart. He had been treated like one of the great Barry West's adoring fans.

"Kid always that rude?" He had red-rimmed, doleful blue eyes.

"The way that lady was looking at him, I'd say he's more smart than rude. Wouldn't you, Red?" Coldiron and Waterbary turned to their wide-mouthed glasses. Down the bar, the woman was looking up at Barry as if she was talking to visiting royalty. In the Four Wall Lounge, a player of West's caliber and record was exactly that.

"Personally, I don't give a shit, Tate. But

your kid's cocky. He's rude." Waterbary played with his glass of beer as he talked. "But, I figure that's your problem. You're his coach. Not me. You gotta handle him."

"Hey. C'mon. You're forgetting who you're talking to, ya redheaded bastard. I'm not some puke-kid who wants to carry your jockstrap around town. We go way back. I remember how you were. Shit, at twenty years old, you figured *you* were the best in the business."

"Maybe I did carry an attitude. That's one thing. Your kid's got lousy manners. There's a difference."

"Aw, let's drop the whole thing. It's goddamned good to see you. You get uglier every year."

"And you get more bourbon-logged. How you been, Tate?"

"Makin' it. How about you?"

"Can't complain. Seen any of the guys in your travels?"

"I run across some. I've seen Petta, Grasso, Zaleski, Uriah the Jew, Fister, and a few more. They hear about the kid and come to see him."

"They say he's excellent."

"The best I've ever seen. Including the old days."

"Horseshit. These kids today don't know whether to fuck, fight, or hold the light. They're all pansies."

"Okay. Okay. *Hee hee.* How about you? Seen anybody?"

"Not really. I don't get around much like I used to. Got an old lady and kids. I did run into Danny in Philly last year. You know the poor kid still feels bad about taking off that night in New Orleans. It's like he never forgave himself. You know he would've rather it'd been his legs than yours?"

"That's crazy. I told him to split. It was the only way. He's a goddamned good kid. I'd like to see him."

"Listen to us. *Kid!* Danny's pushing fifty, like you and me. Things are passing us by. There's a lot of young horses around."

"I know. But like you say, Red, they're different. I'm not saying they're better or worse. Just different."

Red nodded into his beer.

Coldiron continued, "It's all brawn now. They want to blow everyone off the court. You don't see the surgeons anymore. They're a dying breed. Seems like nobody's got the patience to learn the game like it's meant to be. The young guys want to get to the top in a month, or they quit the sport and play golf or that sissy-ass racquetball shit."

"I'm afraid you're right. What about you, Tate? You been playing?"

"A little. Here and there. Mostly to warm up my kid. These old legs are in retirement. It's just that my brain don't know it yet."

"Those fuckers must slosh when you walk.

You ever get shot in the leg, you old fart, and half the city of Boston would get a free drink."

"*Hee hee.*"

"How are your legs treating you?"

"I get by. Don't really need 'em. A couple more months like the last six and I'm gettin' out. I'll have enough to retire."

"Retire? You? To what? A warehouse of Jack Daniel's?"

Just then they looked up from their drinks long enough to see West and the woman leave.

"Ah, maybe you're right. I'm just jealous," Red chuckled. "I need a splint for my dick these days."

"Probably. I'm a little shy myself. About two inches. *Hee hee.*"

"So tell me, what are these retirement plans you got?"

"I got this idea," Coldiron said. He waved to someone down the bar who had just sent him down a Green. He continued, "I want to open a club in Florida. I want to be where it's warm. The place'll be strictly for handballers. Guys could come down for a week or so and play round-robin stakes matches. I'd bring down the best in the game. Be someplace we could all meet once a year."

"You're actually serious, aren't you, Tate? Things have been that good?" Waterbary was facing his old friend.

"Yeh. I almost got the coin. I even picked out the building when I was down there last.

It's a warehouse that could be fixed up just the way I want it."

"How come you've never said anything about it before this?"

"Never thought I'd get there."

"It's a great idea."

"Think so, eh?"

"Fantastic."

"Some days, Red, it's been the only thing that has kept me going. Other days, times I've wanted to lay down and die, I've cursed that fucking dream. It wouldn't let me quit, even when I wanted to."

"I'm glad for you, Tate. Anyone deserves it, you do. Christ, I can see you now, sitting in the sun, sipping Green over ice, and watching all those tight-assed chicks walk by. Shit, you'll get locked up in a month for doing weirdness to some thirteen-year-old in a bikini."

"*Hee hee*. You got it."

"Tell you what. How'd you like me to donate to your place in Florida?"

"Naw. I don't want no investors. I'm gonna own it outright, so's I can kick out any asshole I want. No offense, Red."

"That's not what I mean. I'd like to challenge your horse. One match. Two grand to the winner."

"You shitting me? The construction business must be treating you good."

"I get by. Well, what do you say? I'd be

spotting your kid twenty-five of the best years. You say he's the greatest. Let him prove it.

"And you're lucky I ain't asking for odds. I'm offering you even-up, winner take all. Well?"

"C'mon, man. You don't want to climb in against West."

"What's the matter? You grow a paper asshole or what?"

Coldiron hoisted his drink to eyebrow level, peered under it and said, "You've got yourself a bet, redhead."

"Good. I'd like to delay your retirement a bit and whip that smartass. He can get humility like I did. When guys like you kicked my ass all over the courts." It was Red's turn to laugh.

"I'll drink to that."

"You'd drink to the sun coming up."

"I do. Every day. Whether I can see it or not. It's always coming up somewhere."

Barry was uncommunicative and sullen the following morning in the locker room before his match with Red. The site of the challenge was the old Cambridge Club. It was an athletic temple that went back nearly two hundred years. The shower room was tattered and dim. Lockers hung open like yawning soldiers.

"Waterbary is one of the best. You've moving up a notch playing him." Coldiron was trying his best to keep his feelings out of it. He could hardly take the kid anymore.

Barry looked up from tying his gym shoe and

239

patted his open mouth in a fake yawn. "You just arrange the matches. I'll decide how good they are. I think he's probably moving up a notch playing me."

Coldiron eyes tightened. He turned to head for the courts, and said to himself, "God help me. Just a few more months. Just a few more months."

Waterbary was already on the court when Barry pushed the door open. The jovial redhead threw a big wave at Coldiron and yelled at his friend, "Got your checkbook ready, Tate? I'm the one who's going to Florida. On you."

"Whatever you say. You'd better have the cash on you. I wouldn't take a check from you. Fucker'd probably bounce higher than a fister."

"I got your cash. Right here." Red grabbed his privates and pointed himself at Tate.

Sitting in the gallery, Tate was hoping Red would give the kid a beating. The two grand was nothing. They could win three times that much back in a night. Like Waterbary, Coldiron wanted to see West taught a lesson. Maybe if he got put through a wall, it'd knock some of the arrogance out of him.

If anyone could do it, Waterbary could. His friend had the kind of game that could beat West. Red still had good speed. He could make the ball move around the court like a meteor and could kill it from the upstairs bathroom.

Barry treated Red's offer of good luck with the same poor taste as the night before. He just swept over Waterbary's outstretched hand and turned away, saying, "Let's get under way. I've got a date this afternoon."

Red won first service. He came at Barry early, like a train. He demolished the kid in the first game, 21-7. Barry's stuff started working in the second game. He squeaked by, 21-19.

Something strange happened in that second game. The kid had gotten caught against the front wall, as Red had picked a hard one off the back wall. West had been a target. Coldiron had seen it coming and had held his breath. For a brief instant, he could've sworn Red had lined the kid up. He was going to take a shot at him. Instead, he had killed one in the corner so hard it had sounded like a door slamming.

Barry had looked like he was going to get sick. All the color drained from his face. It had been that close.

The third game was a war, with neither player able to break the back of the other. They were like two cats fighting to the finish.

It had grown into more than a stakes match. Waterbary and West were gambling for more than the two grand. Their honor was on the line. It was the old guard trying to stand off the new. Twice Red had to change gloves, the sweat was running down his arms so heavily. Midway through the final game, Tate had yelled down to him, "Your blood alcohol level is dropping. You might even pass a drunk-driving test."

The smile had left Waterbary's face. His jaw had locked in grim combat. He was out to show the wise-assed kid a thing or two about the game. The score was extended to 26 apiece. Neither man would give anything away.

Coldiron watched with glee. He was seeing a hell of a handball match. It was two flawless champions refusing to budge an inch. Each challenge was met by a counter-challenge, each thrust was thwarted by a return charge. Both men were playing the game with a purity and clarity rarely seen. Handball was being performed the way it had been designed to be played. They were competing without error, without fault, in balanced perfection.

These two men moved around the enclosed box like world champion ballet stars. They made each move count. Their hands moved with the speed of a lightweight boxer's. They were hitting the ball with the force of Arnold Palmer's tee shots. Tate was seeing a duel.

He was also watching Barry's face for any hint of change. With the kid night and day, studying his every move, facial expression, and cue, Coldiron had become able to anticipate the transformation. West telegraphed the change as an epileptic communicates an oncoming seizure. Tate had promised himself to halt the match if he thought the kid was going for the hit. He didn't care about the pretense. He was just going to stop it.

The score reached 30-30; they looked like

they were going to play all day before one of them let up. The kid's face went from the torture of being extended to the limit of his endurance to its sadistic, shining madness in seconds. It happened so fast Coldiron didn't have time to yell a warning to Red.

The kid's chance came with Red off balance from lunging to return a sizzling alley pass. He had landed hard on his shoulder against the wall, bringing a quick grimace as if he had been electrically jolted. Waterbary then pushed himself away from the white surface, spinning to see how Barry played his shot.

When the handballer watches his opponent play a shot, he protects his eyes by extending his arm, so his hand is on the line of flight between his face and the shooter's hand. Because of his shoulder injury, Red was slow in raising his arm. He missed only by a split second blocking the nearly invisible bolt from hitting him in the eye. It was a viciously accurate shot. Red's hand immediately flew to his left eye. His head vibrated and snapped with the concussion and searing pain. He pressed his hand against his eye, compressing the spraying blood.

"*Eeeeeyyyiii*," he screamed.

Coldiron leaped to his feet and shrieked, "Oh, Jesus. Not Red. Not Red."

Waterbary was dazed. He walked around the court, winking his good eye as if there was something in it. The glove that he held against his injured eye was completely scarlet.

The official called down to the injured man, "Red. You all right? You're cut! Take a break."

"Fuck it. I'm okay," he snapped. "Let's finish this thing."

Coldiron stared in disbelief. Waterbary was hurt bad. The eye had already begun to swell, was already pushing the glove grotesquely away from his chin. His forehead was turning purple.

"Red," Coldiron called, "take fifteen. You're cut!"

"Get fucked," was the answer.

Waterbary finished the match one-handed. It took Barry two shots to finish him.

At the end, the kid headed right for Red. This time it was the older man who refused the offer of friendship.

"You okay? Jesus, I'm sorry."

"The fuck you are, man. Get away from me. Your day is coming. Just remember that. Your day is coming."

Red barged out the door. The waiting official didn't bother to look at the eye. He took the injured man directly to the hospital.

Coldiron followed. He took the elevator upstairs, hurried outside to the great cloud of autumn gray and hailed a cab. From the desk clerk, he had learned that the official had driven Red to Queen of Angels Hospital.

Once there, Coldiron limped quickly along the yellow arrows in the floor, which the signs claimed would deposit him in the emergency room. His disgust for West had taken a back seat to his concern for his long-time friend. He reached the nurse's station, a glassed enclosure marked EMERGENCY ROOM. NO ADMITTANCE.

"Is Mr. Waterbary in there?"

"Unless you're a relative, you're not allowed—" the black nurse began. Her tight Afro looked like a nest for her white hat. Coldiron walked right by her.

Waterbary was sitting on the stainless steel table. He was surrounded by a doctor and two nurses. The match official was off to one side. Red was still wearing his handball gear, down to his gloves. The heel of the left one was dark brown.

Coldiron winced when he saw the hip-looking white doctor taking stitches on Red's eye. There was a jagged cut just under the eyebrow. The left side of his friend's face was swollen to twice its normal size. His eyelid was closed over what looked like a torn plum lodged in his eye socket. As if Red's face was soft plastic, the skin followed each suture taken by the doctor. Waterbary spotted Tate.

"Red. Christ, I'm sorry."

"I know you carry a lot of hate, man. I know you want to make up for the broken legs. I know you got that dream of your own club," Red's voice was building. He strained against the nurses' hold. The match official walked over to Coldiron. *"But I never thought you'd walk over the bodies of your friends to do it."*

"It ain't like that, Red. You know that."

"What I know is that I can't see out of my left eye. And your boy did it. He did it on purpose, Coldiron. That we both know. Don't we?"

Coldiron knew his friend was right. There was no sense trying to offer a lame excuse. It hadn't even worked with Susan Burnett. And this was Red Waterbary, one of the best in the game. You didn't even try to bullshit him about a hitter.

Tate left the room. The nurse escorted him out. Red needed medical attention. That would be impossible as long as he was standing and screaming at Coldiron.

"How bad is the eye?"

"We've called in a specialist. The doctor thinks that the retina's been detached." This nurse was quiet, mid-twenties and Irish Catholic fresh-looking.

"That mean he might lose it?"

"There's a good chance Mr. Waterbary might not see out of his left eye again, yes. That's all I can say right now. Why don't you come back later and talk with the doctor?"

"I understand. When will they be done with him?"

"Depends. They may have to operate right away."

"Thanks. I'll call later."

"Mister. . . ?"

"Coldiron."

"Mr. Coldiron, is it true he was hit in the eye playing handball?"

"Yeh."

"I thought that was a nonviolent game."

"Supposed to be." Coldiron hobbled out of the hospital. He decided to walk the mile or so to his hotel, instead of calling for a cab. He needed time to think.

He walked past porno shops, pawn shops, revivalist store-front churches, and run-down clothing and variety stores. He wasn't thinking of the punishment he was giving his legs. His mind was on the monster he had created.

He walked by a schoolyard. He stopped and hooked his hands in the chain-link fence. There were kids, no more than eight or nine years old, banging soft rubber balls about the size of oranges off concrete walls. He watched them play. They were having fun, squealing and driving the ball crazily around the concrete courts. Tate was watching the way many handballers started. Playground one-wall games had spawned some of the great ones. Himself included. And he wondered about what he was leaving these kids. He remembered one of his mother's lessons before she had died. "Tate, always try to leave the campground cleaner than you found it."

He kept thinking about what he would be leaving the youngsters he was watching. He thought about Barry West, the merchant of destruction he had helped spawn.

Coldiron thought of other times, of other players he had seen who had become afflicted with West's ruthless attitude for winning. He thought about how even he had once approached that crazed state when winning became so important that the thought of losing had been unthinkable. The sight of a man hurt, lying in a pool of blood on the hardwood, felled by one of Coldiron's bullets, had always been too much for Tate. His respect for the natural order of things, his reverence for the idea that the best man be victorious, had overridden the compulsive need he had to win at any cost.

There was no sleep for Coldiron that night. He was tortured by what was in front of him. He knew clearly what he had to do, but the idea of destroying the very thing that was lifting him out of the gutter sickened him.

He thought of the man at the top of the triangle, how even he had to realize what had been happening. Coldiron's horse had whipped nearly every player listed on the National Handball Association's ladder of top contenders. The old Indian-Jew was destroying the NHA's credibility by humiliating its best handballers. In turn, Coldiron was single-handedly discrediting its czar. Tate was giving one to the boys.

Now his horse had to be taken out. West was finished as a stakes handball player. Coldiron would have to dismantle one of the greatest handball machines he'd ever seen play. He'd finally surrendered to it. There could be no more delay. He had to turn away from the triangle, from the name at the top. His handball club in Florida would have to wait. If it could ever happen at all.

But how? How could he get West out of the game? He had to try something before *they* took him out, before the group met and appointed someone. There had to be a different way. The old method was too final.

He tore at his brain for an answer. To see his creation destroyed on the court was too horrible to imagine. They might as well take him out, too.

He would try one last-ditch effort. He'd try confronting the kid, talking to him, begging him—anything to get him to quit. Before it was too late. He'd do it the next morning.

Long since rid of the Pinto, the two had been flying to their matches. The plane ride to New York seemed a good time. Before their three scheduled matches at the Gotham Athletic Club ... and before Barry could hurt anyone else.

Chapter Twenty-One

THE PLEA

Despite the brisk autumn Massachusetts day, Barry was clammy nervous on the way to Logan Airport. Over the previous weeks he had grown more agitated. During the one-hour flight from Boston to New York, he seemed bothered and easily irritated.

Coldiron had chosen the plane ride to talk with him. Lately, the only time they spent together was while traveling between matches. The older man had little use for the kid the way he was, and was hardly ever around. Barry had taken to carousing almost every night. It was as if his drive to bed as many women as possible was one manifestation of the storm that raged within West. Tate had even questioned him about it, during their stay in Richmond: "Gettin' a bit carried away with your sportfuckin', ain't you?"

West had replied, "As you once said, 'I need to learn the difference between being in love and being in heat.'"

Cutting through the clouds to La Guardia, Coldiron silently cursed the logic of trying to talk to the kid on the plane. It was a shuttle flight, jammed with commuters. There wasn't an empty seat on the aircraft. Tate hadn't been able to buy first-class tickets so he and West might have had seats alone. A fat guy, coming out of a leather sport jacket like toffee, was wedged into the window seat next to them.

The kid got up to use the lavatory. Coldiron followed him up the aisle. When Barry let himself into the toilet, so did Coldiron. The same one.

"What the fuck? What are you doing?" West said, when his coach jammed against him. There was hardly three inches between their faces. Coldiron slammed and locked the door behind them.

"We're gonna talk."

"Sure. Wouldn't our seats be a more sensible place to do it?"

Coldiron didn't like being that close to him. West had dangerous eyes. They were feverish-looking. The kid appeared to be sick.

"This'll do fine." It was hot in there. The kid started running a sweat. A strange calm came over Coldiron.

"I've known for some time."

"I'll bite. Known what?"

"What you've been doing."

"Tate, what are you talking about? It's boiling hot in here."

"You know exactly what I mean." Coldiron stuck his face even closer to West's. The kid was trying to bend back, get away. There was no room. "Those guys you hit in Mobile, Fredericksburg, Richmond, those other places, and old Red last night. They weren't accidents."

"You crazy or something?" There was no humor in West's voice. It was chilling.

"Wish I was, kid. Wish I was. You're a hitter." Coldiron spit the word as if he had a mouthful of Drano. "You gotta get out of the game."

"The only place I want out of is this fucking can." Barry tried to reach around Tate to unlock the door. The older man blocked his arm. He grabbed the kid's wrist. West tried to squirm free. There was no chance. Coldiron could break a man's hand while shaking it.

"You're gonna hear me out," Coldiron snapped. There was a knock at the door.

"Anything wrong in there?" asked a stewardess in a polite muffle.

"Nothing. Just a little airsick. I'll be okay," Coldiron answered.

"There's a fucking maniac in here," was West's reply.

Outside the door, a look of confusion crossed the stew's face. She had heard two voices. Then came thumping and banging. She walked to the front of the airplane for help.

"You're gonna quit. Go back to Rochester. You've got over fifty grand coming, your half of the stake. Take it and get out of stakes handball."

"Look, man, if you don't like how I'm playing, you're free to hit the road anytime you want. If you don't want to coach me, just say so. I say when I quit. Not you."

"Barry, please. It ain't up to me anymore. Either you get out or someone takes you out."

"The way I see it, that's my business. I'm the one taking the chances. It's my ass. All you do is sit on your butt, sucking up Green and counting money. I don't need you anymore. I got 'em begging to play me. They're standing in line to give me their money. And you're saying quit? You got a spongy brain."

A stronger hand was pulling at the knob of the toilet door from the outside. "Let's go. Get out of there. Don't you know it's a federal offense to lock yourself in the toilet?"

Coldiron ignored the voice and the rattling of the door. "I'm your manager as long as I say I am. If it weren't for me, you'd still be pushing pencils in Rochester."

"Don't forget it, Coldiron. You're responsible for the way I play, too. You taught me the game. Remember?"

A key slipped into the lock. The door was yanked open and Coldiron fell against a large man in a blue flight attendant's uniform.

"What the—what were you two doing in there?" the man asked. He tried to attract as little attention as he could. He had learned that in flight school.

"He's been polishing my knob," Coldiron snapped. "What the fuck you think we been

253

doing in there? You want a little suck of it, too?" He pushed past the startled man.

The flight attendant was knocked off balance, right out from under his hat. He regained his feet long enough to venture another peek around the door. He was just in time for the door to hit him across the neck as it was kicked open. This time Barry stormed by him. The attendant flew into the galley, cross-bodying two startled stews.

Chapter Twenty-Two

THE TAKEOUT

It was their first visit to the Big Apple, their premier invasion of the handball capital of the world. From the squalor of Harlem, from the posh athletic clubs of Manhattan, from the stenched middle-class boredom of the boroughs, came the greatest handball players the game had ever seen.

Through an intricate process of distillation, a natural order of competition and elimination and cross-competition, the four-wall courts of the various Boys' Clubs, Jewish Community Centers, YMCA's, and City Athletic Centers produced the finest in the game. And only the finest of those ended up in the Gotham Athletic Club. It was at this old and prestigious club that the best handball talent in the country played, and where Barry was to be tested.

Coldiron and West endured the hour's cab ride to the Americana Hotel in silence. Each man's mind was locked into its own reality; they were widely different truths, yet closely linked ones.

Coldiron plotted the task that lay in front of him. He was faced with the arrangement of a mercy killing. The kid had to be taken out; Tate's creation had to be destroyed. There was no more question. Coldiron, or the game he loved, could no longer live with what sat next to the old guy in the cab.

There was much to be done. Others had to be consulted. There was an established order about such matters. Evidence needed to be presented. There had to be a vote. Then someone would be appointed. A place would be designated. The takeout would then be set. It would be as good as done.

This procedure was a must. Otherwise guys would be taking each other out at will; the game would be lawless. They policed their own sport. Though it wasn't as strong as it had been in old days, the old guard still had its say. It had been that way for generations.

Coldiron had little time. That had been his out for a while; he had even fooled around with the idea of postponing it, not calling the group together until his own work was finished. He only needed about a month. But even that was no longer possible. The kid had become too dangerous. The sooner the better. For everyone.

Barry sat huddled in the cab's corner. He was concerned with the possibility of his being taken out. It had become an obsession with him, nearly as strong as the one to win.

His inner rage and paranoia were slowly poisoning him. His fear that the takeout was coming mounted with each match. The anxiety was residual. It never went away. It was consuming him. Knowing he was a marked man, knowing somewhere, sometime, there was a player that would be stepping into a court for the sole purpose of maiming him, had pushed Barry to go for the hit sooner. He wanted to get his opponent before he could be set up.

Added to this was his compelling need to rule the game. His bloated ego would not allow him to consider the prospect that he might lose. He had been using the hit also as an offensive tool. It was an insurance policy against being defeated. If it looked as though he'd be beaten, he would take the other guy out first.

He also knew that if it wasn't already out of Coldiron's hands, it soon would be. That the assassin would visit him he was certain. He just didn't know who it would be, where or when it would be. Knowing that at any moment he might be in someone's cross hairs was driving him crazy. And into becoming more unstable.

It was the first Wednesday of December. The day was cold and snowless as the cab pulled up in front of the Americana. They registered for separate rooms and prepared to go their different ways—Tate to the nearest phone, and Barry to connect with some lady.

Before they split, Coldiron said, "We go at seven tomorrow night. I'll give you the book on your opponent in the locker room before the match."

West nodded.

257

"Be at the Gotham Athletic Club by six."

"Yes, *mein capitan*," West laughed and saluted.

Tate walked away. He had gotten to where he despised the kid's attitude. They left each other in the hotel lobby—Tate to take care of what he had to do, the kid in search of someone to spend the night with him, a female companion who might lov. him into liking himself. At least until morning.

The next evening Barry was highly agitated as he rode the elevator to the basement of the club. Even rattling his hotel bed the night before with the woman he had met in the discotheque hadn't soothed his anxiety.

The locker room of the Gotham AC was in the bowels of the ten-story, limestone-faced structure. Though the building was old, 1920s vintage, it was well maintained. There was a lot of money at the GAC. It was old and quiet money. Many memberships were willed from one generation to the next. Some dated back fifty years. There was a two-year wait to join as a new member.

As he dressed, Barry's armpits dripped sweat. His hands were clammy. The steely professional look was gone from his face. In its place was a mask of dangerous fury. As it did everytime he readied for a match lately, Coldiron's warnings about handball justice, explained to West while they were in training in Rochester, played in his ears like "Taps."

When he finished lacing his high-topped shoes, he noticed his hands were trembling slightly. He paused and cupped them together, checking to see if anyone had noticed. Only the locker room was strangely empty. What puzzled the kid was that he had changed clothes in the Gotham Athletic Club, not some small handball garden owned by a couple of wealthy men. The GAC had over two thousand members, most of whom enjoyed a workout after a sedentary day of desk jockeying.

He had seen it like that before. In certain matches, the money people reserved the entire facility for the evening. They wanted no distractions to the betting and the competition. Mostly, they wanted no press coverage. Stakes matches were for gambling, not for glory.

Must be a big one, West thought. He smiled. He liked big, important matches.

Only a Puerto Rican kid wearing rubber gloves, picking up used towels, and a middle-aged white guy running a manual carpet sweeper among the rows of lockers, occasionally passed Barry's line of sight.

He finished dressing. He paced around the locker room. He jumped on the scale and confirmed what he had suspected. He had been losing weight—nine pounds in the last month. He'd sweat off another ten or so in his New York City stand. He promised himself that he'd eat better, get his weight back above 170. If it slipped much lower than it was, he'd start to lose strength.

But he had been eating right. It wasn't his diet that had changed; his metabolism had. It raced. He woke in the night with a sore jaw from grinding his teeth in his sleep. He couldn't sit still during the day. Barry was burning up the food faster than he was replacing it.

Coldiron still hadn't shown by six-thirty. It was getting close to the time he would have to ride the elevator to Court Six and his match. He was playing someone whose name he didn't even know. Let alone have the book on. He didn't like that. It made him even more nervous. Little things, like Coldiron always being late, were bothering him a lot lately. It had been getting so that Barry liked everything in perfect order. He had been having trouble handling surprises of any kind.

The whole thing was getting kind of creepy—the empty locker room, playing against a mysterious opponent, Condiron's absence, all of it.

Where the hell is the old drunk anyway? Didn't he say he'd be here at six? Of course he did. He's probably in some bar, guzzling booze, thought Barry.

Just as he started for the elevator, a short, Latin kid in all-white called to him, "Are you Mr. West?"

"That's right. What is it?"

The kid handed him a note. "Mr. Coldiron left this off around five o'clock. He asked me to give it to you."

"Thanks." Barry dismissed him by patting the sides of his shorts to show he couldn't be carrying any money for a tip. The kid got the idea and split.

West pulled open the sealed envelope. It was from Coldiron, all right. His grade-school-level scroll was easily recognizable. The note read:

Sorry to be late, kid. Got hung up with some scheduling problems. You're playing Lloyd Elm tonight. He's an Indian from Oklahoma. You should handle him easily.

I lined him up first, as a warm-up for later in the week. Just play your game and move the ball around. He doesn't like to run much.

I'll see you at the court at seven.

Tate

Barry crumpled up the note and tossed it over his shoulder. He angrily grabbed his gym bag and snapped to the deserted locker room, "Great coach. Great book. About all I know is that I'm up against some fucking slow-footed Indian."

He cut through the TV room to the elevator waiting area. One car waited with its doors standing open. He stepped in and punched "3," the one marked "Handball Courts."

He jumped off at the third floor and walked down the hallway that ran along the court doors. At the end a man waited. He was dressed completely in white.

The man was balding and, like West, appeared nervous. His tension seemed more natural than West's.

"Hi. You Barry West?"

"Right. Who're you?"

"Name's Biasone. I'm refereeing your match."

"Okay."

"Here's the can of game balls. It ain't been opened." There were three balls to a can. Sometimes one got split open from an excessively hard shot. Or when they struck a wall just so.

West peeled off the top of the can. There was a hiss from the pressure sealed container. He let one roll out onto his hand. "Red balls? You gotta be kidding?"

"They're okay. They're regulation," Biasone said. "New thing adopted by the National Handball Association. To give the game some color."

"Who picked 'em? I don't want to use these fucking things."

"Home man picks the balls, remember. You're the visiting player. You have no choice."

"Fuck it, then. I don't play."

"Up to you. You forfeit if you don't show. From what I hear, this is a big money match. Be too bad to lose all that coin without even

262

playing for it." Biasone had the look of a man who was genuinely concerned. "Don't worry, kid. They play just the same as the black ones. They been approved by the NHA."

"Fuck the NHA." Barry tightened his grip on the can of balls. "Red balls. Jesus Christ. And I'm playing a goddamned Indian. Do I have to wear a cowboy hat, too?"

"I'll be upstairs. Good luck, West."

"Where's Elm. The guy I'm up against?"

"He's already in there. Waiting for you," the official said. He climbed the circular steel stairs that stood in the middle of the hall.

Barry pushed open the heavy door marked Court Six. The place was like a coalshaft inside. He stood in the sliver of light thrown by the hall lights. It was deathly quiet in there. Barry figured it must be a real private match. From the total lack of noise, he guessed that the gallery was deserted. He slammed the door behind him as a call for the lights. Nothing. They didn't snap on. Neither did the fans kick in.

"Hey. What's going on? Am I in the right court?" He could hear someone breathing. Someone to his right. And close.

"You in here, Elm?" He faced the direction where he had heard the breathing. A spooky feeling came over him. He couldn't see his own feet, for the darkness. The whole thing was weird—no one in the locker room, red balls, and now some maniac playing hide-and-seek with him.

"I said, anyone here?"

"Relax, kid," came the official's voice from above him. "You're in the right place. I turn on the lights from up here."

Barry looked up. It was like swimming in a lake of ink. He couldn't see a thing. "Where's Elm?"

"You're in the right place," came a voice from behind him. He jumped about a foot off the floor. "We got a match."

Just then the lights snapped on. Barry's opponent had been standing no more than two feet from the kid. He got a look at the guy. It wasn't a ghost. It was a person, all right. Only his name wasn't Lloyd Elm. He went by the name of Tate Coldiron.

"What the fuck?" The younger man's surprised stare was interrupted by something equally astonishing as seeing Coldiron appear out of the blackness. The four walls and ceiling of the court were all glass. The two men were standing in an aquarium. And surrounding the aquarium were over 2,000 people. The big exhaust fans kicked on. The spectators began to roar with anticipation as they got their first glimpse of the combatants. Only the noise came through the thick glass as a quiet groaning sound.

The kid wheeled in a circle. He was surrounded by humanity. He looked up. High above the court, in kind of a glass basket, sat the official.

Biasone's perch gave him an unobstructed view of the glass box below him. He sat in a revolving chair so he resembled a tailgunner in a World War II bomber. He spoke to the players via microphone.

Two other officials sat at each of the front and back walls of the court. They were to act as spotters to ascertain if a shot was good or not. They each had a button that activated a green or red light. Green meant the questionable shot was good. Red meant that it was a long serve, three-waller serve, that the ball had struck the floor before reaching the front wall, or any other infraction that would end play.

"Take your warm-ups, gentlemen," came Biasone's voice over the loudspeaker.

"Coldiron, would you explain what the fuck is going on here? Where's Elm?" Barry kept shifting his eyes to the packed stands as he talked.

"You're looking at him, kid. Lloyd Elm was my grandfather's name. He was a Cherokee chief in Oklahoma. *Hee hee.*"

"You trying to tell me. . . ?"

"You got it. You and me. Head to head." Coldiron was cinching on his gloves as he talked.

"Here? In this fucking glass coffin?"

"That's right."

West let out a howl. It was the first laugh he had had in a month. "You? Play me? You gotta

265

be fucking crackers. I mean, you aren't too tightly wrapped, Coldiron."

"It ain't my mental health we're talking about here, kid. It goes way deeper than that." Coldiron had suddenly turned solemn.

"What are you talking about?" West had already decided that he didn't like being surrounded by people like this. He kept scanning the stands as he talked. One face caught his attention. He backed up his eyes. It *was* her— Susan!

"What's she doing here? You invited her to this carnival?" West spat.

"You got it, kid."

Hers was the only face in the crowd that didn't shine with anticipation, the festivity, the expectant thrill of what was unfolding that night on Gotham AC's Court Six. Instead of being charged with the growing electricity of upcoming combat, Susan's fine features were caught in question. She was dressed simply, but elegantly, in a double-breasted, brown suit with faint pinstripes coursing through the cloth. Her white satin shirt was open at the throat, and her cleavage was guarded by a gold stay-pin.

Coldiron had called Susan earlier that day. She had nearly hung up on him, so much had she come to resent Coldiron for what he had created. Susan had gamely attempted to put the two men out of her mind, block their very existence from her thoughts, over the past weeks, and she had done a decent job of it, up to when

266

her secretary had announced that a Mr. Coldiron was calling her long distance.

There had been a solemn urgency in the old drunk's voice that caught her from jamming the phone into the cradle. He had said, simply, "Can you come to New York tonight? Barry's going to need you."

"You must be kidding!" had been the acid-washed reply she had offered in attempt to cover the wildness in her heart. "Barry doesn't need anyone. Me especially. He made that quite clear in Florida."

"It's different now. He's gotta be taken out."

A cold shudder had slinked through Susan's body; she had felt her jaw tremble with it. Before he had embarked with Coldiron, Barry had taken the time to explain the term, "to take someone out" to her. West had carefully recounted to Susan the conversation he had had with his mentor that day in training, when Coldiron had explained the laws of his game.

Though she had consented to come, and even as she was sitting in the crowded stands returning Barry's surprised and angry look, Susan wasn't exactly certain why she had bothered to make the trip. Then, as it became apparent to her that Coldiron was to be West's opponent, that it was to be the older man who would take Barry out, confusion poured over Susan's amalgam of emotions. Her trek had made little sense to her in the commuter flight from Rochester to New York. Now it made even less sense.

As the two combatants began waving their arms in warm-up, Susan's allegiance bounded from one to the other, then to neither; she was caught in the crosscut of the events in her life that had begun, months earlier, with West telling her of the stranger he had met at the Rochester Y, and the unusual plan the man had presented to the young accountant.

Since then, Susan Burnett had drifted from distrusting Coldiron, to liking him, even to the point of a vicarious attraction to the roguish old guy, and then, during the period since Florida, to despising Tate for what he had turned Barry into.

Her change of feelings for West had been equally dramatic, but were even less understood by the woman. There was a part of Susan Burnett that hoped Coldiron would paint the walls with her ex-lover's innards, while from somewhere else she was receiving the message of compassion and sympathy for West.

She smiled to herself, in spite of whatever she was feeling, when she remembered Coldiron's comment: "You got more parts than a Broadway musical."

Barry turned away from her direction. Susan watched and wondered what her blond ex-lover was saying to Coldiron. She couldn't make out the words that were being spit from West's tightly drawn lips.

"You couldn't leave her out of this, could you?" Barry said to Coldiron as they passed each other, still rotating their arms in circles to work out any stiffness.

"Nobody made her come. She's here because she wants to be."

All humor had drained from West's face. His jaw muslces went back to jumping.

"Okay, Coldiron. Enough bullshitting. What is this all about? What does it mean?"

"We play a match. Best of three. Winner walks away with everything, all the marbles. You beat me, you take my share of the winnings. Every dime. It comes to over sixty grand. Plus the revenge you've been looking for ever since I kicked your ass through the wall in Rochester."

"And?" West was cinching his gloves on.

"If I beat you, I get your share. Plus your assurance that you don't play stakes handball again. You get out. Stay off the circuit. You're a disgrace to the game. You're a fucking, low-life, sneaking hitter." The words felt sweet and good coming out of Coldiron's mouth.

"That all?"

"We're finished. You win and you get rid of me. You won't have to share your purses with me anymore."

"You're on," Barry smiled tightly. "This is real funny, you know that? A real coincidence."

"Whattya talkin' about?"

"I've signed to play for someone else. I was

going to tell you about it tonight. We were through, anyway."

"Really. Who for? What kind of blood-sucking puke would want a hitter playing for him?" Coldiron kept nicking.

"He's supposed to be here tonight." West wasn't going for it. He knew he had to keep his temper. "I saw him in the first row. In the back right corner. From what I hear, he's an old friend of yours." West was sneering. Whatever respect that had existed between him and Coldiron was gone. They had come to hate each other. They had grown very different.

Coldiron turned slowly to look for the spot where West's new mentor sat.

"Right at the corner, Tate. In the cashmere sport coat. See him?"

There was a man in a cashmere sport coat. But he was looking away. Tate couldn't see who he was.

The man's head turned. Tate froze with horror. His mind showed him an old and yellowed picture from twenty-five years before. Rage blotted the wetness from his mouth. His eyes burned. It was the face of the man who had ordered Coldiron crippled in New Orleans. It was the face of the man who had stepped out of the Buick and taken the money from his pocket. It was the face he had seen every night since he had been pinned against the brick wall. It was the face of Jake Bradford. Coldiron felt his knees going. He fought to stop them from shaking.

Next to Bradford was Dutch Gleason. He had been the driver of the Buick, the car that had finished Tate forever as one of the premier four-wallers in the land. He had done Jake's bidding as commissioner of the National Handball Association to rid the game of the old guard. Bradford wanted to take the sport over. Coldiron and the other vagabond, no-account drunks that had ruled the sport, had stood in the way of Bradford and Gleason's attempts to clean up handball's image.

Most had knuckled under early. Some had been bought off; they had accepted jobs with Bradford's construction company. A few had hung on. Coldiron was one of the old line that didn't roll over and play dead in front of Bradford. They had blocked the NHA from gaining control of the sport by continually putting Jake's best players through the wall. They had made him look foolish. Coldiron, Lowenburg, Grasso, Petta, Zaleski, Reddick, and the others had proven that they were still the best in the land. They had stayed loyal to the old American Handball Association, thus giving its tournaments more popularity than the invitationals sponsored by Bradford's fledgling NHA.

When it had become apparent to him that Coldiron's cadre would not be eliminated by competition, Bradford had decided to take Tate out. By getting rid of their most respected and talented player, Jake would be dealing up his dark notice to the rest of the gypsy-brand, hard-drinking handballers. So the match in New Orleans had been arranged. Coldiron had been taken out, just afterward.

There they sat. Dutch Gleason and Jake Bradford. The years had treated them better than they had Coldiron. Money and prestige had insulated them from the hardships of the road that the penniless drifter Coldiron had faced daily.

Bradford nodded to Coldiron. Coldiron nodded back. It had come full circle. Their hateful combat had reached a new season, maybe the final one. Coldiron had demolished Jake's best horses in the person of Barry West. The venerated National Handball Association's prestige had been shaken by the old, crippled, drunken Indian-Jew. Coldiron had just kept coming at Jake; he'd climbed over the big bumper and up that triangle to settle an old debt.

Jake had been watching him come for some time. He had quietly plotted Coldiron's ascent of the NHA triangle. He had watched as West's name displaced the best of his stable, one by one. A drunken coach and an upstart kid had torn up Jake's private landscape. And West had never known that there had been a rhyme to Tate's scheduling. Only that his mentor had been in a hurry, for some reason.

Then, with the calmness and certainty that comes with the power of money, Jake had stepped in and had bought off Barry West. He had waited until the time was right, when it had become apparent that West was hitting people. Jake had known the break between the kid and his coach was inevitable, that Coldiron had suffered from terminal nobility about his beloved game, that Tate would be incapable of letting the kid continue to hurt people.

Bradford hadn't liked West's methods of winning either. But he had needed the kid. He had to stop Tate.

By his handling of the kid, Coldiron was becoming a legend in the handball world; the entire sport was ringing with the accomplishments of the crippled guy. It had become a matter of Bradford destroying the Coldiron myth, or being consumed by it. Almost like it was twenty-five years earlier.

Tate and the kid were tearing apart a sports cartel. Jake Bradford's personally constructed handball empire was being laid to waste by his old nemesis. It was a game he loved as much as Coldiron did. They just had different ways of expressing that love.

Jake had protected his NHA monopoly on the game the best way he knew how. He bought out the competition. He had signed Barry West to an exclusive contract. The kid would only be participating in NHA-sanctioned tournaments, after his stand in the Big Apple.

The rumor that the old clique had voted to take West out had only reached Bradford hours before the match. He and Dutch had jammed the telephones in his Overland Park office, in an attempt to confirm that their new property was to be maimed that evening in a match at the Gotham Athletic Club. It had been confirmed. That Coldiron had been designated to carry out the assignment was even more startling. Dutch and Jake were on their way to the Kansas City airport before the phone receiver cooled. This was one match that Bradford wanted to see. It was almost too good to believe.

Seeing Bradford in the gallery's front row had indeed shocked Coldiron. But it had also let him know that he had done Jake some heavy damage. Bradford had to be bleeding badly in order to have let the match continue, now that he owned West. Barry was a highly expensive piece of property, much too valuable to run the risk that he might get hurt in a match against Coldiron. Especially one in which Tate had been chosen to act as assassin. Tate was sure that Bradford knew that the kid had been fingered to be taken out. Jake had informants. Even among the old guard.

Tate's hated rival, the gentlemanly predator of the 1940s, had allowed the match to go on. Jake had even showed up to witness the slaughter; he had come to see West demolish the forty-nine-year-old stool bum; he was there to observe the Coldiron myth laid to waste in front of 2,000 rabid supporters of the sport.

The big crowd was charged with excitement.

Kinetic energy throbbed through the gallery as though each spectator was wired to the one next to him. Most had showed up to behold the invincible handball machine that had been burning up the circuit. West's reputation had circulated through the halls of every handball club in the city. The big blond kid from Upstate New York was reputed to rank with the game's all-time greats. He had soundly beaten the thirty-five top-seeded players of the National Handball Association.

But New York City sports fans are snobs. A winner is not a winner until he proves himself in the Big Apple. A champion is not a champion until crowned in New York. A handball great is not considered a handball great until he shows his stuff at the Gotham Athletic Club. This gallery had to be convinced that they were witnessing legendary handball talent.

The main question that circulated through the crowd was, "Who is the kid facing? Who is this gimp, Coldiron?"

There were a handful of guys in attendance from the old days who knew. They were men with graying hair, flat stomachs, and the washed look of athletes still at it. They had pride in their eyes and hope in their hearts. They were scattered throughout the big crowd, smiling at the jeers thrown Coldiron's way.

Derisive comments were harmlessly showered against the glass walls. It was cruelly suggested that the cripple was just bait for the kid, that he was old meat, meant for building West's hunger for the next match, that the main event was still to come, that Coldiron was a warm-up. The crowd was only entertaining itself. Neither player could hear a single word.

Among the Coldiron loyalists was a guy with red hair and a heavily bandaged left eye. When Tate saw him, Waterbary gave his old friend the okay sign. Red understood now. He respected what Coldiron was attempting to do. They went back a long way together.

The look of cold savagery had descended over Barry during warm-ups. He was all business. He had a record to protect. He had only lost three times in almost eight months. He was out to avenge one of those losses tonight.

When he walked by Coldiron, Barry snapped, "Just one question. Why in front of all these people? Do you want them to feel sorry for you? So maybe they'll pass the hat for your retirement fund?"

"Because, punk, I ain't just going to beat you. I'm going to humiliate you. After tonight, there won't be a player in the country that won't know about this. Even if you wanted to break your word and try to get back on the circuit, you couldn't get a match for a cigarette." Coldiron was already sweating hard. His breathing was heavy from warming up. Tate was rundown. He hadn't been getting much sleep in the past weeks. Except for the night before, when he had dozed right off. Things had been decided. But he still looked whipped. Enough Green had been run through that broken body to fill Lake Ontario.

Tate did have a couple of advantages—slim ones. His experience counted for something. He was one of the deans of the sport. He could still make the ball move better than the best. Coldiron was handball. Handball was Coldiron.

There were a couple of other things; there was the red ball. The kid had never seen one before. For the eye trained to pick up a black blur, the change of color could break a player's concentration. That break could cause a slight hesitation. Maybe enough to throw his timing off. Coldiron was banking that it would. He hoped the red ball would confuse the kid for about an hour and a half. For Tate's part he had been working out with the red ball for two weeks. He was used to it.

Then there were the glass walls. Only a handful of such courts existed in the United States. Most of those were out West. He and Barry had not crossed the Mississippi in their swing.

The Gotham AC had been chosen for that reason. Barry had never played on glass walls. Handball was a totally different game on glass. For one, a player was easily distracted by the spectators. A crowd at ground level is in constant motion. It is a movement that can distort a player's vision.

Then there was the business of color contrast. A black ball against a white surface is easily

277

picked up by the eye. A red ball blasting across a swirl of various colors is a different story; it is extremely difficult to pick out its flight against a patchwork of greens, reds, blues, and other street colors. Barry realized it immediately.

"You fucker. You set this up. Glass walls. Red ball. That's what you've been up to." West referred to Coldiron's recent and frequent disappearances; he had been missing sometimes for days at a time. Barry had figured the old guy had been off on drunks.

"This is the reason we've been staying in the East. You've been sneaking in here for practices. We were never more than an hour away from New York by plane."

"I always said you were another Einstein," Coldiron said. He was tossing his red ball side-armed against the front wall.

"*It's not going to help you! You know that, Coldiron?*" Barry was yelling from anger more than to be heard. The two players were hermetically sealed in the big glass box. The crowd's buzzing, the chattering of bets being made across the aisles, and the churning of the fans were all silenced by the thick walls.

West grew more furious by the minute. Instead of warming up slowly, then building, he took to viciously hitting the ball off the front wall. The weeks of seething were showing on the kid. He expelled boiling, paranoid energy in bursts of wild and flailing drills. He was actually standing himself. West moved with the grace and balance of a well-muscled dancer, as he returned his own shots. He uncoiled off his strong legs in explosions that sent the ball moving faster than the untrained eye could pick up. The crowd was loving it; they cheered each time he got off a rocket. He was putting on a show for them.

Coldiron's thin lips formed into a quiet smile. He stood aside and let the kid hot dog it.

That was the other thing Tate had going for him. He was counting on the kid's blazing temper to work against him. Cheap fame had left West with a raw and fuming attitude. And if there was one person who knew how to get to the kid, if there was one player who could nick at West until he came apart like a cheap watch, it was the guy that was in there with him. Tate Coldiron wanted to make him lose control, so the kid's composure would seep through the cracks in the hardwood. The old guy knew that to humiliate an egomaniac was to take the fight out of him.

He knew he could do it. He knew who and what the kid was. He understood West better than the kid understood himself. Coldiron had first torn the kid apart in training, then had built him into what he was. And he figured that the person with the best chance to disarm the dangerous machine was the guy who had first dreamed it up and then constructed it.

Coldiron had one final advantage, probably

the strongest thing he had going for him against his pupil. He had lived with poverty most of his life. In the last twenty-five years, he had been destitute in the worst possible way; he had been left without hope after they had broken his legs. Before he had met West, the only thing Coldiron had had was a score to settle. He had had nothing to lose.

In his match against West, Tate's ultimate power was that he had known hopelessness and poverty of spirit. He had lived through it and promised himself he'd die before he would return to that charred wasteland of indignity. The kid had never walked there, and thus he had no desire to fight his heart out to stay away from it.

From the loudspeaker came Biasone's voice. "You fellows ready to decide first service?"

"I'm ready," the kid said.

Coldiron raised his right arm.

They backed up against the rear wall. Barry readied himself for his throw.

"Hold it, kid. We're gonna toss for this one."

"What do you think I'm doing?"

"No, I mean toss a coin. I brought one."

"Toss a coin? You kidding?" Barry straightened and raised his head toward the official's box.

"He's right," came the reply. "First serve is decided by a coin toss, if there is one available. Otherwise, it's determined by a ball throw against the front wall."

West said through gritted teeth, "Where'd you dig that one up?"

"I told you to read O'Dwyer's book. Page nineteen. *Hee hee.*"

"Okay, asshole, have your fun. Let's see your coin."

It was Coldiron's turn to look up.

"Here you go," from up above. A small hatch opened in the bottom of the official's perch and a heavy-looking coin dropped into Coldiron's wide hand. Tate nodded his approval.

"Here, check it out." Tate flipped it to West.

Barry examined it. It was a medallion. It was heavy. It was solid gold. One side read AMERICAN HANDBALL ASSOCIATION. A figure of a player making a shot was superimposed over the raised letters. West turned it over. Its other side read NATIONAL SINGLES CHAMPION . . . FIVE CONSECUTIVE YEARS . . . 1944-1948 . . . TATE COLDIRON.

"I'm impressed," he said with evident disdain.

"Don't be. Your new boss saw to it that they don't give them away anymore. There is no AHA. Thanks to him."

"It's a tough world."

"It's funny how things work. You guys deserve each other. You and Bradford. You're both lower than whale shit."

"We here to talk or play?"

"The player side of the coin is heads. Toss and call," Coldiron ordered.

281

West flipped it. "Heads," he called, watching the coin turn lazily over in the air. Then he smiled at Coldiron. And never made an attempt to catch the medallion. It sounded like hamburger when it landed. The player side was up.

Coldiron retrieved the medallion and checked it over. The side bearing his name had been scarred when it had hit the floor.

Barry started to say, "My serve." Coldiron's glove got in the way. Tate had peeled it off and had thrown it at him.

"There's nothing sacred to you, is there, you little, miserable fucker," Coldiron spit and grabbed for the kid.

For a short moment his strong fingers had curled themselves around West's throat. He was prepared to crush the kid's windpipe like a stalk of celery. He would've, if the two men hadn't rushed through the door and grabbed him.

"I want you, you little cocksucker," Tate screamed. He and West snatched at each other over the court attendants. The big crowd was on its feet. Outside the glass box the sound was deafening.

"When I get done with you, asshole, you'll be back driving a cab in Kansas City," West gritted. He had Coldiron's shirt and was trying to pull him to the floor.

Tate was clawing after West's bruised throat. Their hatred for each other spewed out over the court. It was an ugly scene. Jake Bradford had lowered his head. For a quarter century he had been attempting to turn the game away from the kind of roughhousing, brawling scene that he was witnessing. The rest of the crowd was loving it. They were screaming for blood.

The attendants finally got the men apart. From up top came the warning, "Any more of that and the match is automatically forfeited. You guys want to box, go to Madison Square Garden. They have a ring there. We're here to play handball. Now, let's get underway."

Coldiron walked slowly along the back wall to calm down. He silently cursed himself for losing control. He was supposedly the one with the cool head.

He promised himself not to let the kid get to him again; it could sink his chances to win the match. He looked up. There was Bradford. His face was less than a foot from Tate's. Though Jake's hair had turned nearly all gray and he had added some wrinkles, it was the same face. Their eyes locked for an instant. Bradford looked away first.

Barry was ready. The student was set to take on his teacher. From above, the voice said, "Begin."

West drove his first serve, low and hard, to Coldiron's left. Tate killed it slick as silk. The animated crowd roared. Blue tobacco smoke and pure excitement congealed around the court. The gladiators had begun.

A respectful calm washed over the faces of

most of the spectators. It had soon become evident that the old man in the glass box was no slouch. They were seeing no warm-up match. The big blond kid was going to have his hands full. The burly unknown with the slicked-down hair knew his way around the slats.

Coldiron's stuff was working well in the first game. He had some powerful junk on the ball. There was enough limber remaining in his wrists and arms that the red spot danced around the court like it was alive. He wouldn't let West get set.

They played without speaking, silently feeling each other out. They probed at one another's game for any hint of a soft underbelly, a vulnerable spot that could be attacked, torn open, and ripped apart for the kill.

Their volleys lasted for what seemed like hours. They slashed, drove, pushed off the walls, dove for low blasts, fought for position and moved over every square foot of the court. Neither would relent an inch. Every point was a war.

The older man lunged to dig out shots that should've gotten by him. He was showing West, Bradford, and all the rest of those in attendance that he had the heart of a jungle full of lions. Coldiron was moving around the court like he was twenty-five years younger, like he had good legs under him.

West was equally compelled. He let nothing

get by him. He refused Coldiron even a second's rest. He made the older man work for everything. While in the server's box, he offered them up one right in back of the other. He kept Tate running. The kid knew that his coach could not keep up the same murderous pace for three games. He'd run out of gas. Or die.

Coldiron had the edge in the first game, 20-19. He won back service by expertly killing a high-bouncing ceiling shot, with a move that Barry, and most of the spectators had never seen before. Tate had gauged exactly where the high shot would drop and timed its descent perfectly. He had begun his swing long before it had seemed sensible and had picked the ball sweetly out of the air. It was a faultless rollout kill. The maneuver was so lovely, the kill so exact and swift, the crowd sat stunned in a second of silence, before they rose to their feet and cheered wildly.

Moving past West to the server's area, Tate shuddered. He had never seen anything like the look in the kid's eyes. West looked drugged. His eyes were filmy. It appeared like he was in another world. Tate turned the other way. West was demonized with his need to rip Coldiron apart.

Tate bent into his serve and skidded the ball along the left wall so it hugged the floor. Barry had to charge the shot. He got too far under it and lifted the ball to the ceiling. It never reached the front wall. The crowd went berserk.

Tate had walked off with the first game. He had drawn first blood. The virtual unknown had whipped the most vaunted handball prospect in the East.

Inside the court, the sensation of not hearing the jubilantly cheering crowd was eerie. If the two men had still been friends, they might've joked about how foolish the fans looked, jumping up and down like mute puppets. The combatants could only feel a slight vibration in the hardwood from the wild celebration just a few feet from where they stood. It felt like a tremor.

As it was, the two players hot-walked around the court to catch their breath for the second game. West tried to conceal his astonishment at being caught completely off guard by his old mentor. The kid had been overconfident. He silently vowed that he wouldn't make the same mistake in the second game.

"Bush leaguer. You're a piece of cake," were Coldiron's words for the kid.

West started for the older guy, but then stopped. If they got into it again, the official might call the match. Which would mean Coldiron would be called the winner. He had one leg up. West retreated to the other side of the court.

The two attendants who had broken up the fight earlier stepped into the court. They brought towels and water containers with them. Barry took the plastic bottle from the Puerto

Rican kid with the overactive shoulders and the curly, full head of dark hair.

Tate said something to his Latin attendant. The kid handed him the towel and ran quickly from the court. Coldiron took to mopping his strands of hair, then peeled off his soaked gloves. He wiped his hands on the towel, carefully drying between his fingers. He had just finished the little ritual when the skinny kid in white reappeared through the court door.

His attendant again had two items with him. He had fetched another pair of gloves for Coldiron. Sweating far more profusely than West, Tate needed a change of mitts. Otherwise, the ball would stain wet each time he struck it. When a ball got a damp spot on it, it skidded erratically. It lost a lot of its bounce.

The other item the kid brought was Coldiron's refreshment. Having waved off the water, Tate had ordered him back downstairs to fill the plastic jug with Green. The container had a hook-shaped straw that squirted liquid directly down into an athlete's mouth as it was squeezed. Coldiron held his rust-colored bottle up in mock triumph. Word had run through the crowd that the old guy had sent down for booze. They loved it. When Coldiron offered a toast for his first-game victory, they gave him a silent roar. He proceeded to press the thing nearly dry with his big hand.

When he pulled on his dry but well-used

gloves, Tate signaled the official that he was ready.

The second game was a different story. Coldiron's legs started to go. They had begun feeling like they were full of lead right after the intermission. He would've done better to have kept playing rather than stopped. The between-game layoff had caused them to tighten up.

In the first game he had beaten West by cutting the court in two. Camping in the center court zone, he had refused to be moved out. Even an occasional elbow in the ribs from the kid hadn't budged him. He had held onto the high percentage shot area with a death grip; he had staked out his claim for that precious six-foot-diameter area behind the server's box like it had been a wealthy gold vein.

Coldiron lost a step in speed in the second game. He was not recovering as fast as he had in the opening tilt. Shots he had picked off in the first game started skidding by him. He was forced to play them off the back wall. In turn he was forced out of the center court zone.

It was a costly concession for Coldiron. He was allowing West to push him into making a fatal mistake. Barry had gotten the older man running.

Coldiron tried everything in the book to slow down the game. He even threw in a few things that were missing from O'Dwyer's text. If he didn't cut back the pace he was dead. He'd collapse in an agonized heap trying to match West's stamina. He'd walked too many miles on those gnarled legs, and Jack Daniel's Green had robbed too much of his wind, for him to attempt to match the perfectly conditioned kid step for step.

Tate drove the ball to the ceiling. He attempted four-wall screaming pass shots. He slammed the red blur with his fist, high off the front wall. All to try and slow the game down. He had to, for survival.

The ball flew away from his big hand like it was supercharged; it bounded high and long; it ran along the walls and circled the court, like he had it attached to his arm with a wire. But West had smelled it. He knew he had the old guy on the ropes.

He refused to let Tate slacken the killer pace. He prodded his mentor with screamers down the alley, nearly invisible bolts the old guy lunged to keep in play, only to then find the kid had given him one down the opposite alley. West taunted Coldiron with shots against the grain. He made the old guy change directions time and time again. Tate felt like his brittle legs would snap. His knees seized as though they were rusty hinges. The dullness in his legs was replaced by a white poker of pain that ran along his inseam to his groin. Each sudden stop and start ran such a stabbing of agony, he felt as though he was impaled on a pointed stake.

West was like a conductor the way he perfectly orchestrated the second game. And the symphony was Coldiron's physical destruction. He knew the old guy would never quit; he'd never lie down. He'd die first.

Coldiron plied his best hustler savvy. Several times, while crossing by each other in the center of the court, Tate reached out with his thumb and forefinger and tugged gently on the kid's shorts. He was careful so the official couldn't detect what he was doing, and didn't pull hard enough so West would claim he had been interfered with and thus be granted a hinder.

It became a game within the game. Barry had to guess whether Coldiron's gloved finger would find its way between the cheeks of his bottom each time they passed each other. Tate alternated his pinch, so Barry never knew when it was coming. Twice, the kid halted play to ask if the official could see what the old guy was doing to him. Which is exactly what Tate wanted. To stop play so he could grab a breather.

West took the second game, 21-18. More importantly, he had stolen the momentum away from Coldiron. The old guy was no longer controlling the rhythm of play, as he had in the first game. West was. And he was stepping up the beat.

The crowd sensed things had turned around. The kid had played a masterful second game. He had the old guy by the throat.

But the crowd's ovation for West, when he

put the last point away, was clearly dampened by their sentiments for Coldiron. Tate was the underdog. He had won their hearts by showing them his. Everyone in the place, save Tate and a few of his loyal friends, knew the old guy had no chance in the third game. They didn't care. They loved the Indian-Jew. He simply hadn't lain down under the most impressive barrage of shots the gallery had ever seen.

West had shown them he was a complete handball player; he would certainly rank, in their eyes, with the best they'd ever seen play the game.

But the crowd had fallen for the old guy who was as durable and ageless as ancient leather. Where West was exhibiting an attitude of arrogant perfection, Coldiron was playing with dignity, even as he was staring defeat straight in the eyes. By his performance and tenacity Coldiron was telling the big and noisy crowd that West was not going to be allowed to walk off the Gotham AC court without being taken to the limit. Even if the old man collapsed doing it.

Which, according to most in the gallery, along with the officials, was a near certainty. Coldiron was out on his feet. During the between-game breather, he fell into the arms of the attendant. Instead of caving in, Tate regained his balance, then just about drove the crowd into an adoring frenzy by doing a little footwork and toasting them with the container filled with booze. He even gave the startled and jabbering Puerto Rican kid a taste.

When Biasone approached him, the official nearly collapsed seeing Coldiron's complexion, which resembled raw clams in color and tone. The player's lips were white from lack of oxygen. His legs were splotched with red. His white gym outfit looked as though he had just climbed out of the shower with it on.

"Tate, you gotta give it up," the official ordered. He had made sure the kid was out of earshot. "You're going under, man."

Out of the tangle of pain and fatigue that was Coldiron's face, his gray eyes glimmered fierce pride. Through his cracked lips, from his mournful mouth, came the words, "No fucking way. We finish it."

"I'm gonna stop it. I can't let it finish you, Tate. Let someone else take the kid out."

"No, Danny. It's my fight." Twenty-five years earlier, on that dark street in New Orleans, he had waved Danny off, so he could make his stand alone. He knew then, as he knew now, that it was him they wanted. He waved his friend off again, for the same reason. "It's up to me. I started this."

Danny shook his head. Next he marched over to West. The kid was standing near the door, mopping the back of his neck with a towel. His attendant was cutting his wet gloves from his hands.

"Let him off the hook, West. You're killing

him." Danny was pleading. "Walk off now and I'll call it a draw. All money stays where it is."

"There are no draws. Let him die." The words fell out of West's mouth like pieces of hate.

"For Chrissakes . . ."

"Let it continue." West turned away. The attendant was wringing his yellow-and-white-striped sweatband into the towel. It ran like a faucet.

Danny walked back to his friend. The old man was massaging his burning thighs. He was trying to get the blood back into his upper legs. His stems looked pathetically thin against the wide-bottomed shorts.

"Just thought you'd like to know. Bradford's been covering everything. He's giving twenty-five to one that the kid puts your ass through the wall this game."

"Tell Red to lay two grand down for me."

"On who? You or West?" Danny couldn't help himself.

Coldiron gave him a thin smile. "You know, Danny, there was nothing else you could do in New Orleans. The only chance we had was to split. We gambled and we lost. I'd do the same thing tonight. So quit looking back, you dildo."

Danny nodded. The record had been rubbed clean. He returned to his perch.

The final game was agony to Coldiron. His legs cramped up. His lungs burned as though he

293

were caught in a fire. If the physical torture wasn't enough, Tate had to endure West's taunts. The kid hurled vile, half-whispered insults at the reeling champion. He was pushing Tate; he was taking him to the limit. He wanted to break Coldiron.

Tate had a few tricks left in that old bag he had been filling for over forty years. The game had been his life; he knew the limits—how far he could go and still be within the rules. He used the judgment call, where one player blocks another's path to the ball. It was considered a hinder and the point is replayed. Coldiron employed the move whenever the kid got him running and he wasn't able to return the younger man's shot. Tate neatly maneuvered so West would be standing between himself and the ball. The voice from above proclaimed a hinder. And Coldiron saved himself a point. Or the service.

He was a master at it. If it were clear he had no play on the shot, couldn't possibly reach the ball for a return, and therefore had no chance for a hinder, he wouldn't use the ploy. Several times it worked nicely, drawing intense, white-angered stares from West, a disgusted look from Bradford, and knowing smiles from the old-timers in the stands.

Barry was in full control of the third and rubber game. He was leading 17-11. But his edge had been hard-earned. Coldiron hadn't given him spit. The kid's knees were bloodied from diving to return his opponent's well-placed shots.

Age, lack of stamina, bad legs, and too much Green had proved to be Tate's undoing. The kid was just too strong for him. It was only a matter of time.

The crowd sensed it. Their sentiments were with the old guy. He was showing nobility and unbelievable tenacity as his game was collapsing. He was a true champion.

The gallery also had a lot of respect for the kid's awesome abilities. He was a player of zenith caliber. He possessed shots and moves rarely seen, and never in the property of one player. He had two of the most equally superb hands that had ever played on the Gotham AC courts.

Some of the old-timers in the stands, hardened guys like Red, Grasso, and Lowenburg, even Danny in the official's box, felt tears move to their eyes. They were witnessing the authorized passing of the torch. Coldiron had been an institution to them. He had never been beaten on the courts by Bradford's faction. It had taken a car bumper to do it. There had always been the question, a rallying point among the old crowd, "Would anyone have been able to beat Coldiron legitimately if he had had two good legs?"

It was always academic. Now it didn't matter. It was the clock, his beloved Green, and a killer kid that were doing it. With each point the kid grabbed off, Coldiron's iron grip on some lonely cliff's edge was loosened. When Tate fell, so would something of the game they loved. They had played it with honor, dignity, and fun-loving camaraderie. They had been an irascible bunch who had toured the country, leaving laughter and high times in their wake.

The blond kid was wiping up the court with their legendary, unofficial leader. Coldiron had been the free one. He was the one who hadn't knuckled under to Bradford's society. And now he was getting put through the wall by the very kid he had trained to take his place. It was the great, undefeated champ coming out of retirement to get his butt kicked by the current titleholder, who couldn't have hired on as a sparring partner in the old days.

The kid knew he had Coldiron. All color was gone from the older guy's face. He rattled when he breathed. His gray eyes were dulled. His legs looked incapable of supporting those proud and wide shoulders, that strong chest, those arms with the power to knock through a brick wall.

Above the court, Danny was silently begging Tate to give it up. He wanted the old guy to drop to one knee, give the signal that he was finished. But Coldiron hung in. It was his fight. He'd take it all the way. He always had.

West could've easily forced the Indian-Jew into a few mistakes, taken the last four points, and walked off with the match. He had long before proven his point. That night, in front of that big screaming crowd, in full view of the old guard, while his new bosses watched, Barry had proven he was the superior of the two gladiators. But that wasn't enough for him. He had to hit the old man.

The play began with a screeching line-drive shot off Coldiron's fist, a return Tate could've easily have killed in the first game. But his timing was gone, along with his energy. He was going on heart alone. He was trying to power everything.

His shot came off the front wall, high and hard. The kid floated through the air, timing his move perfectly to catch the red missile as it came off the rear wall in all its speed.

Coldiron had been spun around with the effort of his play. He found himself facing the kid when the rocket caught him in the face. His neck snapped backward. A fan of sweat flew from his hair. He went down like he had been shot. His hands had instinctively grabbed his head.

The crowd leaped to their feet in gasping horror. Danny threw open the trap door and fell to the court. He ran to his felled friend. Spectators pressed their faces against the glass for a better look. Two thousand people fell quiet. Barry walked to the back of the court. The jabbering Puerto Rican attendants rushed by him.

"Tate," Danny said, bending over Coldiron. "Tate. You okay?"

"Think so. Am I cut bad?" Coldiron stayed down.

"You got it under the eye. Doesn't look too bad. Another half an inch and you would've lost it."

"I saw it coming. Turned enough, just in time, I guess. The fucker only glanced me."

One of the attendants handed Biasone a towel. The official blotted at Tate's face with it. The skin over his cheekbone was split. The cut was about an inch long and to the bone.

"Looks worse than it is. There's a lot of blood."

"The women in the crowd like a little blood. Gets them excited." Tate managed a smile.

Danny worked fast. He tore a piece of adhesive into the shape of a butterfly. Tate pressed the towel hard against his face, trying to coagulate the blood.

"If your fucking blood wasn't sixty percent alcohol, it might clot." Danny smiled down at the injured warrior.

"If it wasn't sixty percent Green, I might be feelin' some pain right now," Tate rasped. His lips were dry and split.

They got the bleeding to slow down enough to get the adhesive tape to stick. Danny and the attendants pulled Coldiron to his feet. He came up in sections.

"You want to call it quits?" Danny asked, adjusting the bandage.

"What do you think? Did you honestly believe I'd let that pansy-palmed punk run me off the slats with a scratch? He'll work for this one."

"You never were smart enough to lie down, you big Indian schmuck," Danny smiled. He turned and signaled that the match was to resume.

Dutch Gleason and Jake Bradford looked around them. What they saw and heard was no respectful clapping for the return of an injured athlete. Tate was receiving a standing ovation. The crowd was nuts about Coldiron. One tall, darkly beautiful woman was standing, the knuckle of her index finger in her mouth, her applause for Coldiron flowing from her eyes.

"Let's go, kid," Coldiron said. "I'm going to teach you how to play this game. You're still bush league. You ain't even a good hitter. I've gotten worse scratches than this in a whorehouse."

Barry glared at him. "You just keep coming, don't you, Coldiron?"

"You got it, punk. Just like I told that lady in Detroit. For this kind of money, you ain't gettin' the easy one."

Suddenly from somewhere deep within that Indian-Jew, bourbon-soaked body, hidden far under his tortured muscles, beyond his conscious level of endurance and good sense, came a wall of strength. It was a pearl of energy that glowed and fired his entire body with one last surge. Coldiron not only fell in step with the game's rhythm, he picked it up some. So great was his burst of raw power and finely honed skill, Coldiron began to play like he was the younger of the two men. It was he who now exhibited the greater staying power.

The momentum shift was in the air. It penetrated the thick glass walls. Coldiron was coming. The old guy was approaching the stretch in full gallop. He was blowing by the startled kid.

West valiantly tried to catch Coldiron's energy and turn it around. He attempted to harness the burst and fight it to a halt. But there was no stopping Coldiron. Twenty-five years of hate generated a lot of power.

Tate was all over the court. He dove for shots. He continually beat the kid to the draw. He pulled even with him. He tied the score at 21 apiece and sent the game into overtime. The crowd went nuts. Barry and Tate stood toe to toe; they were two driving, churning, maddened forces clashing head on. They were locked in a death struggle.

Now the crowd was stilled by the intensity of what they were seeing. Many people stood, as if in solemn prayer. Some waited for one of the two athletes to cave in.

Coldiron managed to pull ahead, 28-27. He had the serve. He stood within striking distance of a colossal comeback. Tate had a chance for an incredible upset.

There was total quiet outside the glass box as

he bent into his serve. All eyes followed the red dot as it skipped low into the left corner. Barry dug it out and drove his answer low against the front wall. Coldiron charged the wall. So did West, anticipating a soft kill attempt.

Coldiron saw him coming; he drove an alley pass along the left sidewall. Barry slammed into a direction change and lunged to his left. He picked the red blur out of the air in a brilliant move. He drove a strong lefthanded shot back to the right front corner. It appeared the ball would skip out of Coldiron's reach and die in the back court.

With a tremendous sideward leap, accompanied by a tortured, guttural scream, Coldiron found the ball. He was parallel to the floor when he made contact. With perfect control, and just before he crashed to the floor, he sliced a shot down the left wall.

The ball had just the right amount of English on it, so it never came away from the glass. Barry raced the twenty feet to the court's opposite side, in a desperate charge to escape defeat.

His arm arched back. Due to the distortion of his depth perception by the glass, he thought the ball was a few inches off the wall. Rather than playing the shot with his hand pointed downward, thinking he had enough room, Barry held his fingers extended rigidly sideways. In that fashion he could get more on the ball; he could slash an alley pass to the left of Coldiron. The old guy was moving right. A shot against the grain would've easily beaten him.

But Barry had guessed wrong on his shot. He made poor contact. Mostly because his fingers collided violently with the glass. He let out a tremendous shriek as the three longest fingers on his right hand snapped at the first joint on impact with the wall. He dropped to his knees, on top of the ball that had fallen at his feet. The match was over. Tate Coldiron had beaten him. The old guy had taken him out.

The crowd went into a frenzy. Strangers were hugging one another. People were banging each other on the back. Hats flew into the thick air. Danny in the official's box was screaming into a microphone he thought he had turned off, *"He did it! He did it! Coldiron did it! Hot damn! The son of a bitch pulled it off!"*

The place was absolutely and totally bonkers. The crowd had witnessed an old man destroy the clock, every principle of good training, and the best in the business. They had been dealt up the impossible. Two thousand people danced and screamed wildly. Coldiron walked around the court with his arms extended in the air, acknowledging the crowd's adulation.

The kid had pushed himself up with his good hand and was ready to leave the court. He grimaced in agony from the injury and the defeat he had suffered. He took his right hand in his left, trying to press back the pain.

Tate stopped his victory walk in the back corner of the court. Unable to exit the stands because of the pandemonium stood Jake Bradford. Coldiron gave the NHA czar a long look. Not only had Coldiron torn down Bradford's triangle, he had just pulled down the extra tier, in the name of Barry West, that Jake had added for insurance. One of the boys had put Jake Bradford through the wall; it had been one of the old-timers. And unknown to Jake, Coldiron had even lightened his hated rival's wallet by $50,000 on a side bet.

Tate made his way to the door, the kid arriving there at almost the same instant. Court attendants and spectators milled between them, the redhead with the big eye bandage among the group. West squeezed his own right hand. Pain, mixed with exhaustion, having found his face, the kid looked like he was on the verge of collapse.

Coldiron stopped him. A thin line of blood ran along the old guy's cheek to his neck, blotting into a circle on his soaked shirt. "You're done, kid. Don't try to play stakes handball again." The words tasted good and right to Coldiron; they had been forming since Fredericksburg, the first time he had been fully aware that West had been hitting people on purpose. "There are a lot of players out there better than this old cripple. The word's out, punk. They'll be gunning for you. They'll eat you up. They'll put your ass through the wall."

303

Then Coldiron left the kid. He stepped out the door into the hall and into a wild melee of backslapping fans. Red tossed Tate's arm over his shoulder and helped him through the pushing throng, only to have Coldiron take his shining limb back as the Indian-Jew warrior saw the tall woman in the brown, pinstriped suit standing in the hallway, away from the crush of people, waiting for him. They looked at each other, their eyes catching, as they had that day in Delaney's Restaurant in Rochester when Susan had consented to front him and Barry the $2,000 for their odyssey, which had brought all three of them here to the Gotham AC.

And for the second time, Coldiron and Susan realized that there was something that linked them, some hidden chemistry of desire, a crying, unfulfilled need in each of them, that would forever remain dormant because of the differing burden of their souls. These two, this man who lived to wager and to run free, and this woman who had been surrounded by her own destructive requirements, had begun from different places at different times, and would, by necessity, have to walk separate paths.

It was Coldiron who spoke first. "He needs you. And I'm a bad risk for love."

"I know it," she said, her dark eyes glistening with tears of confused satisfaction and joy. "Goddamn it all, if I don't know it."

"He's standing on an ugly, lonely shore, he's up to his neck in hate. He'll die with it; it'll consume him," Coldiron said, his voice soft and gentle and exhausted, reaching her and soothing her, despite the din of shouting in the background. "You're his bridge to the other side, his way back. If he stays where he is, it'll only get worse. If Barry walks with you, trusts you, it'll be different. For both of you."

Standing there, dripping sweat and blood, Coldiron looked bigger to the woman. He said, "Good-bye, Susan."

And with that, Coldiron allowed himself to be moved away from her by the crowd, farther down the hall, to the locker room and to some bar well-stocked with Green, though they both took a warm moment to look at each other again, maybe for the last time, and wonder.

Barry came along behind Tate. West received no backpats or hugs, only sorrowful looks reserved for the vanquished. His hand throbbed unmercifully. Tears of humiliation and despair were close to coming. He pushed through the crowd, protecting his twisted and broken fingers as best he could, until he felt the lone, soft hand on his arm that asked him to pause. He looked up and saw Susan.

"Can I help?"

"No. Please. Leave me alone," he said, his prideful words not matching his pain-filled eyes. He tried to pull away, but Susan wouldn't let him. It wouldn't be that easy.

"I said, I want to be left alone." His blond

hair looked shorter and darker because of its wetness.

"Just this once, Barry. Just this once, let go of it. It'll never be any easier than right now."

Barry turned to her. Of course he needed the woman; he always had. It had taken getting hammered and humbled for him finally to be able to admit it. He had wanted out for a long time, but that thing, that unnamed, poisonous greed, had had him too strongly in its grip. Surrender was all over his face; the hate was gone. He started to reach for her, to begin the walk with her across that bridge, but the pain in his hand and in his heart held him back.

"I know," she said. "It's okay. Let me help you. I love you, babe." Susan slipped her arm over his wet shirt sleeve.

"C'mon," Barry said, "I want to get dressed. Let's get out of here. Let's go home."

They both knew it would be different. It had to be. Too much had changed for both of them. The suddenly quiet crowd stepped aside and let them pass. Barry and Susan disappeared down the hallway, the one that could've used stronger lights.

Chapter Twenty-Three

. . . LIKE A BAD PENNY

The best handballers on the Atlantic Coast gathered at the Oceanview Athletic Club, located in Fort Lauderdale, Florida. A big and lean kid, with bushy, brown hair and a centipede moustache was practicing some shots on Court Four. He had just handily won his match. He had stayed on after his opponent had left. There were some things he wanted to work on.

From the darkened gallery above the court's back wall, a gravelly voice blared, "If you had any shots you'd be a decent bush league player."

The young man wheeled around to see an older man step from the shadows, whose wirelike hair was slicked back.

"What the hell are you talking about?" the younger man asked.

"Just what I said, kid. If they hung you for being a handball player, you'd die an innocent man. *Hee hee.*" The guy had his foot propped on the railing like he owned the place.

"If I had this court reserved for the next hour, old man, I'd be happy to kick your butt all over it."

"What a coincidence. So happens I have this

court signed up for the next hour. Would you care for a little stakes match? Say fifty skins a game?"

"My pleasure, friend. C'mon down," the kid said.

"On my way," the old man answered. "Let me go get my gear on. Be right there."

There was something funny about the way he walked. He shuffled up over the gallery seats like he had bad legs—something. The kid wondered whether it might be a cruel joke arranged by one of his friends. They may have paid some wino a few bucks to harass him.

The old guy hurried up to his office. It was the one marked TATE COLDIRON, OWNER. As he shook his gear out, he half sang, "This guy's gonna be a-a-a-ngel food cake."